Kissing Kin

by

Karen Hulene Bartell

Trans-Pecos Series

Dedication

To my best friend, unflagging supporter, and husband,
Peter Bartell!
In memory of Rosie Thornburg, and in appreciation of
Teddy of the loquat trees.

Chapter 1

I'd planned to visit my only living relative in El Paso, but then a packing box and registered letter arrived the day before my discharge.

Harold Baker Law Firm—*Ms. Jackson: it is with deep regret that I inform you of Mildred Taylor's passing. In accordance with her will, please find the assets bequeathed to you—*

I fingered through the box's contents—my grandmother's collection of family journals. Dated 1899, the topmost diary was labeled Fort Lincoln, Texas.

*Fort Lincoln…*The name conjured vague memories of Grandma's stories. Tears stinging my eyes, I checked an online map. The town was three hours from El Paso. *But do I have time for a detour? I'd have to file a DA 31 to request leave…*

A mirthless chuckle escaped. *Tomorrow, I'm getting my discharge. I don't need anyone's permission!*

****

"Our family homesteaded in the Lincoln Mountains." Grandma's bedtime stories echoed through my mind as I sped west on I-10. At an early age, family history had merged with myth until the name Fort Lincoln was as legendary as Avalon or Middle Earth.

But when the snow-covered peaks loomed closer, their reality was undeniable. *Maybe her stories weren't tall tales…*

And what about her proverbs? "Idle hands are the devil's workshop." I winced. *No job and no prospects.* Mustering out after a five-year Army stint, I had to ask myself: *What next?* Where *next?*

Cody slipped into my thoughts, but I dismissed him, refusing to romanticize our breakup.

Though the speed limit was eighty mph, traffic zipped at a brisk ninety, and I approached Fort Stockton just after noon. A troop of cavalry soldiers galloped toward me from the nineteenth century, but a second glance proved the images were metal cutouts—two-dimensional illusions that resembled an officer and guide leading two columns of cavalrymen.

The silhouettes evoked tales of my great-great-grandfather, Ben Williams. Beginning his military career as a scout, he'd been field promoted during combat, then commissioned as Second Lieutenant at Fort Lincoln.

I smiled, proud of our similar career paths. *Maybe Grandma's stories influenced me more than I realized.*

Leaving the Interstate, I turned south. Road signs noted the distance to Fort Lincoln, Terlingua, Lajitas, and Castolon, towns that sounded familiar from family stories but seemed as mythical as Camelot or Tintagel Castle.

Closer now, the mountains' features came into view. No longer mere outlines on the horizon, each craggy palisade and butte towered over the highway.

The forecast had promised sunny skies and temperatures in the sixties. Then an El Niño cold front barreled through. Fog still hugged the mountains—wispy remnants of the blue norther—coating every cactus spine, mesquite thorn, and barbed wire with a fine layer of ice. Fluffy hoarfrost transformed the landscape into an icy spectacle, with flaky, crystal shards overlaying each leaf and every blade of grass.

A frozen fairyland! Just the way Grandma described it. Inspired by the raw beauty, I straightened my shoulders. *Maybe I'm viewing my discharge the wrong way. Instead of adrift, maybe I'm free…*

Crouching forward, I peered through the windshield at the vertically fractured boulders high above. The basalt columns rose like thousands of giant fingers reaching for the sky. Steep bluffs flanked both sides of the road, and as I navigated the pass, another mountain range appeared on the horizon, then another.

Snow flurries swirled about the peaks like confectioners' sugar. A bank of compacted snow lined the twisting highway's shoulders, partially shrouding fallen rocks—proof of a plow's recent sweep—but except for an occasional thin glaze of ice, the road was clear.

As my car continued its climb, another sign came into view: Wild Rose Pass.

A roadrunner sprinted across the road, its neck craned forward and its tailfeathers parallel to the ground.

I grinned at the lucky omen as I rounded the next bend, where a javelina sow and her two piglets scurried onto the highway, directly in my path.

I swerved, but my front wheels caught a patch of black ice, sending the car into a spin as it careened toward a sheer drop-off. My equilibrium off, I pumped the brakes while I steered hand over hand, skidding sideways toward the opposite shoulder, where a solid basalt wall backboarded the emergency lane.

I closed my eyes, clenched the wheel, and braced for impact.

The car crunched through the snowbank and jounced over the rocky debris, but instead of hurtling headlong into the stony barrier, it lurched to a halt, just inches from the mountainside. The hood tilted skyward, and the car's right front tire lifted off the ground.

Rammed against the driver's door and queasy from the spin, I cut the engine, while the javelinas nimbly ducked beneath the railing and scuttled down the hillside. *At least they're safe.*

Thick smoke began filling the car. My lungs burning, I pushed against the wedged door, but it would not give. *I'm not going to die in flames!* Adrenaline pumping, I twisted in my seat and kicked against the armrest with both feet. Millimeter by millimeter, the rim scraped the packed snow until, finally, the metal buckled, and I tumbled out.

Black smoke billowed from the engine. Coughing, I filled my lungs with cold mountain air as I tried to pry open the hood. But with the car nearly leaning on its side, the crumpled metal would not budge. I limped to the passenger side for a better view.

Lodged on a fallen boulder, the right front of the car's undercarriage listed in midair.

That's what saved me from crashing into the wall. Despite February's freezing temperatures, I wiped the perspiration from my brow as I slumped against the solid basalt. Its icy smoothness fortifying, I closed my eyes and mouthed a silent prayer.

"Are you all right?"

"What?" I jumped at the male voice, but the upturned car blocked my vision.

"Are you okay?" The stranger came into view: curly dark hair and long eyelashes framing chocolate-brown eyes.

His warm smile swept over me like a balmy breeze.

I caught my breath as I took in his strong jawline and cleft chin.

Towering above me, he sported a five o'clock shadow. "Are you hurt?"

"I don't think so." Adrenaline flowing, I felt no pain, but I took inventory, inspecting my limbs for blood or protruding bones. "Just shaken and a little sore."

"Understandably. The police are on their way. Do you want to wait in my truck?"

Wary of hopping into a stranger's car, I searched his face but, reading only concern, relaxed. "I'd appreciate it." Then I surveyed the steep snowbank and regretted not wearing boots.

He reached across the bank, palm up.

Using his fingers as leverage, I jumped the piled snow and followed him to his pickup.

"The first step's a doozy." He opened the door and again held out his hand.

"Thanks." Shivering from the cold, I pushed off from his palm and hoisted myself onto the front seat.

He hopped in the driver's seat and turned on the heater full blast, redirecting the vents. "Adjust the temperature however you like."

"This is fine." As the shock wore off, reality hit. *No boots, gloves, or hat.* Aware of my vulnerability alone in the mountains without the car's heater, I took a deep breath. "Glad you came by when you did."

"I was in the right place at the right time." His gaze caught mine. "What happened?"

"I swerved to avoid a family of javelinas and spun out." Frustrated, I stifled a groan. "I can operate an M2

Bradley but can't drive on ice."

"Don't beat yourself up. Ice grabs the wheel."

I ventured a smile, grateful for his support as sirens screeched in the distance. Then turning toward the flashing red, white, and blue lights on the horizon, I recalled another of my grandmother's axioms: "Every event leads to the next." *So, where'll this one steer me?*

****

No Texas twang. He leaned against his truck, listening to the inflection of her voice as the police questioned her. *She's not from here.* He checked her Colorado plates before checking her out.

Despite the puffy vest, her figure beneath was lithe and slender. Her tight jeans emphasized her derriere's curves, and she moved with a dancer's grace. She wore her tawny brown hair in a pixie cut that emphasized her haunting eyes. No makeup, her face was bare except for the freckles on her button nose.

Interest growing, he waited for the police to finish. Then when the wrecker arrived, he joined her. "Can I give you a ride into town?"

Her green eyes probed his. A blink later, she nodded. "I'd appreciate it."

Guess I passed muster. He helped transfer her luggage, then climbed into his truck and followed the wrecker.

"You mentioned an M2 Bradley." He side-glanced. "Are you in the military?"

"I'm stationed at Fort Carson." A pink blush tinged her cheeks. "Sorry, habit. I just mustered out."

"That's an Army installation, right?" His ears perked for confirmation.

"Yup. I belonged to the Fourth Squadron."

"Fourth Squadron?" Barely taking his eyes from the road, he glanced her way. "Isn't that the only Tenth Cavalry Regiment unit still in active service?"

"Yes." Her eyes widened. "How would you know such military minutia?"

"My great-great-grandfather served in the Tenth Cavalry Regiment."

"You're kidding…"

"Nope." He shook his head. "He was stationed right here at Fort Lincoln."

"When?" She came to attention.

"The late 1870s or early 1880s…" Despite the icy patches, he stole a glimpse. "Why?

"Because *my* great-great-grandfather was stationed at Fort Lincoln in 1879."

"What was his name?"

"Ben Williams."

"Seriously?" He pulled off the road to watch her expressions.

"Yup."

Leaning his head against his headrest, he chuckled as he studied her features.

"What's so funny?" A cautious smile fluttered across her face.

"Ben Williams was my great-great-grandfather, too."

"No!" Her full lips formed an O.

"Yeah."

"So, we're third cousins?"

"Kind of…" Mid-nod, he recalled his family's history. "Actually, he's my *adoptive* great-great-grandfather, so we're third cousins on paper only. He raised my great-great-grandmother, Ma—"

"Marianna." She nodded. "My grandmother mentioned her often."

His gaze connecting, he paused a beat. "What are the odds?"

"In fact, I have her journals in my suitcase…" She jerked her thumb toward the back seat. "Grandma was the family historian. She…" Her voice caught. "She left me her collection when she passed away."

"I'm sorry." The words were automatic, but when her eyes bunched, he wished he had offered more than a cliché.

"Thanks, but it's been years since I last saw her." Swallowing, she pressed her lips together. "I've been deployed in Afghanistan."

"Wow." *Who'd have guessed?* He took a second look, unable to imagine her in combat. Nothing about her was fussy or frilly. *Still…* His gaze becoming a stare, he offered his hand. "By the way, I'm Lucas Kaylor, but everyone calls me Luke."

"Maeve Jackson." A quick smile lifted the corner of her lips as she shook hands.

"Maeve." He rolled the word over his tongue, liking the sound. "What's it mean?"

"She who intoxicates." She dimpled.

He again caught himself staring, broke the gaze, and started the engine. "The wrecker's out of sight. Why don't we continue this conversation while we catch up?"

"The driver said he's taking my car to Smitty's."

"The garage is just a few miles up the road"—he gestured with his chin—"next to the fort."

"Fort Lincoln…?"

She spoke with such reverence, he did a double take.

"When I was a kid, Grandma filled my head with so

many tales about Fort Lincoln that it sounded like some fabled kingdom in a storybook." Her eyes dancing, she laughed. "In a few minutes, I'll set foot in this mythical utopia."

He tilted his head to glance from the road. "Fort Lincoln is a beautiful place, but I wouldn't call it utopia."

"Still, it's like being transported to Mu or Atlantis— places you've read about but don't believe exist." Her cheekbones rose in a whimsical smile. "Thinking in those terms, the name's magical."

"When you put it that way, maybe so." Her jade-green eyes mesmerizing, he blinked to break the gaze. *Keep your eyes on the road.* "What brings you here?"

****

"Thought I'd stop on my way to El Paso, spend a day or two looking around, and maybe find my roots."

"You found me, cuz."

Cousin, huh? Taking in his rugged good looks, I studied the man beside me. Tendrils of dark curls dipped artlessly on his smooth brow as if finger-combed into place. When he took his eyes from the road, his gaze was direct, and his warm, coffee-brown eyes—fringed with impossibly long lashes—were captivating. *Maybe third cousins* technically *but not by blood.*

"What are the odds of strangers learning they're related?" His jaw widened into a grin. "Such a coincidence."

"I don't believe in coincidences." I shook my head. "I'd call our meeting a concurrence of events. Synchronicity."

"You're splitting hairs." His jaw stiffening, he turned toward me. "What's the difference between coincidence and synchronicity?"

"Coincidence implies luck. Synchronicity is an arrangement of events. Nothing happens by chance. *Something* caused us to meet." I pressed my lips together. "My grandmother had a saying. 'To everything, there is a purpose.' "

He took his gaze from the road and smiled. "And sometimes, coincidence is just dumb luck."

"I disagr—"

"Here we are." He turned off the road by a sign reading Auto Repairs While You Wait. "And there's Smitty." He pointed to a paunchy man in overalls.

*Already? So close to town. Only a few more miles, and I would've avoided the accident...*Frustrated with myself, I swallowed a groan, then turned toward Luke. "Thanks for the lift."

"My pleasure." His brown eyes glistened in the afternoon sun.

Why was I so confrontational? Dumb...dumb...dumb. My chin dipping, I mumbled into my chest. "Didn't mean to argue."

"Not argued, debated." His lips curled into a slow smile.

Despite my burning cheeks, I couldn't resist returning his smile.

"You own this car, Miss?" Wiping his hands on a rag, the man approached us.

"Maeve, this is Smitty, the best mechanic in town."

"You might not be smiling when I tell you the damages."

"Not good, huh?" Grimacing, I jumped from the truck and followed him.

"Until I get it on the lift, I can't be sure, but for openers, you're looking at a new exhaust system, oil pan, alternator…and possibly transmission and steering."

"Ouch." My shoulders stiffened. "How long will repairs take?"

"Depends on what I find." Smitty shrugged. "But this being the weekend, you can count on at least three days for the parts to be delivered."

"Hopefully, the damages aren't as bad you suspect."

"Time will tell."

Taking a deep breath, I searched for the positive. "I'd planned to spend a day or two here, anyway, researching…"

Smitty took his phone from its holster. "What's a good contact?"

I gave him my cell number.

"Then you're staying in town?"

My options were sparse.

"A hotel's just down the street." Luke pointed. "Near the library if you want to research while you're here."

"Good to know." Once again indebted, I nodded my appreciation. "Thanks, cuz."

"You're related?" Smitty's brow puckered as he looked from one to the other. "Not much family resemblance…"

"You might say we're *distant* relations." I caught Luke's gaze.

"Third cousins." His arms crossing over his broad chest, he winked. "Barely kissing kin."

Smitty gave me another once over. "I'll call when I know the damages."

"Fair enough."

"Can I drop you off at the hotel?" Luke straightened his spine. "Your bags are still in my truck."

"Oh, sorry. I'm holding you up." I winced. "You must've been on your way somewhere when you stopped…"

"No worries, but"—his lips curled in a leisurely smile—"I *did* promise to deliver the *masa* tonight. My aunt's making tamales."

"And I kept you." I shrank into my vest. "Please give her my apologies, and just point me toward the hotel. If it's down the street, I can manage my bags. Thanks, you've—"

"Trust me, five minutes won't matter. I'll drive. Besides, it's starting to snow again, and sundown comes early in the mountains."

I glanced at the surroundings. With the Lincoln Mountains as the backdrop, the sky had faded from brilliant blue to dusky twilight. Stars glimmered in the early evening's velvet canopy, and—*sure enough*—fluffy snowflakes wafted through the crisp air.

This scene could be one of Grandma's tales come to life. I breathed in the beauty.

"Ready?"

Luke's voice roused me from my reverie. "I can't help admiring the view."

"No place like it."

Watching the sun lose its grip behind the mountains, I shook my head. "No wonder our families settled here."

His warmth radiated as he smiled, opened the truck door, and held out his hand. "Summer Swallows Hotel is at the other end of town."

"Thanks." Again, pushing off from his palm, I hopped into the front seat. "What's the story behind its name?"

"The way northerners wintering in the south are

called *snowbirds*, in the 1800s, people escaping the heat were called *summer swallows*. A mile high, Fort Lincoln has one of the balmiest summers in Texas."

The passing storefronts' façades grabbed my attention. "The buildings look like something from the old west. I feel we're riding through a time warp into the 1880s."

Signaling a left turn, Luke nodded as he waited at the courthouse's intersection.

The clock tower chimed five times, and I turned toward the sound, glimpsing the structure's octagonal turret. "What a charming building, especially its pink stonework."

"The material is rhyolite tuff, a local volcanic stone." He turned onto a driveway. "Here we are— Summer Swallows Hotel, also constructed with tuff."

The two-story, pink-stone inn sported wide porticoes with white railings on both levels. A heart-shaped wreath adorned the front door.

"It's so welcoming." As I stepped from the truck, the Texas Historical Commission plaque caught my gaze. "This place was built in 1880?"

"Some folks say Quanah Parker stayed here."

"In this hotel…?" I glanced at the structure, reevaluating the events that had led me here. Then Luke caught my gaze. *If I hadn't had the accident, would we have met?*

"And if you want to explore local history, the library's only a few steps away." He pointed to a limestone building across the drive.

"Talk about convenient…" *For the first time in five years, my time's my own. And with no orders or assignments to interrupt, I can research to my heart's content.* A vague sense of mission began to gel.

"Let me grab your bags from the back."

"I've got 'em—"

"Too late." His arms weighed down with my luggage, he laughed. "Why don't you get that box?"

"Thanks." Knowing the bags' weight, I breathed a sigh, grateful for someone to share the load. *It's been a while…*

I lifted the box of journals, recalling the past five years' self-reliance, and my grandmother's adage echoed through my mind: "If you constantly have to prove yourself, you've forgotten your value." My arms full, I struggled with the doorknob.

But Luke propped open the door with his leg, in addition to carrying my luggage.

"Chivalry's not dead." Impressed, I rewarded him with a bashful smile.

"Ma'am." Speaking in an exaggerated cowboy drawl, he pretended to tip his hat.

Inside, the open fireplace welcomed me with the tangy scent of mesquite. Its cozy dry heat shook off the early evening's chill as it embraced me.

Painted a cheery yellow and white, the old-fashioned wainscoted hall with its ten-foot, tin ceiling offset the front desk's dark wood. Sturdy antique furniture graced the lobby, and a winding stairway rose to the second floor.

"Mamie"—Luke called from behind me—"have you got a room for family?"

The gray-haired woman greeted us with a cordial smile. "Sure do for any family of yours."

"I'd like you to meet my long-lost cousin, Maeve." He set down my bags. "This is Mamie, the unofficial town historian if you need help researching family genealogy."

"Glad to meet you." I set the box on the desktop and held out my hand.

"Let me know if you have any questions. Always glad to help." Mamie grasped my hand in a firm shake. "How long are you staying?"

I glanced at Luke before answering. "Depends on what Smitty finds and how soon the parts are delivered, but at least three nights."

"Car trouble?"

"More like javelina and ice trouble." I snickered, annoyed by the accident.

"The longer your stay, the better." Mamie passed a key to Luke. "Why don't you put your cousin's luggage across the hall in room 117, while I check her in?"

As I finished registering, Luke returned with the key. "I have to drop off the *masa*, but—"

"Oh, sorry to keep you so long." Reluctant to say goodbye yet resigned, I muffled a groan. "Thanks again for your help. I'm so glad we met."

"Actually"—wearing a silly grin, he rubbed his chin—"I was going to ask what you're doing for dinner. Figured I'd drop off the *masa* and get back about the same time you've settled in your room."

Well, now…cousin or date? Caught off-guard, I gazed into his eyes. "I don't have any plans…" I shrugged. "Sure."

"Great." He flashed an easy smile. "Meet you at the front desk in a half hour."

"Sounds good." My pulse accelerating, I returned a cautious smile, excited at the prospect of seeing him again yet self-conscious and out of my element.

His broad back to me, he strode away in his tooled leather boots and thigh-hugging jeans. Then just before shutting the door, he turned and caught my gaze.

The heat rose to my cheeks as my blood pressure spiked.

"Cousins, huh?" Her eyes twinkling, Mamie chuckled while she pointed to the X and handed me the pen. "Sign here."

"Third cousins…by adoption." Uncomfortable at being caught flirting, I mumbled. "We just met this afternoon."

"What a coincidence…"

I shook my head at the woman's ironic tone. "Everything happens for a reason."

"Whatever the reason, you couldn't meet a nicer guy."

"Really?" My ears perked. "How do you know Luke?"

"We've met at Chamber of Commerce meetings." Mamie's smile warmed. "He's got a head on his shoulders."

"Chamber of Commerce…so he owns a busin—"

"It's a *blizzard*—not *flurries!*" The door opened, and a couple burst inside, along with a blast of frigid air. "I'm *not* driving twenty-four miles through the mountains. *In. The. Snow!*"

"We have reservations." The woman slammed the door. "*In Alpine!*"

"Do you have any rooms available?" The red-faced man turned toward Mamie.

"You're in luck—one's left." After greeting the couple with a magnanimous smile, Mamie gave me a wink. "Excuse me."

"No worries." Carrying my box of journals, I crossed the hall into my room and nearly tripped as a red rubber ball rolled in my path.

Where'd that come from? I glanced up and down the hall but saw no children or open doors. I toed the ball against the wall, pushed open the room's door, and flipped on the lights.

In addition to the high, pressed-tin ceiling, the room sported tall windows, draped with pleated, double-layered fabric that faced the town's main street.

Snug inside the room, I peeked at the swirling snow outdoors. Then I set the box on the Victorian desk as I eyed the two sumptuous queen beds, swathed in bleached white linen.

Undressing, I stepped into the contemporary bath, its fixtures updated, except for the vintage pedestal sink. And after a quick shower, I caught myself smiling in the mirror as I slipped on jeans and an angora-wool sweater. *What'll tonight bring?*

Chapter 2

A good night to stay home. Second-guessing himself, Luke blew on his hands, warming them as he entered the hotel lobby.

Then Maeve stepped into the hall. With the soft blue sweater clinging to her silhouette like contour feathers, she was as eye-catching as an indigo bunting.

He caught his breath, reminded of why he'd ventured out in the storm. "Good timing."

"Hey." Her smile lit up the lobby. "Been waiting long?"

"Just got here." He shook his head as his gaze swept her from head to toe. "But I wouldn't have minded waiting an hour. You look terrific."

"Thanks." Blushing, she tilted her head in a shy smile.

Good looking but doesn't know it. His gaze lingered, and the pause lengthened. Then the puffy vest on her arm registered. "Let me help you with your jacket."

"Thanks." Relinquishing her vest, she slipped her arms through its sleeves.

He breathed in the fresh, lemony scent of her shampoo. "Thought you might like some company for dinner—being new in town and all."

"That's especially thoughtful on a night like this." She glanced at the snow outside.

"Not really. Selfish is more like it." He laughed at

himself. "Might as well be honest."

"As long as we're being honest…" Turning toward him, she lowered her voice. "I hate eating alone in restaurants."

"It isn't every day I stumble on a long-lost cousin."

"Third cousin"—her green eyes danced—"by adoption."

His gaze caught hers and held it a beat too long. Recovering, he gestured toward the café next door. "Hope you're hungry. The bistro makes a mean beef bourguignon."

"You mean beef stew?"

"Hey, it's a small-town restaurant trying to be chic." Pretending indignation, he opened the door, and a blast of frigid air sucked away his breath.

"Brisk." She shivered as the wind swept back her hair.

"And icy." He stepped over the downspout's ice flow, where the snow had melted and refrozen beneath the snow. "Watch your st—"

She shrieked as she slipped.

He caught her, then keeping a protective arm around her shoulders, guided her beneath the strung lights. Relentless snowflakes swirled about them, weighing down the giant oak boughs overhead and collecting in drifts along the hedges. *If this snow freezes, will the roads close?*

"This storm's turning into a blizzard."

"You read my mind, but we'll be cozy inside." He opened the restaurant's door, and the aromas of flame-broiled steak and smoked brisket filled his senses. Dismissing the uncertainties, he breathed deeply, and his optimism returned.

"Table for two, Luke?" The grinning host grabbed two menus.

"Yup. Charlie, I'd like you to meet my cousin, Maeve."

"Do you live in the area, Maeve?" Speaking over his shoulder, he guided them to a window booth beneath an antler chandelier.

"Nope, just visiting a few days, at least 'til my car's repaired."

"Hope you enjoy your stay." He handed her a menu. "Can I get you two something to drink?"

"Would you like wine?" Curious about her tastes, Luke turned toward her. "Red or white?"

"I like a good cabernet or tempranillo now and then."

Luke exchanged a grin with Charlie. "A woman after my own heart."

"What's so funny?" She looked from one to the other.

"Luke's winery makes cabernet sauvignon and tempranillo."

"What a coinci—" Her eyes sparkled. "Synchronicity."

"Which would you prefer? A cab or tempranillo?"

"Tempranillo, especially if we're having beef bourguignon." She smiled at the host. "Which I hear is the house specialty."

"*Definitely* a woman of refined tastes." Luke exchanged another look with Charlie. "A bottle of tempranillo and beef bourguignon for two."

"Be back in a minute with the wine."

"You own a winery?" Head back, she appraised Luke.

"A vineyard that I'm"—he stifled a sigh—"*slowly* expanding into a winery."

"How'd you get started?"

"I worked summers at my grandfather's boutique winery. Then I changed my major to viticulture."

"The study of grapes, right?"

"Grape cultivation." He nodded. "And I took a double major in enology."

"Which is…?"

"The study of wines and winemaking."

She cocked her head as if interested. "What led you to that field?"

Recalling the sequence of events, he took a deep breath. "That's a longer story—"

"Honey, I'm home." Wearing an impish grin, Charlie brandished the wine's label in front of Maeve. "Chateau Mont Bleu, Luke's winery." After opening the bottle, he handed Luke the cork and splashed a taste in his glass.

Luke breathed in its bouquet as he swirled the silky, deep-red liquid. Then sipping, he rolled the wine over his tongue. "I detect tones of cherry, dried fig, and cedar, with just a *trace* of dill." His tone tongue-in-cheek, he winked.

"My, what a developed palate you have, sir." Charlie's smile broadened as he poured a glass for Maeve and refilled Luke's. "The beef will be out in a minute."

"Thanks." Luke lifted his glass. "To meeting new kin."

"I'll drink to that." She clinked glasses and inhaled before sipping the tempranillo.

"Well, what do you think?" He watched her lips, still

red from the wine.

She sipped again. "Full-bodied, yet light...delicious."

"Glad you like it." He breathed a sigh, then gave a self-conscious laugh. "Guess I take wine personally."

"What do you mean?"

"Just realized I was holding my breath, waiting for your verdict." His sniff passed for a laugh. "Apparently, I confuse people's opinion of me with my wine."

"I can relate. Wine's your career. You're not confusing the two. You're *fusing* your results to your self-esteem."

"What are you in your spare time? A psychologist?" Relaxing, he leaned back.

"Far from it. For the past five years, I've done nothing but push myself, always trying to prove myself, yet never quite measuring up." She snickered. "Now that I've mustered out of the Army, I have to ask myself, where's that drive gotten me? What do I have to show for it?"

So, she has self-doubts, too. "You did what you had to do—kept on keeping on, and it's gotten you to this point—gotten you *here.*" He tapped the table for emphasis. "For that, I'm glad." Recognizing a kindred soul, he held out his glass. "To persistence."

"You mean, pigheadedness." Her smile crooked, she clinked glasses.

A server set a basket of warm sourdough bread on the table, its sharp, yeasty scent rising with the steam.

"Bread?" Luke offered her the basket.

"No thanks." Shaking her head, she paused while Charlie placed individual cassoulets before them.

"Smells wonderful." Luke glanced at the buttery

mashed potatoes piped around the terra-cotta bowl's edge, then closed his eyes to better appreciate the rich meld of aromas: beef brisket, pearl onions, cremini mushrooms, and hickory-smoked bacon.

"Let me know if you need anything." Charlie topped off their wine and, with a friendly nod, stepped away.

"I don't know whether to take a picture or dig in." Maeve leaned over the steaming dish and breathed in its bouquet. "My mouth's watering, but the presentation's perfect."

"Don't stand on ceremony. Enjoy." Leading by example, Luke speared a brisket cube and popped it in his mouth. "Melts on your tongue." He ate leisurely, savoring the textures of the velvety mashed potatoes and *al dente* chewiness of the fork-tender brisket as much as the stew's taste.

She tried a forkful and groaned. "Delicious." Smiling, she raised her glass. "I'd like to propose a toast for this fabulous meal. May neighbors respect you, trouble neglect you, angels protect you, and heaven accept you."

After clinking glasses, he leaned forward and cupped his mouth with his hand. "I have a confession to make."

"Why are you whispering?"

"Since Charlie sells our wine exclusively, I feel obligated to bring in new customers."

Her eyes glistened beneath the chandelier's muted glow. "This restaurant doesn't need your help. The food is great." As she tipped back her head sipping her wine, her delicate neck arched from her sweater's cowl neckline.

His gaze traveled the length of her torso, and he

caught his breath at the swell of her breasts. Clearing his throat, he took a long draught of wine.

"You never finished telling me how you became a vintner." Stabbing a beef chunk, she attacked her food like a starving model.

"After graduation, I interned at a major winery—didn't pay much, but it gave me firsthand experience." He scooped a forkful of the beef.

"What kind of experience?" She met his gaze. "Specifically."

"Winery design, wine-processing technologies, fermentation, and my personal favorite"—he winked—"*flavor* chemistry. But the most important takeaway was what I learned about grapevine diseases."

"Why's that?" Her fork suspended mid-air, she paused, her green eyes wide.

"Because I learned how to prevent Pierce's Disease, which attacks grapevines from Florida to California. It's what destroyed my grandfather's vineyard."

"Pierce's Disease…never heard of it." She shook her head, her shiny hair swinging with each movement. "What causes it?"

"Insects spread the bacteria, and in my grandfather's case, sharpshooter leafhoppers destroyed his vines."

Her brow bunched. "If he knew Texas vineyards sat in the middle of this zone, why did he start a vineyard here?"

"Because…"

She speared another beef cube and used her teeth to slide it from her fork.

Her gesture was strangely arousing; he lost his train of thought. Then covering, he sipped his wine. "*Because* experts misled him into believing the area's high altitude and snowy winters would protect his vines from leafhoppers."

"How sad." Staring at her cassoulet, she seemed lost in thought. Then brightening, she leaned across the table. "How could he have prevented Pierce's Disease?"

"The industry's developed better practices and pesticides." He scowled at the irony. "If my grandfather knew in the seventies what I know now, he wouldn't have lost his shirt—or the vineyard."

She arched her left brow. "What are the workarounds?"

Is she interested or just being polite? "I won't bore you with details, but prevention boils down to pruning and pesticides."

Nodding, she peeked through her eyelashes. "So, you've hit upon the magic combination?"

He shrugged. "The proof is in the yield."

Shaking her head, she raised her glass. "The proof is in the *wine,* as this tempranillo attests. To your continued success."

"Thank you, ma'am." As he clinked glasses, he caught her gaze. "You mentioned you were headed to El Paso. What takes you there?"

"Originally, I was going to visit my grandmother." She shrugged. "But now I'm just relocating."

"Any particular…reason…?" *Person?* He left his words hanging.

Her smile distant, she shook her head. "No, I'm not seeing anyone if that's what you're asking."

"Glad to hear it." He leaned across the table. "Though it's hard to believe you aren't taken."

"I *was* engaged." Grimacing, she glanced at her plate before meeting his gaze. "But long story short, just when I mustered out, he was deployed. I was collateral damage."

"Wow." He sat back. "Three of the top five."

"Top five what?"

"Most stressful life events: leaving a job, moving, and ending a relationship."

"Never thought of it that way." She stared out the window as if lost in thought, then came to attention. "The storm's getting worse. All I see is white."

"You're not kidding. Visibility's zero." A groan escaped as he rubbed his chin. "Just wondering about the roads."

"Where do you live?"

"A couple miles from here"—his laugh was dry—"vertically."

"Maybe we should call it a night." She checked her watch. "If it weren't for me, you'd be safe at home."

"No worries." *Let's see where this evening leads.* "I'll be fine."

"I'd be responsible if anything happened to you." She slipped her arms through her vest. "Thank you for a lovely meal and terrific company, *but* you'd better leave before the storm gets any worse."

"Can I get you folks anything else? Coffee? Dessert?" Charlie set an open menu between them.

"Their coconut cream pie melts in your mouth." Luke appealed with a smile.

"Thanks, but I couldn't eat another mouthful." She shook her head. "Besides, we should leave, so you can beat the storm."

Hiding his disappointment behind a smile, he turned to the host. "You heard the lady."

"Here's your check."

"That was fast."

"In case you haven't noticed, you're my last customers."

"What?" Luke eyed the empty tables and booths before glancing at his watch. *How long have we been here?*

"Everyone else had the good sense to leave. You may be my supplier and best customer but *get out*"—Charlie laughed—"so I can lock up."

Chuckling, Luke placed several bills inside the folder.

"Be right back with your change."

"Keep it. It's the least I can do for keeping you late." Then standing, he offered her his hand. "Don't know about you, but I've been kicked out of better places than this." He winked. "Ready?"

****

Ready for what? My pulse spiked as he helped me to my feet. Despite meeting him just hours before, I liked his hand's warm grip around mine. I studied his profile as we crossed the room, taking in his long eyelashes, hint of sideburns, bristling five-o'clock shadow, and thick shock of hair that invited tousling.

His arm brushed mine as he opened the door.

Goose bumps broke out, then the blast of frigid wind sent chills up my spine. *Or was he the cause?*

Snow covered the courtyard in a thick mantle of white. Knee-deep drifts between the bistro and hotel hid the path, and beneath the snow was ice.

Sleet stung my eyes and burned my cheeks as the wind whipped at my hair.

"Whiteout." He draped his arm around my shoulders and guided me through the wet, driving snow.

I side-glanced. His lashes were so long, they caught snowflakes. "Somehow, the courtyard didn't seem as wide walking here as going back."

"Almost home."

"*I'm* almost home, but what about you?" I stared into the frenetic white. "I can barely see my feet. You can't drive in this storm."

"That's why they invented windshield wipers." He turned toward me with a grin.

Blaming myself, I drew a deep breath. "Seriously—"

"*Seriously*, here we are."

As he opened the door, the warm, dry heat of the hotel's cheery fireplace surrounded me. Inviting armchairs faced the open, stone hearth. "Why don't we sit by the fire until the storm passes?"

He glanced at the crackling fire, peeked out the door's window, and a slow smile lifted a corner of his mouth. "You talked me into it—just until the snow lets up—but first…" His dark eyes twinkling, he held up his index finger. "Back in a sec."

Where's he going? I peered through the window as he disappeared into the white.

Two minutes later, he returned with a bottle.

"Where'd you get that wine?"

"Never know when I'll have to make a delivery, so I keep a case in my pickup." The label facing me, he held up a bottle of cabernet sauvignon.

"Always prepared, huh?" I chuckled.

"Not really…no wine opener." Grinning, he turned to the desk clerk. "Do you have a corkscrew we could borrow?"

"Sure." The night clerk dug behind the desk and

produced an opener and two plastic cups. Then he offered a napkin-lined basket of cookies. "Help yourselves."

"Thanks." His hands full, Luke's dark eyes appealed for help.

Responding to his body language, I snatched two cookies with a napkin and set them on a tea table between overstuffed chairs in front of the fire. *What a cozy setting*. I dropped my guard, unwinding for the first time in months…years. "All the comforts of home."

"Home away from home." The wine cork came out with a pop.

While Luke poured, I got an idea. "Be right back."

I rushed to my room, grabbed the most dilapidated diary from the box, and caught my windblown reflection in the mirror. *Yikes*. After exchanging my puffy vest for a silky, merino-wool wrap, I ran a brush through my hair and added a touch of lipstick.

Five minutes later, I returned with a water-stained, antique composition book.

His gaze embraced me from head to toe as he rose to his feet.

Butterflies tickled the pit of my stomach, and I squirmed beneath his stare. "Thought you might like to page through one of Marianna's journals."

"I would, but first, a toast to new friends." He handed me a plastic glass as he raised his.

I tapped my glass against his with a nonmusical thud, then sipped the cabernet, rolling it over my tongue and letting it linger. "This cab's even better than the tempranillo."

"Thank you, ma'am. That's what I like to hear." He gestured to the armchairs. "Have a seat."

"I haven't sorted through the diaries yet, but this one looks the oldest."

Its stained, cloth covers unraveling, the notebook's narrow spine hung by a thread.

Though the disintegrating book had no market value, I cherished its sentimental value. *This belonged to Grandma and, before her, Marianna.* I placed the journal in his hands as gently as if it were eggshell art.

He opened the front cover, smiled, and lightly traced a child's penciled scrawl. *"Marianna Rodriguez.* My great-great-grandmother."

Beneath the childish print, *Mrs. Ramon Garcia* was written in an ornate cursive font.

His eyes glistening in the firelight, he turned the lined, yellowed page. *"November sixteenth, eighteen-ninety-nine, Castolon, Texas. Henrietta discovered cinnabar."*

"Seventeen."

"What?"

"Page seventeen." Pointing to the ink stamp on each page, I thumbed through the notebook. "The numbers are consecutive, but they start at seventeen. What happened to the first sixteen pages?"

"Maybe they were so worn, they fell out of the binding." He rubbed the edge of the crumbling, dog-eared page between his fingers.

"The stitching's loose, but I don't think they fell out." I fingered through the missing pages' straight-edged stubs. "See the neatly sliced edges? Someone used a ruler to tear these off."

"Wonder why?"

****

Marianna Garcia examined the blood-red crystal. As

the mid-morning sun poured through the window, the mineral lit up like frozen fire.

"Where'd you find that stone?" Ramon hung his hat on the wall peg, gave his wife a peck on the cheek, and sat at the table.

"Henrietta flew the coop again this morning. I found her near the arroyo, sitting on this stone like she was hatching eggs." Chuckling, Marianna handed him the crystal before ladling three-bean chili into terracotta bowls.

"She's broody." Studying the rock, he spoke over his shoulder.

"*Loco*, you mean." She set lunch on the pine-plank table and sat across from her husband. "But she made a discovery."

"What do you mean?" He handed back the stone.

"I think that's cinnabar, though I've never seen it crystalized before." Gesturing to it with a nod, she passed him the basket of warm corn tortillas. "Usually it's a dull, brick-red, so I'm not sure."

He helped himself to a tortilla, then spooning thick chili on it, rolled it into a *taco*. "What are you going to do with it?"

"Add it to my rock collection." Shrugging, Marianna glanced across the table. "Why?"

****

Luke sipped his cabernet before resuming. "*November twenty-third.*" He chuckled. "*Treatment of chicken lice. Paint the upper edges of roost perches with small amount of nicotine-sulfate.*"

"Wait a minute." Maeve's fingertips grazed his wrist. "Did you skip several entries?"

"No."

"Are the pages stuck together?"

"Nope." Turning the tattered page, he shook his head and pointed to the ink stamp. "Page eighteen."

"That's *it?* Marianna skipped a week, then left a cure for chicken lice?"

"That's all she wrote." He held the journal closer to the dim firelight. "See?"

Maeve's Irish-green eyes danced in the flames' reflection as she read silently, then glanced up. "Marianna doesn't say much the next day, either."

"Why don't you read a while?" Swallowing a smile, he handed her the diary, rested his head against the back of the chair, and watched her bow-shaped lips move as she read aloud. *How would those feel?*

"*November twenty-fifth. Henrietta flew the coop again.*"

Maeve smiled as she turned the page and glanced from the diary. "Finally—longer entries.

"*November thirtieth. Today, the storekeeper dropped by with an offer on the ranch. Told him no.*

"*December second. Ramon surprised me on my Saint's Day with a pendant made from the cinnabar. When I told him it was too expensive, he called it an early Christmas present.*

"*December fourth. Mr. Barnes stopped by with another offer.*"

****

"We're not selling." Ramon exchanged a glance with Marianna. "This is our home."

"Don't force my hand." Teeth gritted, Mr. Barnes slammed out the door.

"What's he talking about?" Concerned by the man's tone, Marianna turned to Ramon.

"Remember the day you found the stone?"

"You mean, the day Henrietta found it." She fingered the pendant at her neck.

"I'd seen necklaces at the general store, so I asked Mr. Barnes if the vendor could wire wrap the crystal."

"So that's how you arranged it." She grinned at his ingenuity, then puckered her brow. "But what's this have to do with him wanting our land?"

"When he saw the cinnabar, he opened his ledger and reminded me how he's carried us on his books."

"We'll pay our bills at harvest, just like all the other ranchers." Marianna stiffened at the man's gall. "Did you tell him we have good crops of corn and cotton planted?"

"Yes, and I told him the goats have started dropping their lambs. Cabrito sales will cover the bills until July, when the corn comes in."

"And…?"

"He said July is five months off and asked how I had 'money for trinkets' when we're three months behind in bills, and the taxes are due. Then he slammed the ledger, saying he *tries* not to foreclose…but if we squander money instead of paying our bills, he'll be forced to reconsider."

She swallowed hard. *He wouldn't evict us, would he?*

"If it weren't for the boll weevils, we wouldn't be in debt." Ramon's shoulders slumped.

"The cabrito and corn will get us through. We'll be fine!" Marianna flashed a smile, but a chill seeped into her bones. *Won't we?*

****

"*December twelfth. Henrietta flew the coop again. This time, a chicken hawk got her—found her feathers at the arroyo.*"

Maeve clicked her teeth. "Poor Henrietta.

"*Also found footprints and churned-up caliche. Someone's been digging on our property.*

"*December twenty-fifth. Tried the recipe for Simple Sponge Cake. Beat six eggs long and well with a teaspoon salt. Then slowly add one cup sugar, and in the same manner one cup flour. Flavor to suit the taste.*"

Shaking her head, Maeve glanced from the journal. "No oven temperature or baking time. I'd be lost.

"*January fourth, nineteen hundred, Castolon, Texas. Mr. Barnes stopped by with a final offer. Said he'd be back in the morning for our answer.*"

"What a persistent son of a gun." Snickering at the man's relentlessness, Luke topped off her glass.

"Thanks." Maeve raised it in a toast. "To Marianna's resistance—hope she doesn't cave."

Luke studied her as he clinked glasses. The flickering firelight lent her skin a soft, rosy glow, accenting the red highlights of her tawny hair. Then he settled back in his chair, enjoying the camaraderie. "Want me to read a while, or are you okay?"

"I'm fine." Her lips curled in a smile. "Besides, I'm curious what happens to Marianna.

"*January fifth. Mr. Barnes returned this morning with Mr. Holden. When we refused to sell, they threatened us.*"

****

"I've purchased your debt from Mr. Barnes, and I'm within my rights to collect the full balance—forty-seven dollars and seventy-nine cents."

"We'll pay when everyone else does, Mr. Holden, just as soon as we bring in the harvest." Ramon straightened his shoulders.

"You'll pay *today*." The corners of the man's thin lips dipped in a sneer. "Or I place a lien on your property."

His forehead wrinkling, Ramon repeated his installment plan. "Cabrito sales will cover the bills until July—"

"Payment is due *today*…with interest." Holden peered down his nose.

"We can make monthly payments against it." Marianna twisted her apron's ruffle between her fingers. "Weekly, if you like, now that—"

"You've been in arrears for three months." Mr. Barnes gestured toward her pendant. "And what did you do when you had a few dollars? Spent them on trinkets."

"Before the boll weevils destroyed the cotton, we weren't in debt." Marianna bristled. "And now that lambing season's here, money's coming in again. We can make weekly payments until the corn's ripe. Then we'll pay you in full."

"*Not* July." Mr. Holden jabbed the air with his finger. "*Not* next week." He jabbed again. "*Today*. Pay me in full today—with interest—or I'm placing a lien on your property."

"Don't you use that tone with my wife." Ramon jumped between them, shielding her as he shoved the men out the door. "Get out of our home. Both of you!"

Mr. Holden threw the letter in his face. "These aren't idle words. They're my *rights*. And you—"

"Get out and stay out." Ramon pushed the men onto the porch and bolted the lock.

Holden shouted through the door. "You haven't heard the last of this."

Marianna froze until the porch boards creaked with the men's retreating steps. Then she ran into Ramon's arms. "What'll we do?"

****

"*January sixth. I woke Ramon early with a solution.*"

****

"They want the cinnabar, not our ranch."

"What?" Ramon rubbed the sleep from his eyes.

"They just want the mineral rights—not the land." Marianna jumped to her feet. "Get dressed."

****

"Mr. Barnes, we'd like a moment of your time." Marianna straightened her shoulders.

"Come to your senses, have you?" The storekeeper smirked.

"We've come to a decision." She tossed her chin. "Do you have a place to speak privately?"

"Fetch Mr. Holden from the hotel." Grabbing the ledger, he barked orders over his shoulder.

"Yes, sir." His clerk scrambled from behind the counter.

"This way." Mr. Barnes led them to the inner office, plunked himself behind an oversized desk, and opened the ledger. "Do you have the forty-seven dollars and seventy-nine cents?"

Marianna exchanged glances with her husband.

"Well? Be quick about it." He tapped his fingers on the wide, deep oak desk. "I'm a busy man."

"We prefer to wait for Mr. Holden." Uninvited, she sat across from him.

Following her lead, Ramon pulled up a chair.

Minutes later, Mr. Holden joined them. "Got the

money?"

"Let's lay our cards on the table." She flashed a smile. "You don't want the ranch. You want the cinnabar. Why buy the cow when we'd happily sell you the milk?"

****

"I don't recall any family stories about a mine." Luke leaned across the lamp table and peered at the journal.

"Here." Maeve passed him the diary before snuggling into the upholstered chair. "Your turn to strain your eyes." Then after a languid stretch, she leaned back.

"Tired?"

"Nope, just relaxing."

"Maybe I should let—"

"No, I want to see how this works out." She came to attention. "Don't you?"

****

Marianna swallowed, summoning her courage. "We'll lease you the minerals under our land, Mr. Holden."

"Why should I pay you royalties, when I can buy your property outright?"

"Simple." She met his jeer. "Because our ranch isn't for sale."

"Then I'll place a lien against your property." He snickered.

"A lien would cost you legal fees, as well as time…" She glanced at her husband, gambling she was right.

"What makes you think time is of any concern?" His pupils became tiny black flecks.

"Because of your sudden demands *after* Mr. Barnes learned of cinnabar on our land." She stared him down.

"Coincidence." He scowled at the storekeeper before turning back.

"I don't believe in coincidences."

"And I don't believe in leases." Mr. Holden turned to leave. "I *do* not, and I *will* not pay royalties. Good day."

"Since we have a stalemate"—Ramon sprang from his chair—"I suggest a compromise."

Mr. Holden turned. "I'm listening."

Chapter 3

"Brrr." Luke shivered from the draft created as the wind howled down the chimney.

Maeve's breathing was steady and shallow.

"Are you awake? Maybe I should let—"

"No, I'm just resting my eyes." She gave him a sleepy smile. "Don't you want to know what Marianna does?"

"Yes, but you seem tired."

"I'm fine."

Luke grinned.

"What?" Maeve's eyelids flickered.

"You're dozing. I really should be—"

"No, I'm just relaxing." Rotating her shoulders, she yawned. "The fire's so cozy, and listening to you read Marianna's diary, I can visualize her defending their rights." Waving him on, she leaned back. "Keep reading."

Over the wind whistling through the chimney and the fire crackling and hissing, Luke detected another rhythmic sound. He glanced from the journal to Maeve and smothered a chuckle. *She's snoring—if I can call it that*.

Her rosebud lips were slightly parted, and she gave a faint sigh each time she exhaled. Her body armor at rest as she slept, her face was as peaceful as moonlight on freshly fallen snow.

Snow... Careful not to wake her, he crossed to the window and peeked out.

Gale-force winds whipped the blustering snow, driving it into steep drifts that swallowed the hedges and hid the sidewalks. A car parked along Main Street was nearly buried beneath a white mantle.

Thinking of his truck, Luke groaned. *How long will it take to dig out?* He tiptoed behind her chair and into the lobby, where the night clerk watched captions on a muted television. "Any weather updates?"

The man glanced from the screen. "Blizzard's worse. Between the snow, icy roads, and a three-car collision on route seventeen, all highways are shut down."

"Doesn't look like I'm getting home tonight." Luke stifled a sigh. "Got any rooms left?"

"Nope. Sorry." The clerk shook his head. "We're booked solid."

Luke ran his hand across his chin. Then he gestured to the armchairs with his thumb. "Mind if I camp out 'til the roads clear?"

"Under the circumstances? Not a problem."

"Thanks." He started toward the sitting room and nearly bumped into Maeve, leaning against the wall. "Sorry, didn't mean to wake you."

"You didn't." She tossed her chin. "I was cat-napping."

"Right." He compared her guarded veneer to her sleeping-beauty persona. *Which is closer to her true self?*

"Couldn't help overhearing." Gesturing toward the clerk with her chin, she grimaced. "I'm responsible for you being out tonight—"

"No." He shook his head. "This is just a freak

storm."

"You don't have to sleep in a chair." She took a deep breath and gave a quick, tight-lipped smile. "My room has two queen beds, and you're welcome to one of 'em."

Unsure of the extent of her invitation, he did a double take.

"Just so we understand each other, this is a bunk, a place to sack out. Period. Amen." She spoke in a low-pitched, no-nonsense voice. "Nothing more, so don't get any—"

"Got it." He covered his disappointment with a laugh. "Thanks, I appreciate the offer, but I'll be fine dozing by the fire."

"Hey, I've bivouacked with soldiers in Afghanistan. I don't mind sharing a room. We do what's necessary under extenuating circumstances." Shrugging, she glanced at the door. "And this blizzard qualifies." Her face relaxed into a smile.

Her offer tempting; he compared sitting up all night to stretching out in a bed. Then he glimpsed the clerk. *Her room's right across from the front desk.*

"If you're worried about my reputation, don't be. I'm just passing through. Besides, people would talk even if they caught us napping by the fire." Jerking her thumb toward the sitting room, she laughed, the sound like sleigh bells tinkling on a crisp, wintry night.

What is it about her that conjures thoughts of other times—other eras?

"Look, if you're afraid of small-town gossip, we'll wait 'til the clerk steps out." Her eyes glistening merrily, she grinned.

On cue, a microwave beeped, and the clerk slipped into the back room.

"Quick! The coast is clear." Turning, she grabbed the wine and glasses, strode toward her room, unlocked the door, and waved him in.

He swallowed hard. *Now what?*

****

Was this a dumb idea? Second guessing myself, I closed the door. *What would Cody say?* Exasperated that he crossed my mind, I sighed. *Who cares? What I do is none of his business.*

Luke crossed to the far end of the room, clasping the diary to his chest like a shield. Shifting from one foot to the other, he studied the décor as his gaze moved from the door to the window, to the vintage desk, to the beds.

He looks as nervous as I feel. My knuckles white from clutching the handle, I hugged the door as I mentally tallied his actions. After stopping to help me, he called the police, gave me a lift into town, found me a hotel room, and bought me dinner. *If anyone's trustworthy,* he *is.* Relaxing, I let go the doorknob and stepped into the room.

He took a step back, bumped against the desk, and caught the teetering lamp moments before it crashed to the floor. "Sorry."

"No worries." I pointed at the windows. "Hey, a storm's raging outside. We're dealing with extenuating circumstances." *I already said that...* What started as a chuckle came out a high-pitched giggle. "We're both adults. We're just being sensible."

"Absolutely." He nodded emphatically. "Consenting—" He cleared his throat. "*Sensible* adults."

"Have a seat." I gestured to the desk chair. "And since you're holding the journal, why don't you read another entry or two?" As I backed toward the chair nearest the door, I realized I was still holding the bottle and glasses. "Want any more wine?"

"Actually…yes." He tugged his jacket into place, zipping, then immediately unzipping it. "I could use it."

His tone had a self-conscious ring, and I chuckled, empathizing. "So could I." Handing him one, I filled both glasses and raised mine in a toast. His thoughtfulness that afternoon reminded me of a story. "Be the sun, not the blizzard."

"What?" His glass mid-air, he cocked his head.

"I read about a traveler stranded in a blizzard and how his host's hospitality impressed him. Can't recall the details, but the moral was 'Be the sun, not the blizzard.' "

"Good words to live by." He laughed deep in his throat as he clunked his plastic glass against mine, sipped, then opened the journal. "How much of *this* story do you remember while you were catnapping?"

"Ramon had just suggested a compromise, and Mr. Holden was listening." Pretending to be insulted, I arched my brow. "Fooled you, didn't I?"

"So, you *were* listening." He made a mock bow as he took his seat. "My abject apologies for doubting you."

I settled into a chair and closed my eyes, letting the journal's entries come alive in my imagination.

****

"Since you won't lease the minerals under our land, Mr. Holden, I recommend—"

"You're in no position—"

"That we sell you the plat south of the arroyo but keep the tillable land to the north." Ramon caught his wife's glance. "That way, you get what you want, and we keep our ranch."

Tweaking his mustache, Holden leaned forward. "How much you want for it?"

****

"*January seventh. Sold the south section. Own the ranch free and clear.*

"*January twenty-ninth. Can't keep anything down except Mother's Soft Gingerbread.*

"*February fourteenth. Fainted while chopping wood.*

"*March fourth. I may be pregnant.*"

A crying baby yanked me from a semi-doze.

"Wonder who the baby was?" Luke cocked his head.

"You heard it, too?" Half-asleep, I blinked.

"Heard what?"

"The crying baby." I shook my head to clear it. *I must've nodded off.* "What baby are you talking about?"

"My great-great-grandmother's." He tapped his index finger against his lips. "Bet Aunt Rosie knows."

"Good…" Drowsy, I felt myself slipping into a twilit dream of gingerbread, Henrietta, and crying babies…

"If your eyelids were any heavier, you'd fall flat on your face."

I woke with a jerk. "I'm just resting my eyes."

"You're dozing again." He chuckled. "Why don't we call it a night?"

"It's a night." Slaphappy, I grinned.

"Seriously, let's get some shut-eye."

"I'm not tired." Like a stubborn child refusing to go to bed, I shook my head while hiding a yawn. "I want to hear what happens to Marianna." I kicked off my shoes, lifted my knees to my chest as I curled into the chair, then rested my cheek on my hand. "Keep reading."

"Five more minutes." Wearing a stern frown, he made a growling sound in his throat. "Then I'm hitting the hay. Which reminds me. Which bed's mine?"

My eyes snapped open, and I pointed to the one nearest the window. "That one." *Mine's closer to the door.* I planned escape routes as I swung my feet on the floor. "Want me to read a while?"

"Sure." He crossed the room and handed me the diary. "Reading might keep you awake."

"I wasn't asleep!" Chuckling at the banter, I turned the page.

"*April third. Told Ramon the good news.*"

****

"You're sure?"

"Yes." Marianna nodded. "I've suspected for months, but now, I'm positive."

Ramon lifted her in the air and twirled her around.

Her skirt and petticoats flying, she laughed, glad she had delayed sharing the news until she was certain. "We've been disappointed before, but *this* time…" She swallowed to keep her lips from trembling. The premature birth and miscarriage still haunted her, and after two unsuccessful years of trying, she had all but given up hope of having a baby.

He took her in his arms and held her close.

Responding to his tender grip, she drew strength. "*This* time, I'm sure."

****

"*September first. Brought in a good crop of cotton. No boll weevils.*

"*October fourth. Gave birth to Ramona, a beautiful, healthy girl.*

"*October eleventh. Ramon carved our initials in a*

cottonwood near the spring."
****

A week after their daughter's birth, Marianna and Ramon strolled about their property.

Dressed in their autumn finery, the cottonwoods' buttery yellow and gold leaves rustled in the evening breeze, sounding like rain on a tin roof. The Texas sage nearby exploded with purple and mauve blossoms, perfuming the air with their spicy-sweet fragrance.

Her heart bursting with love for her husband and new daughter, Marianna breathed in the scene as she inhaled the scented air.

"Let's remember this moment." Ramon unsheathed his hunting knife, carved the initials M & R into a tree, and etched a heart around them.
****

"I wonder if they're still there."

"If who are still there?" Luke opened his droopy eyes and blinked.

"Not who—*what*—Marianna and Ramon's initials."

"Why don't we find out?"

"You mean, look for their old homestead?" Scrunching my eyes, I tried to remember the settings of my grandmother's bedtime stories. "Castolon is nowhere near here, is it?"

"It's only two hours south in what's *now* Big Bend National Park."

Physically connect with what I thought were fairytales? The idea appealed to my sense of family as much as my taste for adventure. "What time do we leave?"
****

The next morning, Luke woke to voices outside the

door. *Who's that?* He threw off the covers and sprang from the bed. *Why am I dressed? Where…?* Half asleep, he glanced about the room. Then he spotted Maeve in the next bed, and the evening's events whooshed back.

Tiptoeing into the bath, he eased the door shut to avoid its squeak. After a quick shower, he found a toothbrush and razor in the hotel's amenities, brushed his teeth, and shaved.

The hinges objected as he opened the bathroom door, and he froze until Maeve's chest rhythmically rose and fell with each breath. Then catlike, he slunk to the window to check the weather.

Outside, the sun shone brightly. Clear blue skies above, the snow-topped peaks of the Lincoln Mountains glistened in the distance.

The snowplows had cleared Main Street but buried the parked car in salty slush.

That poor owner. Then suppressing a groan, he estimated the shoveling it would take to dig out his truck.

He scribbled a note from the hotel's pad and stuck it in the mirror's corner.

Luke—*Gone home to change. Back at eight to see the homestead—*

Barefoot, he tiptoed past Maeve's sleeping form, and her artless beauty stopped him. Her face as serene as dawn on a still lake, she seemed to shed her military exterior when she slept. Her brow untroubled, she looked as vulnerable as a newborn, and a protective impulse overtook him. *Good thing I happened along when I did yesterday.*

Boots in hand, he cracked the door, checking if the clerk stood guard at the front desk. All clear, he popped into the hall.

"Luke?"

He recognized the voice, and the hairs on his neck bristled. "Bea."

"What're you doing here?" Her raised eyebrows silently reproached as she bobbed her head left and right, rubbernecking to see into the room.

He shut the door behind him, accidentally slamming it. *So much for a silent retreat.* Then he leaned against the wall to pull on his boots.

"Isn't February a little early to go barefoot?" Her cold eyes glittered. "What *are* you doing here?"

"Family research." With a tight-lipped smile, he stepped toward the exit.

"Research?" Her posture shrieking, *I don't think so,* she planted her legs wide and grabbed his arm, blocking his exit.

As her manicured talons dug into his flannel shirt, his back stiffened.

"Your Aunt Rosie is the family historian." Her grip loosening, her fingers slid down his arm and interlaced with his. "Why not ask her instead of sneaking around hotel rooms?"

"Why don't you mind your own business?" Shrugging her off, he stepped around her. *Great.* His shoulders tensed as her gaze burned into his back. *Now the rumors will fly.*

"Have a good night's rest?" The night clerk's sly grin suggested more.

Luke swept by with a noncommittal grunt, caught in the man's trap no matter how he answered.

"They plowed this morning." The clerk raised his voice, calling after him. "Bea made it through the roads okay…"

Luke pictured her wheedling the details from the man, then twisting the facts.

****

The door slammed like a detonated bomb.

IED strike! Snatching my knife from beneath the pillow, I vaulted from bed and scanned the area for terrorists. *Oh, yeah.* As I got my bearings, I gulped air. *This is Texas, not Afghanistan. Adapting to civilian life may take longer than I thought.*

Then the night's details slammed through my mind. *Luke! Where…?* Glancing from his empty bed to the note, I caught myself smiling in the mirror. *What am I grinning about?*

I analyzed my reflection. *Meeting Luke yesterday…seeing him again today…* and *exploring one of Grandma's "fairytales." What's not to smile about?*

I studied the knife in my hands—a precaution against sharing a room with a stranger. *Glad I didn't need this.* Then, eyeing the clock, I hopped in the shower.

Steam hung thick in the bathroom as the water vapor fogged the air.

Suddenly, a child's laughter penetrated the haze.

"Who's there?" I peeked from behind the shower curtain into the billowing steam.

Another high-pitched giggle—like a little girl muffling her laughter—invaded my privacy.

"Hello?" My skin crawling, I turned off the water, but only a hollow drip, drip, drip echoed in the drain.

"Anyone there?" I reached for a towel and stepped from the shower into the steamy room. A smiley face materialized on the mirror as condensation dripped from it like transparent blood.

The hinges squeaked as the bathroom door cracked

open.

"Luke?" *He doesn't have a key.* "Hello…?" I kicked open the door and burst into the bedroom.

Silence.

Unnerved, I scoured the room, testing the locked door and windows. Then crouching, I checked beneath the beds.

Nothing moved or seemed out of place.

"Who's there?"

****

He pulled into the same parking spot he had left an hour earlier and texted Maeve as he entered the hotel.

Luke—*I'm in the lobby*—

"Good morning." The day clerk smiled from behind the desk.

Relieved to see her instead of the night clerk, he returned the smile. "Morning."

"Here you are, Miss Mamie, cream and two sugars." Her syrupy voice preceding her, Bea emerged from the back room, carrying two mugs. As she handed one to the clerk, she stopped short. "Luke, what a pleasant surprise…*again*. Can I interest you in a cup of coffee?" She took a sip before offering him the mug, leaving a lipstick kiss on the rim. "Just the way you like it…hot and sweet."

Her voice like satin, she all but purred. Recognizing the tone, he suppressed the urge to roll his eyes. "No, thanks."

"What brings you…back?"

Though her lips curled in a smile, the pupils of her eyes narrowed like a cat's ready to pounce.

The door opened across the hall, and Maeve emerged in cropped hiking boots and tight black jeans that hugged her bottom.

"Morning." Her face brightening as she met his gaze, she slipped her arms through her vest.

"You must be Luke's…cousin." Sprinting around the desk, Bea held out her hand. "I'm Beatrice Perkins but call me Bea. Everyone does."

Maeve's gaze again brushed his before she shook hands. "Maeve Jackson."

"Any friend of Luke's is a friend of mine." Wearing a wide smile, Bea sidled next to him, linking arms. "We're all one big happy family here."

His spine stiffening, he stepped toward the door as discreetly as possible.

Bea snatched at his hand, her long nails tearing the keys from his grip while she grazed his palm.

As the keys clattered to the floor, he stooped to retrieve them, pulling away.

"A little edgy this morning, are we?" Her eyes narrow slits, Bea smiled sweetly. "Maybe you didn't sleep well last night." Not missing a beat, she turned to the newcomer with a lipstick smile. "How long will you be staying?"

"Sorry to interrupt, ladies, but we're running late." He opened the door. "All set?"

"Yup." Zipping her vest, Maeve nodded. "Just as—"

"Not leaving so soon, I hope!" Her smile painted on, Bea stepped between them, blocking the exit.

"Excuse me." Maeve arched her brow as she shifted sideways, squeezing past the woman.

****

Bea sulked at the window.

"What's that about?" I took a deep breath, the brisk

mountain air constricting my lungs. When I exhaled, my breath steamed.

"Don't mind her." He shook his head. "Some people are territorial even on neutral turf." He grimaced as he opened the truck's door and offered me a hand.

"Thanks." Appreciating the boost, I pushed off from his palm, propelling myself onto the front seat. The tingle of his touch shot up my arm and catapulted down my spine like a hot flash.

He hopped in the driver's side. "Thought we could check on your car, then grab a bite to eat."

"Sounds good. I could use a cup of coffee." *Or a cold shower.* Despite the frigid temperatures, I unzipped my vest as I studied his profile. His five-o'clock shadow was already shading his strong jawline, reminding me how I'd studied his profile last night in the moonlight.

After showering for bed, I'd slipped my knife under my pillow, then crawled between the sheets. Uncomfortable about sharing my room with a stranger, I lay awake, alert for footsteps or the slightest creak of his bed, but only his steady breathing broke the silence. Against the moonlight streaming through the window, I watched the shallow rise and fall of his chest and fought the temptation to brush his curly tendrils of hair from his forehead.

What's his relationship with Bea? Just as I was about to ask, he pulled into the auto shop.

He rolled down the windows and called to Smitty. "What's the good word?"

"Not good." The mechanic wiped his hands on an oily rag as he came around to the passenger side. "You definitely sheared off the exhaust system and damaged the oil pan, alternator, cooling system, brake lines, fuel lines, and drive shafts. But what I'm worried about is the transmission and steering."

"What *isn't* damaged?" I managed a weak smile.

"The trunk." Smitty chuckled. "Have you called your insurance company?"

"Not yet." Glimpsing Luke, I winced. In the excitement, insurance had slipped my mind.

"You may be looking at a totaled vehicle." Smitty pointed to my car on the lift.

So much for getting to El Paso any time soon.

"When will you know the damages?" Luke's voice splintered my thoughts.

The man shook his head. "Not 'til the parts arrive to test if the transmission and steering work. Then if more repairs are needed, it's up to the insurer whether to give the go-ahead."

"Thanks." *How much will a replacement car cost?* I weighed the guesstimate against my bank balance. *And how could I forget to call the adjuster? What was I thinking?* A glance at Luke answered my question. *I wasn't. Girl, get your head on straight.*

Excusing myself, I jumped from the cab and called my insurance company. Five minutes later, I hoisted myself back in the cab. "The adjuster will stop by this afternoon to assess the damage. The good news is she's already received the police report."

"Nothing more you can do at this point." Luke shrugged. "How 'bout breakfast?"

Worried about transportation and car payments, all I could muster was a detached nod. "Sure."

"Hey." He gently shook my shoulder. "This'll work out whatever way it's meant." His eyes twinkled. "What was your phrase? To everything, there is a purpose."

Is he poking fun? I peered into his chocolate-brown eyes. *Or trying to cheer me?* His reassuring smile put my doubts to rest.

"Thanks." *What would I have done if he hadn't come along yesterday?* Appetite returning, I gave him a twisted grin. "Breakfast sounds great."

"I know a terrific *taqueria*. Like Mexican food?"

"*Love* it." My stomach growled at the thought. "I haven't had authentic *huevos rancheros* since the last time I visited Grandma."

Ten minutes later, we sat across from each other in the café. Drinking freshly brewed coffee from an oversized cup, I breathed in the rich, nutty aroma as I scanned the décor.

Rows of low-hanging, multicolored *papel picado* lined the ceiling, and each time a person walked beneath, the tissue-papers fluttered. The glossy walls were painted a vivid mustard yellow above their red-brick wainscoting. Colorful, relief-painted chairs portrayed macaws, calla lilies, wide-brimmed sombreros, saguaro cactus, and Mariachi musicians.

How good to be back in a taqueria. I inhaled the scents wafting from the kitchen: sautéed garlic and onions, cilantro, oregano, cumin, and chilies. The mouthwatering aromas triggered memories of past meals with Grandma.

"They make their own tortillas and tamales here."

"No wonder they are such a booming business on a snowy morning." The door chimed as two more customers walked in and another left. "That door's open more than it's shut." I chuckled at the counter's steady queue.

"Lucas." Holding a tray piled high with empty

dishes, a grinning, gray-haired woman in her early sixties paused at our table. "What brings you out this snowy morning?"

"A cousin to taste your cooking."

"Cousin?" She set down the platter as she regarded me. "Why don't I know you?"

"Aunt Rosie, I'd like you to meet Maeve Jackson."

Running the name over her tongue, the woman tilted her head as she glanced into space. Then a light flashed in her dark eyes. "You're not related to Milly Taylor, are you?"

"Yes." I gasped, shocked to find another connection. "She's my grandmother."

"Call me Aunt Rosie." Holding out her arms, she stepped toward me.

I stood to return the woman's hug.

"I met Milly at a family reunion"—letting go the embrace, Rosie paused, again glancing into space— "maybe ten years ago, but I remember her well. She wore glasses, wound her long hair in a bun, and mentioned a granddaughter named Maeve." Her lined face warmed in a smile. "How is she?"

"Grandma passed away two weeks ago." Swallowing the sudden lump in my throat, I forced a tight smile.

"I'm so sorry for your loss." The lines deepened on Rosie's forehead before a sympathetic smile brightened her face. "What brings you to Fort Lincoln?"

Luke caught my gaze. "Maeve's researching her family tree."

"You don't say. Bring her to supper tomorrow night." Rosie brushed her hands as if that were that. "Let her meet the rest of the family."

"From what I understand, we're only related by marriage. I'm from—"

"Cadence and Ben's side." Living up to her name, Rosie flashed another smile. "Like I said, meet the *rest* of the family."

A warmth began in my chest, thawing parts I didn't know had iced over. "What can I bring?"

Chapter 4

Supper…with Bea there… Luke took a sharp intake of air. *Knowing her, she'll 'slip' about me leaving Maeve's room. Doesn't matter that nothing happened. Bea gets too much pleasure skewing facts, then watching people squirm.*

The waitress delivered their orders.

"That's my cue to let you young people enjoy breakfast. See you both tomorrow." Rosie retrieved her tray, then navigated the steady streams of customers coming and going, all the while trading pleasantries and balancing the overloaded platter in one hand.

Maeve leaned across the table. "Your aunt's such a warm person."

"She's a born nurturer—always feeding or encouraging someone, whether here or at home."

"And she makes it look easy."

"She invented multi-tasking." He eyed his plate of grilled chorizo, crispy corn tortillas, eggs sunny-side up, homemade guacamole, and refried black beans, all lightly sprinkled with crumbled *cotija* cheese. "How are your *huevos rancheros?*"

"Picture perfect and they smell heavenly."

"Dig in." His stomach rumbling, he inhaled the intoxicating aromas of his *chilaquiles verdes*, the lemony floral fragrance of cilantro balancing the sausage's spicy scent. "Nobody cooks like Aunt Rosie."

Her mouth full, Maeve groaned and nodded, enjoying her breakfast.

His fork poised mid-air, he opened his mouth to speak, then stifled a sigh.

She cocked her head. "Something on your mind?"

"Yeah." He gave a wry chuckle. "About last night—"

"Everything all right?" The waitress leaned between them as she refilled their coffee cups.

Flinching, Maeve clattered her fork against the dish.

"Delicious. Thanks." He nodded, waiting until the waitress moved to the next table. "You and I know nothing happened, but—"

"Then let's keep it our secret."

"If only it were that simple. This morning, Bea caught me leaving your room." He stifled an uneasy sigh. "At the very least, she and the night clerk suspect..." Growling in his throat, he shook his head. "There's no delicate way to put this."

"I get the picture." Her smile was crooked. "Like you said, nothing happened. The roads were closed, and we did the only sensible thing. That's all there was to it."

Was it? He remembered faking sleep when she emerged from the bath, smelling of lemon and vanilla. More than part of him hoped she would choose his bed, but she had slipped into hers. *Fantasies don't count.* He repositioned himself on the chair. "You're absolutely right, that's all it was, but I wanted you to know in case...*anyone*...brings it up."

"*Anyone*...do you mean Bea?" She arched her brow. "Which reminds me, why did you call her territorial? Are you two seeing each other?"

Her directness startling, he ran his hand across his

mouth. "No."

"That wasn't my impression." Maeve's eyes twinkled.

"We dated a while back, but we've gone our separate ways." *No need for details*. He drew a cleansing breath before nibbling the sausage.

"Maybe…"

"Maybe what?" He washed down the food with coffee.

"Maybe you've gone your way, but Bea hasn't." She dipped her fork into the *pico de gallo*.

"What makes you say that?"

"*Subtle* details"—she chuckled—"like her death-grip on your arm or her blocking my exit or glaring through the window when you helped me into the truck."

"Didn't realize she was that obvious." He wolfed down the refried beans with a toasted tortilla. "I only mentioned this topic because…" His mouth went dry. "She'll be at my aunt's tomorrow for supper."

"Isn't tomorrow's supper a family gathering?"

"Yeah."

"Then why's she coming?" She squinted. "If Bea's not your 'friend,' is she another cousin?"

"No." He laughed at the notion. "But for some reason, Aunt Rosie always includes her—considers her family." He shrugged, wanting to end the topic. "We'd better eat before the eggs get cold." He shoveled a forkful into his mouth, then remembered his plans. "After breakfast, how'd you like to drive to the park and see Marianna's old homestead?"

"I'd love it." Her green eyes lit up, then dimmed. "But I don't want to keep you from whatever you'd planned."

"This is the slow season. Besides, with the snow, I can't work in the vineyard, anyway." Enjoying her company, he looked forward to the day's plans. "The park's only two hours from here. We'll be back before dark."

"I'd really like to connect with Grandma's stories—walk in my ancestors' footsteps, touch something they handled." Her shoulders hunching, she chewed her lip. "But what if the insurance company calls?"

"Smitty will take care of it." *Is she stalling?* "Or maybe you'd rather not go…?"

"No, I just don't want to step on"—she winced—"*anyone's* toes."

Is that all? "Trust me. You're not stepping on Bea's toes." The morning brightening, he dug into his *chilaquiles* with renewed gusto. *Yesterday brought Maeve. What'll today bring?*

****

We pulled into Big Bend National Park just as the sun climbed above the mountains. The sky was cobalt blue, and the snow capping the peaks contrasted against the flame-colored rocks. Despite the frosty temperatures, the mountains' rugged beauty was inviting.

"Want to go for a hike?" Confined to the passenger's seat for two hours, I jumped at the opportunity to stretch my legs. "This path's calling me." I gestured toward the trailhead with my thumb.

"You sure you're up for a three-mile hike through creosote and cat's claw?"

I took in the austere beauty, then laughed. "Three miles is just a warmup."

Luke parked near a narrow caliche path. "The morning is still chilly, but when the sun's overhead, it can take its toll. I'll bring water just in case."

"I'm not new to desert conditions." I met his gaze. "Don't forget I spent time in Afghanistan."

"I did forget." He dipped his chin while he fished two water bottles from the back seat. "Ready?"

As I stepped from the warm cab, the icy mountain morning jolted me awake. My senses reeled from the bracing freshness, and the cobwebs cleared. For the second time since my discharge, I sensed a purpose—a mission. *What it is, I haven't a clue, but I'm* not *adrift.*

The frosty air filling my lungs, I closed my eyes and tilted my face to the sun, letting its warm rays penetrate every thought and cell. A sense of place permeated me, and I wrapped my arms across my chest, hugging myself. *I've come home.*

When I opened my eyes, I caught Luke watching and gave a sheepish laugh. "I *love* the high desert."

"Apparently."

"Didn't realize how much until this moment."

"Why?" He cocked his head.

Taking in the craggy splendor as I scanned the horizon, I spoke in a whisper. "Its raw beauty…" Then I flung out my arms, encompassing the magnitude of the land. "But the sense of freedom is what I love most." I pointed to the prickly-pear cactus and yucca dotting the chaparral. "Even the plants give each other space. Here, I'm not restricted, not boxed in. I have room to grow."

"They practice social distancing."

I laughed. "That and the desert offers a oneness with nature—a solidarity. Here, I'm free…*yet* I belong."

"I feel the same way." His gaze steady, he nodded. "This land beckons with a melody few hear."

"*Beckons*—yes, that's the word." Sensing a kindred

spirit, I took a second look, homing in on his inviting lips. His chest hair peeked from his V-neck shirt, and my pulse quickened. Then Cody's face flashed before my eyes, and I skidded to an emotional halt. "Want to continue this discussion while we hike?"

"Good idea. Do you like petroglyphs?"

"Absolutely, I love anything to do with history. Why?" I started on the caliche trail.

"That formation has ancient petroglyphs." He pointed to the rocky crest on the left. "If you don't mind scrambling up rocks and know where to look..." His eyes twinkled in the morning sun.

"A challenge? You're on." Tossing my chin, I pushed past him to lead the way. Twenty-five minutes later, I reached the base of the cliff, then scrambled up the steep slope.

He pointed to a ledge several feet above the sheer rock wall. "That's where you'll find the rock carvings." Nodding toward the rise, he cupped his hands to give me a boost.

"Thanks." I pushed off, reached for the ledge with my other hand, and hoisted myself the rest of the way. "Your turn." I caught his hand and pulled as he scaled the smooth rock face.

The ledge was so narrow, we sat shoulder to shoulder, facing the desert's expanse with the petroglyphs at our backs. To see the weatherworn lines and circles, I had to twist my torso. Some figures were etched into the rock wall; other pictographs were painted on its surface. "I wonder what these symbols mean."

"I've heard the zigzag lines indicate lightning *or* they warn of snakes." He shrugged. "I'm not sure of their meanings, but from their sheer number, I'd guess this place was important."

"Maybe sacred." Our shoulders rubbed each time we moved. The downy hairs on the back of my neck tickling from the electricity passing between us, I shivered as the currents barreled down my spine.

"Cold?" Eyes wide, he caught my gaze.

I opened my mouth to speak but, forgetting what I meant to say, lost myself in his inviting brown eyes and could only nod.

He reached his arm around my shoulders and pulled me close, sharing his body warmth.

With the faint scents of leather and saddle soap wafting from his jacket, his nearness was intoxicating, and I was tempted to lean into a kiss. Yet huddled together on the bone-chilling ledge, I gazed instead at the rugged wilderness surrounding us, content to savor the sweet ache of longing. *If more is meant to be, it'll happen.*

Then thoughts of Cody froze me like a blue norther. *Why did* he *come to mind?*

****

So close, Luke felt the rise and fall of her chest each time she breathed. Her hair tickled his ear, raising goosebumps—and possibilities. *If she turns toward me or gives any sign…*But her sigh signaled something else. He side-glanced to read her mood, but she stared at the scenery, apparently oblivious of his rising libido.

"Want…" His voice cracked. Clearing his throat, he tried again. "Want some water?"

"Sure." She turned her head quickly, her hair brushing his cheek with a citrus scent.

He reached into his vest pocket, pulled out a bottle, and opening it, handed it over.

She took a long swig, then returned it with a smile. "Thanks."

Not wiping off the bottle, he took a long swallow, sending a subtle signal. Then he offered it to her, watching her response.

Her cheekbones rose, and her lips curved in a half-smile. Her green eyes sparkling like fireworks, she reached for the bottle, drank it dry, and handed it back. Then with a snicker, she jumped off the ledge. "Weren't we going to the homestead?"

Surprised by her mixed signals, he laughed. "Your command is my wish. Lead on."

A half-hour later, they were back in the truck, heading south along the Ross Maxwell Scenic Drive.

"Mule Ears Viewpoint." Reading the signpost, she peered at the twin mountaintops rising from the chaparral.

"Want to stop?"

"Absolutely."

He parked facing the two peaks, then tilted his head left and right. "If you get the right angle, you can see a mule's head and ears."

"I think some of us read more into scenes *and situations* than others..." Her lips twitched.

The shared water bottle came to mind. *Busted.* He swallowed a sheepish smile before pulling back onto the road. "Next stop—the old homestead."

"When did Marianna and Ramon's ranch become part of Big Bend?"

"The government began buying land for the park during the thirties. From what I heard, they had mixed feelings about selling, but the Depression and Dust Bowl decided for them." He parked near the trailhead. "What's left of their farmhouse is less than a half mile from here."

As the dusty trail descended into a narrow valley between the foothills, the flora changed from Spanish dagger and yucca to spindly trees and native grass punching through the rocky soil.

"Is that a chokecherry?"

"Yeah, they say Marianna planted the first tree, and it's reseeded itself."

"To think this is the offshoot of something she planted, and it's still going…still growing." She lightly drew her fingers along a branch. "It's almost like touching her, physically connecting."

He reached for her hand. "*Now* you're touching the offshoot of something she planted."

She pulled away, stiffening. "Let's see the homestead."

Chastened, he led the way to the adobe ruins, then stepped inside the roofless cottage. "The door's long gone. These walls are all that's left."

"Imagine living here…" She caressed the crumbling adobe. "I love reaching through time and connecting with the past." She spun toward him. "Just think. We're standing where they did…why, Marianna could've touched *this* brick, right *here*…"

"Never thought of rubble that way." Impressed by his cousin's fresh perspective, he recalled the reason for their journey. "Think their initials are still here?"

"Maybe. Wouldn't it be great to find them?" Her eyes lit up like green fire. "The journal said Ramon carved them in a cottonwood near the spring. Where's the spring?"

"This way." He led her along a narrow path lined with trees and teeming with birds, then paused. "Listen."

Songbirds trilled and sang as they flitted among the branches.

He turned toward a tall ashe juniper and crooked his head. "That slurred whistle is from a Say's phoebe, and that single chirp is from an ash-throated flycatcher." He pointed out the golden-breasted bird as it took flight. "In the desert, water is life. This spring's created an oasis in a wilderness."

Stepping toward a mature tree, he estimated its width with his hands and shook his head. "This one's not old enough."

He searched from tree to tree until he found a granddaddy of a cottonwood. "This one might've been here in Marianna's time."

"How can you tell?

"Look at its width." He tried spreading his arms around it, estimating its girth. "It has to be eighteen, maybe nineteen feet in diameter. This tree's well over a hundred years old." Stepping over a mud puddle, he walked around the tree but saw no initials. "Do you see anything?"

"Nope."

Then his gaze followed the trunk to the upper branches. "What's that?" He pointed to a slight deviation in the bark's pattern. "Maybe forty or fifty feet up...see it?"

"I see something." She squinted. "But I can't make it out."

"Give me a sec." He hoisted himself to the nearest branch, and climbed, limb from limb, until he got a clear view. Grinning, he gave a thumb's up and snapped a photo with his phone. Five minutes later, he swung down from the lowest bough.

"What'd you see?" Her eyes flashed.

She's like a kid on Christmas morning. He chuckled at Maeve's enthusiasm as he brought up the picture. "Look for yourself."

The bark had grown around the carved heart over the decades, and the two initials had lightened over time.

"M & R." She cooed like a mourning dove. "They're still here."

"Just a little higher off the ground than they were a hundred and twenty years ago."

The color of spring leaves, her eyes flashed in the stippled sunlight. "Be right back." She attacked the climb as if it were a military maneuver, but when she reached the initials, she traced the heart with her finger, pausing as if in silent communication with the carver.

After a moment, she started down. Her cheeks ruddy from the exertion, she grinned from ear to ear as she jumped from the lowest branch. "I connected with them. We *know* Ramon's fingers carved *this* tree."

"All right, you've 'touched' the characters in your grandmother's stories and walked in their footsteps." Her enthusiasm contagious, he chuckled at her obvious delight, glad to contribute. "Now is your bucket list complete?"

"Complete? Hah!" She tossed her chin. "Nowhere near!"

"Then what's next?"

****

"Is it possible to see Marianna's cinnabar mine?"

"I don't—"

"And did I see a sign in Lajitas?" Another thought took hold, and I grabbed his arm as I raised up on my toes. "Something about *horse stables*?"

Luke grinned. "To answer your first question, the park includes several abandoned mines, but I doubt any of those were on Ramon and Marianna's land. *However*, you asked about horses…" His eyes flashed. "Do you like trail riding?"

"Love it. Why?"

"A friend of mine offers trail rides to an abandoned quicksilver mine." He cocked his head. "Interested?"

"Heck, yeah." Returning his grin, I fought the urge to let out a Texas whoop. "Are his stables nearby?"

"A half-hour drive." He glanced at his watch. "It's almost one now. Are you hungry?"

"Not really. I'm still full from breakfast."

"Same here." He nodded as he scrolled through his phone's contacts, then pressed a key. "Let's see if he has room for two more riders on the next tour."

****

Hoisting myself from the stirrup, I mounted the dappled-gray mare. *Feels good to have a horse beneath me again.* I breathed deeply, inhaling the moment as much as the mustang's earthy scent. "I love the smell of horses."

"Maybe that's alfalfa you smell." Grinning, the stable's owner, Joel, gestured to the nearby bale of hay as he and Luke approached on quarter horses. "It's a richer, more complex scent than coastal hay."

"You sound like you're describing wine." Luke snickered. "Next you'll say it has a tangy, pungent bouquet, and you'll comment about its legs."

"Nope, I'm more a beer man, myself." Joel chuckled as he led us from the corral into the pasture. "Love the grainy whiff of a good microbrew. You don't just smell the rye, oats, and malted barley—you *drink* 'em. Beer's a feedstore in a bottle."

"Well, I love this horse's scent." I crouched forward, burying my face in the mare's mane, and inhaled the fragrance. "It's organic—something between freshly mown grass and warm tomatoes on the vine. I could breathe it all day."

Pointing, Joel reined his gelding. "The mineshaft is in those hills. See the pink mounds? They're tailings from the abandoned mercury mine." He guided us toward a rocky trail, then gestured to an earthen knoll. "That's where they stored the dynamite."

I regarded the ridges of caliche and loose rocks. "These dunes look like a scene from a moon landing."

Joel smiled over his shoulder as he pointed to the left. "That's Maverick Mountain."

The undulating foothills at the base of the mountain rose, fell, and then climbed higher on the next ridge and the next. After a half hour, the mine's abandoned buildings came into view.

"The ruins look so stark out in the middle of…nothing." I stood in my saddle, taking in the three-hundred-sixty-degree lunarscape. "How did they mine and refine the cinnabar in such a remote area?"

"Through sweat equity and sheer determination." Luke's lips set in a thin line as he peered into the distance.

What's he thinking?

"This was one of the mineshafts." Joel pointed to an entrance blocked with heavy-duty wire mesh. "If you think life was tough topside, imagine the miners tunneling below."

Luke reined his horse closer to the opening and peered in. "The heat must've been unbearable."

"Like burrowing to hell." I shook my head.

"That's cinnabar." Joel pointed out the brick-red rocks strewn about. "The story goes that this area was so rich in deposits that the heat from a campfire would form drops of quicksilver."

"Isn't it poisonous?"

"Mercury sulfide's the most toxic mineral on earth." Joel nodded. "Miners inhaling its dust or furnace workers breathing its vapors led short lives."

Peering into the dark hole, I took a deep breath, glad to be topside.

Joel clicked his teeth as he reined his horse around. "Let's find some better scenery." Riding past several roofless shanties of stacked limestone and adobe, he led us down a steep ravine. Then he guided us across a narrow trickle of water flowing through a wide riverbed. "This is Rough Run Creek. Looks peaceful now, but you wouldn't want to be here in a flash flood."

The horses climbed a vertical incline to one of the highest peaks, and as the path widened onto a broad butte, he pointed northeast. "Those are the Christmas Mountains, the highlight of the tour before we start back."

The majestic range extended to the horizon, with only sparse vegetation dotting the miles of stony terrain.

"Xeriscaping on a grand scale." Using my chin, I pointed toward the nearest vegetation. "What kinds of shrubs are those?"

"A mix of mesquite, ocotillo, lechuguilla, cholla, and prickly-pear cactus." Luke spread his arm across the expanse. "To survive here, everything needs thorns, spines, or quills."

"A protective shell." I nodded, relating. "Yet in their

own way, each is beautiful. Maybe that's why I love the desert."

"A prickly kind of love, like between a porcupine and a cactus." Luke turned toward me with a languid smile, his smoldering brown eyes sweeping over me like a desert breeze.

I held his gaze a beat too long, then to cover, checked the time. "Four-thirty? Are you getting hungry? Because I sure am."

"No wonder. Breakfast is nothing but a dim memory."

"Terlingua has a restaurant that opens at five." Joel glanced from one to the other.

"I have no pressing engagements." *Or timetables, or orders.* Enjoying the day as it unfolded, I shrugged.

"Works for me. Otherwise, it's another two hours to Fort Lincoln." Luke caught my gaze. "You game?"

****

"The wait for a table's thirty-minutes." The hostess took Luke's name, then pointed to the old-time saloon. "But the bar's open, or you're welcome to sit on the front porch and watch the sunset."

"Thanks." He turned to Maeve. "How 'bout something to drink?"

"After Joel gushed about microbrews and 'a feedstore in a bottle,' I could go for a beer."

"A cold draft it is." Luke held the door while a steady stream of people entered and exited. "Why don't you grab us seats on the porch. This may take a while."

He joined her several minutes later, handing her a bottle just as the sun set behind them, casting long shadows. "To tranquil sunsets and new dawns."

"I'll drink to that." She clinked her bottle against his.

Enjoying her nearness, he leaned back against the weatherworn bench, while the evening sky morphed from crimson and gold into plum and amethyst. The reflection of the last sunrays transformed the Chisos mountains into a glowing spectacle of ginger and crimson. "This is the only place I know where you watch the sun go down in the east."

Her gaze on the mirrored sunset, she chuckled in her throat.

Someone strummed a guitar, and he relaxed into a comfortable camaraderie. "After we get back, want to read more of Marianna's journal?"

****

Luke found packets of spiced apple-cider mix by the hotel lobby's coffee machine and brewed two cups of mulled cider.

A substitute clerk slid a basket of heart-shaped cookies across the front desk. "Help yourself."

"Thanks." *It isn't Valentine's Day, is it?* He checked his phone's calendar. *February eighth. Will she still be here on the fourteenth?* Juggling the cups with one hand, he snagged two cookies with the other, then settled into the same armchair as the night before.

"The dates don't follow the first chronologically, but here's a later diary." Waving the journal as she entered the sitting room, Maeve sported a pink crewneck sweater with a red-heart pattern. Though a bulky weave, the wool sweater hugged her like a kid glove, tapering at her slim waistline.

"You look like a Valentine."

"Too much?" She pivoted as if to return to her room and change. "I was a little chilly—"

"No, you look terrific—and very seasonal." *Chilly?*

Rising to his feet, he considered sharing his body heat in a hug but, instead, offered her the steaming cup. "Maybe this cider will warm you."

"Good thinking."

Seven. He counted the freckles on her button nose. Then becoming aware of the pause, he tilted his head toward the treats. "Speaking of seasonal, have a cookie."

"How cute." She nibbled one as she took her seat.

He sank into his chair and gestured toward the notebook. "You say this is a later journal?"

"It's dated nineteen-eighteen. I'm guessing Marianna would've been in her early forties at this point." As she faced him, the fire's glow outlined her high cheekbones. "Isn't it strange to peek in and out of people's lives, tapping in years or decades later?"

"Last night, we read about her life in nineteen hundred. Now tonight, it's nineteen- nineteen. How time flies." Swallowing a smile, he deadpanned. "Whose turn to read?"

"Yours." She handed him the diary.

"Okay." He sneezed as he opened the composition book's water-stained cover.

"*Gesundheit.*" A smile played at her lips.

"What microbes and dust mites did I just inhale from the past?"

"Who knows, but that diary holds more than a century's worth."

"And on that thought…" He turned to the first entry. "*September twenty-second, nineteen-nineteen. Ramon has influenza.*"

Recoiling as he speculated about infectious viruses, he took his gaze from the diary. "Wasn't that about the time of the Spanish Flu?"

"Yikes." She grimaced. "What happened?"

"*September twenty-third. Ramon was too weak to get out of bed. Ramona came home to spend time together.*"

"Ramona…wasn't she the baby born in nineteen hundred?"

Maeve nodded. "If she 'came home,' does that mean she'd married?"

"*September twenty-fifth. Ramon's better—kept down toast and chaparral tea. Ramona stayed as long as she could, but the children need her.*"

"Guess she was." As Luke sipped his cider, an idea formed. "What're you doing tomorrow for lunch?" Then second thoughts surfaced, and he flinched. *Am I moving too fast? Coming on too strong?*

"Not a darned thing." Her face lit up.

Responding to her smile, he leaned closer. "I know a 'quaint place.' How 'bout I pick you up at noon?"

Chapter 5

"Between 'quaint place' for lunch and 'supper' at your aunt's, I wasn't sure what to wear." Wearing an off-the-shoulder sweater over skinny pants, I climbed into his truck's front seat. "Hope I'm dressy enough yet not over-dressed."

"You look great. Actually"—he side-glanced—"terrific."

"Thanks." Squirming at the compliment, I buckled my seatbelt. "Where are we headed?"

"You'll see in a minute." He turned off the main road onto a climbing, two-lane highway through the mountains. "This route is part of the Scenic Loop Drive, one of the most scenic in Texas."

Unfamiliar with the rugged landscape, I studied an imposing rock formation ahead. "What's that?"

"Mount Livermore, more familiarly known as 'Old Baldy.' At over eight-thousand feet, it's the tallest peak in the Lincoln Mountains—the second highest range in the state. Only the Guadalupe Mountains are taller." Keeping his eyes on the road, he smiled over his shoulder. "In fact, this whole area is called a 'sky island.' "

I rolled the words over my tongue. "Sounds like a paradox—an island in the sky, not water."

"If you think of the desert as an ocean, the mountains rise above it like an island."

I glimpsed the peaks poking through the clouds. "Yes, here, the name makes sense."

He turned right onto a steep, caliche drive.

The sun flashed, its glaring brilliance like the reflection of a splintered mirror.

Just before I shut my eyes against the blaze of light, a man appeared in a vintage uniform—brown trousers, blue shirt, and white suspenders.

When I opened them, the image was gone. *A mirage?* Orderly rows of vines came into view. "That's your vineyard?" Bobbing my head left and right, I strained to see past Luke.

"Yup." As if suppressing a proud smile, his cheeks dimpled. "Chateau Mont Bleu. Thought you might like to see it."

"Absolutely. I love vineyards. I went to a grape-stomp once as part of a harvest festival." I chuckled at the memory. "We picked grapes, trampled them with our bare feet, and then made purple footprints on souvenir t-shirts."

"So, you're an expert vintner, huh?" Tongue-in-cheek, he turned toward me as he slowed the truck.

"Hardly. That's the extent of my expertise—other than in wineries' tasting rooms."

"Let me know if you ever want to pick up a few hours—or weeks—of work." He scratched his chin, his five o'clock shadow sounding like sandpaper. "It's hard to find experienced help in these parts."

"Thanks, but I'd be more a hindrance than help. What I know about winemaking I learned in a five-minute how-to."

"If you picked it up that quickly, you're a fast learner." Cutting the engine, he gestured through the windshield. "Home sweet home. Want a tour before lunch?"

"Definitely." A quick glance took in an adobe cabin, a lean-to that sheltered a vintage tractor, and a DIY structure with rough, untreated siding.

He pointed out the buildings as we strolled the grounds. "This hunting cabin and lean-to were here when I bought the property, though a bit worse for wear. After restoring the cabin, I lived in it while I converted the old root cellar into a wine cellar"—his cheek dimpled in a smile—"actually, a warehouse with living quarters in the back." He thumped an unfinished, poured-cement wall. "Later this spring, I'd like to add an open-air tasting room."

"Here?" Walking closer, I studied the modest building.

Pacing off from the structure's side, he faced me and held his arms wide. "This'll be the edge of the covered patio. I'll put a load-bearing column in this corner to support the roof and place the bar in the opposite corner, against the wall." A spring in his step, he sped across the space, demonstrating his plans.

"Sounds ambitious." Visualizing his design, I followed after him.

"With a shoestring budget, I'm hoping sweat equity makes up for lack of capital."

"I'm sure you'll realize your dreams, sooner or later."

He stopped in front of a pueblo-style house.

Viga beams projected through the adobe walls. Built-in steps led to a roof terrace, and rough-wood columns supported the overhang that acted as the front entrance's portico.

"You said this cabin is original to the property?"

"Yes, it was renovated in the early fifties but was originally built in the late eighteen-nineties. It's small but comfortable. Want to see inside?"

"I'd love to." I jumped at the opportunity to connect with history.

He punched the code in the keyless lock, opened the sturdy wooden door, and stepped aside. "After you."

The viga beams spanned the length of the cabin, their dark wood contrasting against the whitewashed tongue and groove ceiling. A kiva fireplace was the room's focal point, while skylights flooded the space with sunlight. The floors were gray slate, and the walls were white plaster with dark wood trim. A double bed, desk, table, antique cedar chest, refinished rocking chair, and two chairs furnished the main room, while a breakfast bar separated it from the kitchenette.

"Entering this cabin is like being transported back in time." The longer I examined the main room, the more details I found to admire. I pushed open a heavy wooden door, and light streamed through the bath's glass-tiled windows, while colorful, Mexican Talavera tile lined the shower's walls, vanity, sink, and backsplash. Modern copper fixtures completed the updated yet rustic look and feel. "I love this cabin. It's so inviting."

"This is how it looked when I bought it." He pointed to a framed photo near the fireplace, showing the same room, but with crumbling plaster walls, warped linoleum, and a broken door. "The restoration turned out all right…"

He sounded unconvinced as he regarded the room.

Doesn't he realize what a fantastic job he did? I chuckled at the irony. "Talk about understatement. If your expansion plans work out even half as well, your winery's bound to succeed."

"Thanks. Appreciate your vote of confidence." He gestured toward the door. "Now, how 'bout lunch?"

"Absolutely, I'm starved." My stomach growled at the mention of food, and I started toward the truck. "Where are we going?"

"To my favorite restaurant, but no need to drive." Wearing a mysterious grin, he waved me back. "We can walk."

"Okay…"

"Are you up for a picnic?"

"In February?" Glancing at the remaining patches of snow, I squinted.

He ushered me toward a small, concrete patio between the vineyard and wine cellar.

A linen-covered table beneath a wooden arbor displayed vintage china, silverware, crystal wine glasses, a vase of pink roses, several covered platters, and an ice bucket holding a carton of orange juice and a bottle of champagne. Beside the table were two cushioned chairs and a gas heater.

"Lunch is served." Wearing a grin, he pulled out my chair. "And you're seated in front of the heater."

"All the comforts of home." *How romantic*.

"Would you like a mimosa?"

"This day just keeps getting better."

He blended the sparkling wine and juice, handed me a glass, and lifted his in a toast. "To…what?" His eyes flashing in the sunlight, he tweaked a brow.

A smile tickled my lips. "How 'bout to fresh starts and new beginnings?"

"I'll drink to that." He clinked glasses. Then one by

one, he lifted the covers from the chafing dishes. "This is sautéed mushrooms and asparagus, and that's grilled chicken." He pointed to the plastic-covered salad bowl. "Maybe you'd like to start with the fresh strawberry and spinach salad? Or would you rather begin with cheese and bread?"

"It's a hard choice." I blinked at the unexpected feast. "You made all this yourself?"

"Yup." His cheekbones lifted in a grin. "Everything but the cheese, champagne, and OJ."

"You're a Renaissance man." Impressed, I studied him. "What can't you do?"

He bunched his lips as if uncomfortable, then offered me the cutting board with a wheel of brie and a round loaf of bread. "The brie's so creamy, it melts into the bread."

I tried cutting the crusty loaf with my knife.

"Don't stand on ceremony. Pull it apart." He gave me a lop-sided smile. "Bread tastes better pulled apart than sliced."

I ripped off a piece, crispy on the outside and yielding on the inside. "This is a real treat." After inhaling the bread's yeasty fragrance, I added cheese, then bit into the buttery and crunchy textures. "Delicious."

"That's just the appetizer." He laughed.

Is there nothing he can't do? "You should open a restaurant."

"Maybe someday." He held up his hands as if fending off the idea. "But for now, I'd be happy just to get the winery going."

"Understandable." I nodded my encouragement. Then leaning toward the roses, I closed my eyes and inhaled their subtle scent. "Pink for Valentine's Day?"

"Wish I'd thought of that." A grin ghosted his face. "Actually, pink because we met on Wild Rose Pass."

****

After lunch, he showed me the vineyard. "The vines are dormant now, so I need to start pruning them this week."

"They're so brown and reedy. They look dead." I gently bent the tip of the nearest vine, and it snapped off in my hand. "Will they come back?"

He nodded. "Grapes only grow on year-old wood, so ninety percent of what you see needs to be lopped off."

I gazed across the acres of vines and gave a low whistle. "You must have thousands to trim."

"Which is why I need help." He gave a dry laugh. "The best time to prune is now, while the vines are inactive. Ideally, a crew of workers would clip them in a week, but with just me pruning, the process takes longer, and if I don't finish in time, I risk cutting into the vines' growing season." He grinned. "Pun intended."

"You certainly have your work *cut out* for you." I recalled the one time I'd harvested grapes. Clipping grapes was backbreaking work. "Can't you hire a crew?"

"Sure, that is, *if* I could find experienced trimmers, and *if* I could afford to pay them." The gleam in his eyes dimmed.

"If I were staying, I'd offer to help." I bunched my lips. "But I'm leaving in a few days."

"Yeah, I know." He drew a deep breath before gesturing to the furthest edge of the vineyards. "Want to see Dry Gulch Creek?"

At my nod, we followed an intermittent stream's

gravel bed to where three huge cottonwoods towered above us, their branches bare in the wintry sun.

He leaned against the tallest. "According to the National Register of Big Trees, this is the largest Rio Grande cottonwood in the nation at seventy-nine feet tall and twenty-nine feet around its trunk."

I gave a low whistle as I trailed my fingers over the tree's deeply furrowed bark. "And I thought Marianna's cottonwood was big."

"Imagine the stories if this tree could talk."

On cue, the wind soughed through the branches as if murmuring a subtle message.

More sensed than heard, a word seemed to waft on the breeze. *Stay.*

I perked my ears.

Stay.

"Are you up for a walk?"

Deep in concentration, I flinched. "Always."

"This path loops around the vineyard in a three-mile circle." He offered his hand as we climbed the steep incline.

I hesitated. *Don't start something you can't finish.* But despite my travel plans, I linked fingers. *El Paso's only three hours away…hardly a long-distance relationship.*

Relationship? This is nothing but a chance encounter. Yet nothing happens by chance, so why did we meet? And why am I so attracted?

I side-glanced at his profile—a basalt jaw and cheekbones so angular they seemed chiseled. Watching his features instead of my step, I stumbled.

His hand around mine, he slipped his other arm behind my waist and caught me in a pose like a dip in a dance.

Suspended in his arms, I held my breath as I gazed into his expressive eyes.

He leaned forward slowly, pausing millimeters from my lips as if asking permission.

His breath tickled, and I arched my neck to meet him in a sweet, exploratory kiss.

Hormones revving from zero to sixty, I flung my arms around his neck, took the kiss, and ran with it.

Then Cody's face flashed before me, and I froze. *Whoa. What am I doing?*

****

As she tensed, he regretted his lapse of judgment. *But she did respond...* Still tasting her lips, he held back his head to read her eyes. "Sorry." He lifted her to her feet. "Didn't mean for that to happen."

"You literally swept me off my feet." She laughed as if making a joke. Then she slapped at her thighs, brushing off imaginary dust.

Or is she brushing me off? Keeping his hands to himself, he gestured to the path ahead. "Still about a mile to finish the loop, then would you like to see the wine cellar?" He glanced at the time. "We have an hour 'til we leave for Aunt Rosie's."

"Already?" She checked her phone. "Seems like we just ate."

It does. He picked up the pace and, twenty minutes later, led her into the wine cellar.

The temperature dropped abruptly.

He flipped on the lights as he shut the vault door, its sound echoing off the cement walls.

Stacked, wooden barrels neatly lined the rectangular, temperature-controlled room, while several

A-frame wine racks held green bottles tipped on their sides.

"This is quite a production." She studied the casks and ran her fingers over the bottles before turning toward him. "Did you make all this wine from your own grapes?"

"Yup, last year, I hauled ten tons to a custom crush facility to vinify them into wine." He grimaced. "It took four separate trips and cost more than it was worth, but that qualified me to apply for Federal and State licenses to operate as a winery. *Voila!* Chateau Mont Bleu was born."

"Impressive." Again, she eyed the barrels and bottles.

"Want to sample a young merlot?" A pipette in hand, he hovered over one of the casks.

"You mean from the barrel?" Her eyes opened wider. "I'd love to."

"This is my first attempt at a merlot." He took two oversized red wine glasses from a cabinet, removed the cask's bung, plunged the glass cylinder into the barrel, and expressed a small sample into each glass. After replacing the bung, he handed her a glass. "To young wines and new beginnings."

She clinked glasses, the sound resonating in the chamber, and she took a tentative sip, swishing it in her mouth before swallowing.

"What do you think?"

She swirled the pomegranate-red liquid in her glass, holding it up to the light. She inhaled its fragrance. Then she sipped slowly, rolling the wine over her tongue, as if letting its flavors linger.

Again, he found himself holding his breath, waiting

for her approval. He raised his brow. "Verdict?"

"Reminds me of a young Chianti." She ran the tip of her tongue over her lips. "Light and refreshing."

Dismissing his uneasiness about the wine's quality, he stared at the moist, inviting lips he had just kissed, tempted to taste the wine from her perspective. Instead, he held up his glass in another toast. "To wine—grape juice with experience."

Clinking glasses, she grinned, this time sipping rather than sampling.

"Did you know, wine contains nearly *all* the essential minerals, antioxidants, and B-vitamins?" He held back his head while he appraised her. "Coincidence?"

"Nope, nothing's coincidental, but I'll happily drink to wine's health benefits."

"In that case, let's also drink to its trace minerals: calcium, chloride, chromium, copper, fluoride, iron, magnesium, manganese, molybdenum, phosphorus, potassium, selenium, sodium, sulfur, zinc, and—"

****

"Show off." Enjoying his company, I grinned.

"Another toast?"

"Wine not?"

"Oh, you're *on*." As if tickled by my challenge, he raised his glass. "To wine…liquid therapy."

I wracked my brain as we clinked and sipped. "In case of emergency"—I held up my glass—"call nine wine wine."

Smothering a chuckle, he swallowed, then held up his glass. "To making *pour* decisions."

"A groaner."

He glanced at his watch. "We should leave for

Rosie's soon." Then, a smile twitching at his lips, he raised his glass. "Time to wine down."

"Let me drink about it and get back to you." Clinking, I giggled and drained my glass.

A small disk flashed beneath the overhead track lighting as it rolled along the vault's center aisle.

He retrieved the coin and placed it in my hand. "Where'd this come from?"

I traced my finger over the tapering neck of Liberty. "I don't remember the last time I saw a Mercury dime."

"Then keep it as a souvenir."

"You're sure? Because if I recall correctly, they're collectors' items."

"A dime isn't going to make or break me." He shrugged.

"Thanks." I dropped it in my pocket as a memento. "I'll research it later."

"Before we leave for Rosie's, would you like a quick tour of the living space?"

"Lead on." Palm up, I gestured toward the door.

The door opened into an efficiency apartment.

"Home, sweet home. The bath and office are in the back." He pointed toward two open doors at the far end, then gestured to the mini fridge, bar sink, wall oven, and microwave. "This is the kitchen."

He made that fabulous meal in this tiny kitchenette?

A white, faux-brick backsplash ran from the counter to the ceiling, and track lighting lit the silver-gray granite countertops from above.

"That's the formal dining room." Tongue-in-cheek, he nodded toward the breakfast bar, separating the kitchen area from the seating area. "And this is the master bedroom." He deadpanned as he pointed to a loveseat facing two armchairs with a coffee table between them.

I glanced about the space. "Where…?"

"It's a convertible sofa. Nothing fancy, but it's home."

"What more do you need?"

****

Knocking as he opened Rosie's front door, Luke called. "Anyone home?"

A chorus of greetings welcomed us.

The tantalizing aroma of homemade tamales filled my nostrils as I followed him inside.

Two dozen or more people lounged on sofas, easy chairs, and folding chairs, apparently added for the gathering.

After growing up with no family but my grandmother, I smiled at the friendly faces, eager to meet my cousins.

"Come in. Come in." Rosie bustled toward us, hugging me. "I'm so glad you could come. Make yourselves at home." Rushing off, she called over her shoulder. "Lucas, introduce Maeve to the family. I have to check on the barbacoa."

More people passed through the living room on their way to a buffet table laden with tortilla chips, salsa, salsa *verde*, and *pico de gallo*.

A mustachioed man standing by a frozen margarita machine held up a full pitcher of lime-green slush. "Luke, would you and your friend like a margarita?"

Luke's raised brow an unvoiced question, he turned toward me.

I grinned. "Why not?"

Leading me by the hand, he squeezed between the

clusters of people toward the bartender. "This is Ricky, Rosie's husband, and this is Maeve, your second cousin once removed."

"Welcome." A salt-rimmed glass in each hand, Ricky gave me a partial hug before handing over our drinks. As another couple queued behind us, he patted Luke's shoulder. "Make sure you introduce Maeve around." Then turning to the next duo, he dispensed two more frozen margaritas.

I chuckled, impressed by the man's friendly efficiency.

"Want some chips and salsa?" Luke gestured toward the other end of the buffet table with his chin.

"Sure." I stepped toward the fresh bowls of *pico*, salsa, and thick tortilla chips. "Are these homemade?"

"Aunt Rosie makes everything from scratch."

"Must be where you inherited your kitchen skills." Bumped from behind, I slopped my drink.

"Sorry!" A chubby tween pushed his glasses up the bridge of his nose.

"No harm done." I pulled a packet of tissues from my pocket, and the dime slipped out with it, rolling beneath the buffet table. Groaning, I wiped my sticky glass.

"I'll get it." The youngster crawled under the table to retrieve the coin and handed it back. "Here you go."

Reflecting the overhead lights, the dime flashed in my hand.

"You know what they say." The woman behind me spoke in a sing-song voice. "Dimes appear when angels are near."

"Could I see that coin again?" The boy pushed up his glasses.

"Sure."

"This is a 1919-D Mercury dime." His eyes opening wide, he pulled out his phone and scrolled to an app. "Whoa!"

"What?" Unsure what to think, I shared a blank look with Luke.

"You hit the jackpot. This dime could be worth up to twenty-five thousand dollars."

"Right…" Unconvinced, I squinted.

"See for yourself." He held out his phone as he returned the coin.

Sharing the screen with Luke, I read the app's statistics and gulped. *What couldn't I do with that money?* Thinking of the possibilities, I closed my fingers around the dime. *If my car's totaled, this and insurance might cover a new one.* Then taking a deep breath, I handed Luke the coin. "You found this dime. It's yours."

He shook his head as he gently pushed away my hand. "Like I said, a dime isn't going to make or break me."

"Maybe not ten cents." Meeting his gaze, I grimaced. "But twenty-five thousand dollars would finance your patio bar." I returned the boy's phone. "Thanks for the tip." Then I pulled Luke from the food line, retreated to the far corner of the room, and again tried to press the dime into his hand. "Take it."

"No, I gave it to you." His hand a fist, he refused to accept it. "It's yours."

"Lovers' spat already?"

I flinched at the saccharine tones.

Her eyes steely, Bea smiled like a spinster at a wedding. "Shouldn't the honeymoon last more than a day or two?" Her eyes narrowing to slits, she turned to

Luke. "After sneaking out of her hotel room yesterd—"

"You and I need to talk." Grabbing Bea by her wrist, Luke hustled her out the door.

Chapter 6

"Getting rough in your old age?" Outside, Bea pressed her body against his as she nipped his ear. "I like it rough."

He pushed her away. "Keep your mouth shut, and I'll do the same."

"What do you mean?" Bea's eyes narrowed.

"I've kept quiet about your fling—"

"What fling?" She stiffened.

"Double-dealing on me, you threw yourself at Neuman. Then after he ditched you, you came crawling back—that's what 'fling.' " His chest heaving, he fumed. "I've kept your secret, but if you spread rumors about Maeve, I swear I'll make your humiliation public. Is that what you want?"

"What I *want*"—running her talons along his chest, she sidled up to him—"is for us to be together again."

Her spidery touch made his skin crawl. "You ended anything we had."

"I made a mistake—one tiny indiscretion."

"Indiscretion?" He spat out the word like sour milk. "When Neuman's oil wells came in at a thousand barrels a day, you ghosted me—wouldn't even return my calls."

She slithered against him. "I may have misjudged the situ—"

"You ran after him, and he dumped you." He shoved her away. "To let you save face, I've kept quiet. Don't make me change my mind." Turning, he strode in the house.

****

Maeve joined him. "What was that about?"

"You and I know nothing happened between us." Remembering their recent embrace, he shifted feet, then frowned. "I just don't want Bea starting rumors."

"Don't worry about my reputation." She shook her head. "I'm leaving in a few days, *but* while you were outside, I figured out how the Mercury dime could benefit us both."

"It's yours." He crossed his arms. "Subject closed."

"Nope." She shook her head, her shiny hair swinging with each movement. "But you are right about one thing…"

****

"It's mine."

"Damned straight, it is." Planting his legs wide apart, he gave an affirming nod.

"To do with as I please"—I smothered a grin—"right?" *Got him.*

His eyes narrowing, he hesitated. "Meaning…"

"I want to invest it."

"I'll probably regret asking"—he took a slow, deep breath—" but invest it where?"

"In your winery."

"No." Uncrossing his arms, he stood to his full height.

"It's my money to do with as I please." Straightening my spine, I stood up to him.

"Chateau Mont Bleu isn't a public offering."

"Maybe not, but that doesn't mean I can't invest in it."

"Not if the owner doesn't agree."

"Why wouldn't you?" I threw up my hands, frustrated that he'd balk at my offer.

"Trouble in paradise?" Her last word a hiss, Bea strolled past, her smile a lingering sneer.

Luke's eyes blazed, then narrowed to slits.

I rested a light hand on his forearm, redirecting his attention. "This is the only fair solution. A dime appeared from nowhere on *your* property, in *your* wine cellar."

"Coincidental."

"I don't believe in coincidences, remember?" I shook my head. "Everything happens for a reason, and if I ever recognized divine intervention, this is it."

His stiff jaw softened. "What do you mean?"

"Call it the spirit of cooperation"—I shrugged—"or the spirit of fair play or—"

"Maybe the spirit of a common ancestor?" His eyes twinkled.

"Now you're making fun of me." I took a deep breath. "Look, I'm making you a business offer. I say we find out what the Mercury dime brings on the market and invest it in the winery. You get your patio bar. I get a share of the winery." I raised my chin to meet his gaze. "What do you say?"

He stared silently, the pause growing painful.

Thinking he hadn't heard, I raised my voice. "What do—"

"Put 'er there." He held out his right hand.

As I shook hands, my fingers tingled. Despite my resolve to stay detached, a twinge dashed up my arm and catapulted down my spine, ending deep in my belly. I took a breath to steady myself. "This makes it official, right?"

"That's right"—his grip tightened—"partner."

"Isn't this cozy?" Her voice syrupy, Bea approached with Rosie. "What're you two plotting?"

"What are you insinuating?" Luke spun toward the voice, dropping my hand.

"You two certainly had your heads together." Rosie smiled as she gestured toward the groaning buffet table and long queue. "Didn't mean to interrupt, but supper's served. Better get in line before the barbacoa's gone."

"When have you ever run out of food?" Luke gave his aunt a skeptical grin before turning toward me. "She always makes enough to feed an army."

"Flatterer." Rosie playfully tapped his shoulder, then gave me a friendly smile as she half-turned toward Bea. "Have you two met?"

"Maeve's had the pleasure." His face soured.

Rosie quirked a brow, side glimpsed Bea, then gestured toward the crowded dining-room table and packed living room. "If you can't find empty chairs, the back porch and gazebo have plenty of seating." She squeezed my hand. "Make yourself at home."

"Thank you for inviting me." Then remembering the diary, I pulled the thin notebook from my purse and pressed it into her hand. "This was Marianna's journal, and I'd like you to have it."

"No." Rosie's jaw dropped. "I can't take something so valuable."

"It's hardly valuable." I eyed the water-stained diary.

"Because it was Marianna's, its sentimental value is priceless."

"This is just one of many, and we've already read it.

Now it's yours."

"Thank you." Rosie clasped the booklet to her chest.

"Thank *you* for welcoming me."

"Of course. You're family." She gestured toward the buffet table. "Now, go eat and enjoy yourselves. Meet the rest of the family."

Bea's mouth opened as if to remark.

Luke flicked her a sharp glance.

Intervening, I tugged his hand as I inhaled the smoky, mouthwatering aromas wafting from the table. "The barbacoa smells wonderful. Let's get in line."

He turned toward me, his face relaxing, then gave Rosie a hug. "Being the family historian, you'll enjoy the diary."

As we walked away, I spoke under my breath. "What was that exchange about with Bea?"

"What exchange?" His eyes innocent, he shrugged.

"Don't play dumb." I wrinkled my nose. "If looks could kill, you'd be arrested for homicide."

"I don't trust her." He took a deep breath. "But I *am* hungry, so, yes, let's get in line."

Five minutes later, I set my overloaded plate on the metal table and glanced about the octagonal gazebo. "Everyone else is on the porch or inside."

"Good." He grinned. "I've got you all to myself."

"How am I supposed to meet the family?" Hunching my shoulders, I lifted my hands.

"You will…later, but I want to be sure you've thought through this winery investment."

"The dime was yours from the start. I shouldn't have phrased it as an *investment*."

"That's the only reason I considered your offer." He met my gaze. "I'd rather you put the money toward a car."

"Splitting this windfall is the only reasonable solution. Besides…" I laughed at myself for not questioning the online quote earlier. "The *estimated value* and the *going rate* may be as different as chalk and cheese."

"Good point."

Then from the corner of my eye, I caught movement at the edge of the backyard. "Is that a roadrunner?"

****

He turned his head, following her gaze.

The unmistakable gait of the brown and white-streaked bird gave it away. Stopping mid-stride, the roadrunner puffed its head crest like a cockatoo.

"Yup." He turned back. "Why?"

"I've always liked them." She gave a hesitant smile. "But when I visited a sweat lodge a few months ago, I learned it was a lucky omen. What began as relaxation therapy ended in a vision quest." She spread her hands wide on the table. "In my mind's eye, I saw a roadrunner. The leader told me it's my totem animal with the message to think on my feet and hit the ground running."

"Then why did you just roll your eyes?"

"Because the last time I saw a roadrunner was right before I lost control of my car."

"Maybe its appearance was a heads up. You did some fancy footwork to avoid sliding over that ledge. Besides, if not for that accident, you'd never have connected with your family." Homing in on her seven freckles, he offered his hand. "And we might never have met."

She reached across the table to clasp it. "That's true."

"Is this a private party, or can anyone join?"

Luke flinched at Bea's voice. "It's a free country."

She pulled a chair so close, her elbow brushed his arm. "Aunt Rosie always has the best get-togethers, doesn't she?"

"*Aunt* Rosie?" Her familiarity irked him. "Since when is Rosie your aunt?"

"Figure of speech." Bea waived away his question with a flick of her wrist, wafting cologne fumes.

The heavy perfume irritated his nose, and he sneezed. Its sickly-sweet scent reminded him of Copper Canyon daisies. The first time he smelled them, he inhaled deeply, enjoying their fragrance, but after an allergic reaction, even a casual whiff churned his stomach.

How much perfume did she use? Did she spill the bottle? His eyes watering, he wrinkled his nose. "Just remembered something." Breathing through his mouth, he grabbed his plate, pushed back his chair, and stepped away to inhale. "Maeve, can you help me?"

She paused momentarily, studying his face, then gathered her plate and joined him. "Sure."

"Leaving so soon?" Bea's eyes flashed, then narrowed. "Lovers' tryst?"

He opened his mouth, then snapped it shut. "Enjoy your meal." Turning to Maeve, he gestured toward the house with a nod, then strode away, not stopping until they were out of hearing. "Sorry, but her perfume was so strong, it took away my breath. Hope you didn't mind moving."

"Not at all." She shook her head. "A match could've set off the charged atmosphere."

Relieved that she understood, he sighed. "But I *did*

forget the wine." Balancing his plate on the porch railing, he gestured with his chin. "Can you find us seats, while I run out to the truck?"

****

When he returned, I moved over to make room. "It wasn't easy finding a place. Rosie's suppers are popular."

He glanced at the cramped seating. "Before I squeeze in, let me get a wine opener."

A second later, Rosie appeared with a twist corkscrew. "Where's Luke?"

"Just missed him." I grinned at the irony. "He's looking for an opener."

"Seek and ye shall find." Rosie handed it to me.

I removed the metal wrapper and started opening the wine.

"I'll do that." Bea grabbed the corkscrew and bottle from my hands.

"What?" Surprised by the rough jerk, I gripped the bottle, worried it would drop in an exchange.

"You don't know how to pull a cork." Bea yanked harder, nearly wrenching the bottle from my hands.

What is this woman's problem? Not letting go, I held tighter. "I've already start—"

"Give it to me!"

Not wanting to make a scene, I let go. *"Winning" isn't worth stooping to her childish behavior.*

"*This* is how to open a bottle." Speaking with an air of authority, Bea turned the bottle counter-clockwise while she held the opener stationary.

I rolled my eyes.

The cork came out with a loud pop.

"Now"—pulling out the cork, Bea held the bottle

high, brandishing her trophy—"who wants wine?"

"I'll have some." A man from the other end of the porch held up his glass.

"You got it." Wearing a victorious grin, Bea sashayed toward him, trailing her perfume.

I sneezed. *Is she scent marking her territory?*

"Couldn't find a corkscrew." Luke squeezed in beside me.

"Rosie brought one." I scowled as I presented the opener, the cork still on its tip.

His brow wrinkling, he studied me. "What happened?"

"Your friend…" Swallowing a groan, I shook my head. "Nothing."

"No, tell me."

"I don't want to sound like a tattletale."

"What happened?" Straightening his spine, he spoke in carefully controlled tones.

"Bea *insisted* on opening the bottle—in fact, jerked it from my hands."

"I'll talk to her." His face and ears red, he started to rise.

"No, please don't." I placed a light hand on his forearm. "It's not important."

"You're sure?"

"Just let it go."

He shook his head. "I don't know why Rosie includes her at the family gatherings."

"Doesn't matter. Why rock the boat? I'm leaving soon, anyway…" The thought triggered others, and I reached for the Mercury dime in my pocket. *Am I leaving? It isn't likely my car will be ready any time soon—and I* did *offer to partner in the winery…*The impact of the dime deal hit home.

"You're leaving?"

"You sound surprised." I forced an uneasy grin. "Yeah, when—*if*—I can drive my car."

"That's right." His smile sagged. "Somehow, I thought…"

"I'm just passing through." I homed in on his lips, recalling their gentle insistence. *I've got to be honest.*

"Seems longer than two days since we met—maybe because we've spent every waking moment together."

"And then some…" Bea leaned over in a sibilant whisper as she swept past, her perfume's stench fanning behind her.

I began to cough. My eyes tearing, I dabbed them with a tissue and breathed through my mouth until the fumes dissipated.

"Let's eat somewhere Bea can't follow."

"Where?" I blinked through watering eyes.

"My truck. It's the only place we'll have any privacy." He gave me a crooked smile. "If you'll grab our drinks, I'll get the plates."

A few minutes later, we sat in his pickup. Windows open, I breathed in the fresh air. "Much better."

"Sorry about Bea." He grimaced. "I'll have a talk with Rosie."

"Please don't make waves."

"You mean, don't 'make a stink?' " His eyes twinkled. "Too late. Bea's already done that."

"She has, hasn't she?" Chuckling, I nodded. "That cinnamon smell's stronger than sulfur."

"Cinnamon…that's it." He pulled out his phone, checking online. "As I recall, her cologne is custom made with something that not only smells like but *sounds* like cinnamon. Here it is…cinnamaldehyde, a common fragrance in perfumes…and mosquito repellant. Yup, it's *her* essence, all right." Shaking his head, he tucked away his phone and turned on the radio.

A country-western tune came on the air.

"Do you two-step?"

"Not really." I shook my head. "Never learned."

"If you're still here Friday night, I know a place with live music." He leaned toward me. "And I'd be happy to teach you."

Tempted, I entertained the idea but shook my head. *Don't start something you can't finish.* "Thanks, but if the car's ready, I'll be long gone."

"And if the parts haven't come in or the car's totaled, then what?"

"I take life one day at a time."

"So, you're waiting for a 'sign,' is that it?" He sat back, as if challenging me.

"Not necessarily." I pursed my lips, annoyed he reduced my agenda to superstition. "I'm trying to squeeze the plans I'd made before the accident to fit the current circumstances—cram square pegs into round holes."

"What about the Mercury dime?" He caught my gaze. "Wasn't that you who proposed I get the patio bar, while you get a share of the winery? And now you're walking out on our deal?"

"No." My shoulders slumping, I groaned. "I didn't say that."

"So, you're *not* leaving?"

"I didn't say that, either." Sighing, I reached into my pocket and handed him the coin. "Here. Take it." Then pulling back my shoulders, I held up my hands. "It's *no* part mine, anymore."

"Oh, no, you don't." He shook his head as he grinned from ear to ear. "You're not weaseling out of our agreement. *No, ma'am!* A deal's a deal, *and* we shook on it."

"Okay, I'll play along..." I gave a begrudging chuckle. "But only until the car's fixed, then I'm out of here."

*Despite my bravado, my words sounded hollow, even to me. Deep down, I was glad for this delay. I've known him what—forty-eight hours? Yet...*Losing myself, I leaned closer.

"Not leaving already, are you?" Rosie approached the driver's window, wearing a pout.

I flinched.

Luke gave me a subtle wink before turning to his aunt. "No, the porch was crowded, so we ate here."

"Come in when you're done." Rosie waved us inside. "I have something for Maeve."

****

"Good, you're back." Fifteen minutes later, Rosie bustled toward us and pressed a small, velveteen pouch into my hands. "Gifts should go full circle."

I glanced from the gift to the beaming woman. "What do you mean?"

"After a hundred and twenty years, the gift should be returned to the giver"—Rosie folded her hands as if in prayer and held them to her lips—"returned to where its journey began. Open it."

As I undid the drawstring and tipped the bag, a cameo brooch slid into my hand. "What—"

"This is the pin Cadence gave Marianna the day they met."

Mentally replaying Grandma's repertoire of stories, nothing came to mind, and I shook my head.

"This brooch has been in Marianna's family for a hundred and twenty years. It's time to return it to Cadence's family."

I studied the cream-colored carving on an orange-pink background. "What kind of material is this?"

"A conch shell."

"I can't accept this heirloom. It belongs in a museum." I held out my hand, returning the pin.

"Nonsense, it's back where it rightfully belongs." Rosie folded my palm over the brooch. "When you gave me Marianna's journal, I knew it was time to make this exchange."

I pressed the brooch against my heart, then hugged Rosie. "Thank you so much. Until now, I'd had only stories—nothing tangible of my great-great-grandmother."

"Hope it brings you luck." Rosie's smile included us both.

"Which reminds me…have you seen this dime?" Luke shared its story.

"Seems like fortune's already smiling on you." Rosie's lips lifted in a half-grin. "That or you have an angel on your shoulder."

"That's the second time someone's mentioned angels." I pulled back my head, watching her. "What's their connection with dimes?"

"Angels are messengers. Finding a dime means an angel or departed loved one is reaching out."

Departed loved one…who?

"And the number ten symbolizes completion, coming full circle."

I squinted, trying to follow. "Can you give me an example?"

"Cycles are personal—achievements or realized potentials that only you would recognize." Rosie raised her index finger. "But *maybe* by coming here to find your roots, you've come back to where your ancestors started."

"Or maybe I'm completing a journey that began in my imagination." Memories of my grandmother raced through my mind. "First hearing bedtime stories about Fort Lincoln, and now seeing and experiencing it."

"So, by *closing* one circle, you spiral to the next."

"Like the threads of a screw, gradually rising." I grasped her idea.

Luke flashed the coin. "Maybe finding this dime is the start of a new cycle."

"Whatever the message, whatever the journey, keep your options open." Rosie gave an emphatic nod. "Listen with your heart."

****

Luke side-glanced as he drove Maeve back to town. "What're your plans for tomorrow?"

"Other than checking on my car and researching the family history at the library, I haven't any." She canted her head. "Why?"

"The wind's changing with a warming trend, which means I've got to start pruning the vines tomorrow morning, but in the afternoon, I'd like to check out that dime in Fort Stockton." He took his gaze from the road. "Want to go with me?"

"Sure." She shrugged. "Why not?"

"We won't know whether it's worth more than ten cents until we speak with a coin dealer, but in case it has any value, I thought you might like a taste of partnering in a winery."

"What do you mean?" Her head spun toward him.

"Want to learn how to trim vines?" He tried to keep a straight face.

She groaned. "What am I getting into?"

"Exactly." He grinned. "After four hours' working in the vineyards tomorrow, you'll have firsthand knowledge of how much work's involved. No surprises. Then when—*if*—we sell the dime, you can make an informed decision about whether to go ahead with our deal."

"Good idea." She nodded. "But can we stop at the repair shop on the way?"

"Of course."

"I'm not looking forward to hearing the damages, but I *am* curious." She wrinkled her nose.

"Look, I gave you that dime." He pressed his lips together. "If you need the money to fix your car, it's yours."

"I appreciate the offer, but we shook, remember? A deal's a deal...*though* I have a confession to make." She gave a wry chuckle. "Vineyards have always intrigued me, even if my only experience has been an hour or two of picking and stomping grapes."

He caught her gaze. *So, she* is *interested in the business...*"You were part of the harvest crew then—the back end of production."

She nodded. "And I earned a souvenir t-shirt for my efforts, but after slaving in your fields tomorrow, I may have second thoughts about wineries."

"Consider it field training, where you'll learn the front end—vine pruning." He parked at her hotel, then turning toward her, he stared at her lips, recalling their ice-wine sweetness. *Should I kiss her good—*

"Time?"

"What?"

"What time will you come by?" Her chin down, she watched him through uptilted eyes.

"Sunrise." Embarrassed by his fantasizing, he bunched his lips. "I'll meet you here at seven."

" 'Til then." She cracked the door but, before bolting out, grazed his cheek with a kiss. "See ya." With an impish grin, she was gone.

What just happened?

Chapter 7

I sprinted to my room, threw the deadbolt, and leaned against the door, laughing until I hugged my sides. *The look on his face was priceless*. Still giggling, I stepped into the room and grinned at the mirror. *Who'd have thought a car accident and getting stranded could be so much fun?*

I lifted the velveteen bag from my purse, undid the drawstring, and tipped the cameo into my hand. Then I held the carved brooch to my neckline and checked my reflection. *Do I look anything like my great-great-grandmother? Though she must've had long hair*. Staring, I scrutinized my ear-length, tawny brown hair, freckled nose, and green eyes.

Gradually, my mirrored image seemed to transform beneath the room's overhead lights. Instead of my usual tan, my complexion paled to buttermilk, and as my hair caught the light, it suggested an upswept, *Gibson Girl* hairdo instead of a short bob. Only the brooch at my throat remained the same…but it adorned the high collar of a postbellum, wedding dress.

"What the…?" I jumped away from the image. Then swallowing hard, I stepped back to peek.

My reflection back to normal, I chuckled at my imagination. *What was in that margarita?* Setting the brooch on the dresser, I turned on the shower and undressed while the bathroom steamed.

THUMP…Thump…thump. A shiny, red ball bounced into the room.

How did that rubber ball get in here? Did I leave the door unlocked? Panicking, I grabbed a towel and tested the deadbolt. Though it was secure, I slipped the night latch into place. As an added precaution, I checked the closet, looked under the bed, and flung open the draperies. *No one.* I checked the windows. *Locked.*

At a loss as to the ball's source, I squeezed it between my fingers. Springy and elastic, it was new—not a long-forgotten toy lost behind a dresser. Then I recalled seeing it in the hall the night I registered. *Maybe it rolled in when I opened the door?*

Good thing I'm not superstitious. I tried to laugh it off, but even after showering, I was anxious. Instead of counting sheep, I replayed the weekend's list of firsts. *Survived the car accident. Met Luke.* Kissed *Luke. Read the journals. Visited Marianna's homestead. Met Rosie. Inherited the brooch…*

I slipped into an uneasy dream, where a wisp of a girl dropped her red ball and threw her arms around my waist, hugging me.

"*Quédate un poco más.*" As the ball rolled away, the girl's dark eyes filled with tears.

"What's she saying?" In my dream, I looked about for an interpreter. I placed my hands on the girl's thin shoulders. "Can you speak English? What are you saying?"

"*Quédate.*" The girl held tighter, her long dark hair framing her angular face. "*Quédate.*"

I woke repeating the word over and over. Switching on the bed lamp, I grabbed my phone, found an online Spanish-to-English translating app, and punched in my best guess at the word's spelling. "*Quédate.* Stay." *Stay?*

I turned off the lamp and stared at the ceiling. *Who was that little girl? Why would she want me to stay? And stay* where? *And what's with the red ball?*

Again, I fell into a troubled sleep. This time, a woman's face with a buttermilk complexion and upswept hair appeared—the same face as in the mirror. The woman wore the cameo brooch above a lacy, floor-length, wedding dress.

"Please stay," said a male's disembodied voice.

In the dream, I *was* the woman. *Do I stay, or do I go?* The words echoing as I woke, I glanced at the nightstand—SOS. *The distress signal? What?* Bolting upright with a yelp, I double-checked the digital alarm clock and laughed at my fears: *5:05, not SOS.*

****

I watched through the hotel lobby window with my fourth cup of coffee in hand. The moment I saw Luke's truck, I ran out and hammered on the passenger window.

"You're up bright and early."

Jumping in, I leaned against the headrest and breathed a sigh of relief. "I've been up since five. In fact, I barely slept at all."

"Why?" His eyes bunched.

He'll think I'm crazy. I paused, debating how to tell him. "I'm seeing 'ghosts.' "

"What?" He smothered a laugh. "Did something go bump in the night?"

"More like *thump* in the night." I handed him the rubber ball. "Here's the 'proof.' Though the door was locked, this rolled into the bathroom while I showered."

"That's it?"

"No, I saw…for lack of a better word, apparitions."

109

Frowning as he eyed the ball, he bunched his lips. "You mean the hotel's haunted?"

"Not exactly. I saw an image in the mirror. Then after I went to bed, I saw the same image in my dream." I stiffened, remembering. "Grandma always said dreams were thin veils between our world and the next—gateways where messages can slip through." I shook off the chill. "I'm trying to stay objective, but last night's encounters were spooky."

"How do you know all the 'encounters' weren't dreams?" Brow wrinkled, he dropped the ball in the cupholder.

"The first was so vivid, I'd swear I was awake." I paused, absorbing the idea. "And the other dreams spoke to me—literally."

"Some cultures believe dreams are a means to communicate with the dead." He shrugged. "I suppose anything's possible."

"I'm just *so* glad the night's over." A deep sigh escaped.

"You sure you're up for working in the vineyards?" He scrutinized me.

"Absolutely." As we pulled onto the street, I eyed the hotel. "But I don't want to stay in that room any longer than I have to."

"So, you *do* think the hotel's haunted."

"Not really." Wrinkling my nose, I tried to determine what made me uncomfortable. "Maybe it isn't the room as much as something that's *in* the room…"

"Did you sense it before last night?" He glanced my way.

"That first morning, I saw a smiley face in the steamed mirror, and…Why are you wearing that silly grin?"

"Sorry, my bad." His lips twitched with a suppressed smile. "I made that doodle after I showered but thought it'd disappear." His smile fading, his forehead puckered. "Did you see anything else?"

The giggle and squeaking door came to mind, but I dismissed them to an overactive imagination. "Nothing until last night."

"Besides the rubber ball, what was in the room that wasn't there the other nights?"

What was different...new? Hands folded, I tapped my index fingers against my lips, mentally taking inventory. *The cameo...* "The brooch appeared in both the mirrored image and my dreams." I glanced at Luke for confirmation. "Could the cameo be the trigger?"

"It's been in my family for a hundred and twenty years." He scratched his ear. "Aunt Rosie never mentioned anything odd, and I don't recall hearing any stories."

"I don't know. Maybe I'm grasping at straws, but I get the feeling someone or something is trying to communicate." *But what are they telling me?*

****

Twenty minutes later, Luke pulled clippers from his pocket as he led her into the vineyard. "To get the best grape production, you have to cut back last year's vines to the shape of the wire trellis. Leave only two or three green buds with about six inches in between."

"What percentage should I remove?" She shrugged. "Maybe ten?"

"More like ninety. Trim any growth that points down or has insect or weather damage." After demonstrating, he turned toward her. "Get the idea?"

"I think so, but could you watch me clip a vine or two, just to be sure? I don't want to ruin this year's production."

"As long as you don't cut the vine's main trunk or permanent extension, you're fine." He chuckled. "But if you're more comfortable with me watching, sure, I'd be happy to look over your shoulder."

"Does that make you an angel on my shoulder?"

"Not quite." He stepped to the next vine. "Try this one."

She knelt and clipped one spur. "Like that?"

"That's a good start but clip off this spur"—he pointed—"this one, this one, and these two." He lifted his lips in a half smile. "Be ruthless. Don't trim ten percent. *Leave* ten percent."

He monitored her next attempt, watching her nimble body angle and twist while she trimmed the vine. *So, she doesn't want to stay in her hotel room any longer than necessary.* As her earlier words came to mind, he got an idea. *But will she go for it?*

****

A bird cheeped overhead, repeating the same notes, over and over, as if singing *stay, stay, stay, stay*.

I tracked the song to a nearby tree.

Its black crest erect, a bird warbled *stay, stay, stay, stay*.

The refrain reminded me of the little girl in my dream, repeating Quédate…*Stay. Am I hearing things now?* Rosie came to mind. *Or listening with my heart?*

****

After four hours of stooping and bending, I stretched before I grabbed a quick sandwich in the arbor.

"Nothing fancy, but these should hold us until

dinner. Maybe you'd like to eat in Fort Stockton?"

"Sounds great." I glanced at my rumpled clothes. "But first I have to shower, change, and call the insurance company."

****

"What did the adjuster say?"

"It's totaled." Her shoulders slumping, she climbed into the truck. "The car would cost more to repair than replace."

She looks so vulnerable. His protective instincts stirring, Luke spoke before he thought. "You keep the Mercury dime. You need—"

"No, a deal's a deal. Besides, insurance will cover *most* of the costs"—she grimaced—"minus the deductible and depreciation."

"In other words, the payout won't replace your car."

"It's all right." She pressed her lips into a grim line. "I don't need anything fancy, just something to get me from point A to point B."

As they left Smitty's, the wrecker hauled away her car.

"Its last ride." The corners of her mouth sagged.

If she won't take the dime, how can I help? He turned toward Fort Stockton, wracking his brain.

At Wild Rose Pass, she pointed at the roadside. "That's where I slammed into the mountain."

"And *that's* the ledge you would've gone over if you'd steered in the opposite direction." He gestured to the drop-off on her right. "Your guardian angel was working overtime."

She stared over the cliff. "He was, wasn't he?"

****

A half-hour later, Luke handed the coin dealer the

dime. "Could you give us an estimate?"

"A Winged Liberty Head." The man examined it through the loupe hanging from his lanyard. Then drawing a sharp breath, he pulled a stereo microscope from under the counter and studied the coin beneath its lenses. Finally, he peered at Luke. "I see a few scratches but no defects. You know its history?"

"Not really." Luke shook his head. "I recently built onto an old root cellar. My guess is the coin was trapped in the original wall. Then when I renovated, the dime slipped out."

"Do you know what you have here?" The dealer arched his brow.

"I know it's a 1919-D Mercury dime." Luke shrugged. "But nothing else."

"And one that's virtually uncirculated, *but* did you see this?" The dealer stepped away from the microscope and waved him over. "Not only is it in mint condition, but the dime has a doubled die obverse."

"Which means…?" Tilting his head, Luke squinted.

"In the right hands, this coin could bring a decent price."

"Why?" Maeve leaned in.

"See how the words in god we trust were partially printed twice, one over the other?"

Luke stepped away to let her see.

"Yes…" She gave a surprised laugh as she peered through the eyepiece, then stepped aside.

"That's a doubled die obverse—a rare occurrence."

"How did that happen?" Luke studied the coin's motto under the microscope.

"When the dime was printed, the first hubbing was incomplete. Only part of the letters were cast. Then when the hub was repositioned for a second strike, the letters were at a slightly different angle, creating a ghost image beneath the motto."

"I never would've seen that detail without the microscope." Luke shook his head.

"I may have an interested party. Let me make a quick call." The dealer scrolled through his phone's contact list and pressed a key as he stepped away. "Excuse me."

"What do you think?" Luke searched her face.

"Your guess is as good as mine." Her forehead wrinkling, she shrugged. "I don't know anything about numismatics."

"Me, neither." Despite being across the room, Luke caught snippets of the dealer's conversation.

"MS sixty…uncirculated…some luster."

After several minutes, the dealer returned, smiling. "I believe I've found a buyer."

"Can't *you* buy the dime?" Maeve wore a hopeful smile.

"This coin's out of my league." He shook his head. "As a retailer, I can't afford to tie up my inventory, but if you can wait a few minutes, a wholesaler's on his way here." Then squinting, he peered at the brooch on her turtleneck. "Now, *this* interests me. Is your cameo for sale?"

"Sorry." Catching Luke's gaze, she shook her head. "This is a family keepsake."

"If you ever change your mind, I have a ready market for mourning brooches."

"You mean as in good morning?" Maeve tilted her head.

"No, m-o-u, as in grief." He stared at her brooch.

"Did you notice the oak sprays in the gold filigree?"

"No, I didn't." She removed the pin from her collar.

"The pattern looks decorative, but it's symbolic." The dealer lightly ran his finger around the metal design. "An empty acorn cup represents an empty shell—a death—and those lilies-of-the-valley symbolize a reunion with a departed loved. Both motifs were popular mourning symbols in the mid-to-late nineteenth century."

Maeve's brows shot up.

"Could I see the brooch?"

"Of course." The bar pin safely on top, she placed the cameo in his hand.

He pressed a node at the side, and the back sprang open, revealing a glossy fabric. "Just as I thought—a secret compartment."

Maeve gave a surprised cry as she fingered the shiny material inside. "Such a fine weave…is that flax?"

"No, ma'am." He shook his head. "That's plaited hair."

"Human hair?" Recoiling, Maeve turned toward Luke. "Whose?"

"No idea." He shrugged. "This is the first I've heard of any lock of hair."

"Sometimes family bibles show birth and death records." The dealer closed the hinge and returned the pin.

"If anyone has a family bible, it'd be Aunt Rosie." He glanced at Maeve. "We'll have to ask the next time we see her."

A gray-haired man entered the shop.

"This is George Dawson, an estate wholesaler, who may be interested in your Winged Liberty Head."

After introductions, the man examined the dime beneath the microscope. He rubbed his chin, made several calculations on his phone app, then turned to Luke. "This your coin?"

"No, it belongs to—"

"Yes, it's his." Maeve shot Luke a dirty look.

"Doubled die obverse coins don't come on the market often…"

Luke frowned before turning his attention toward the dealer. "Go on."

"I represent a national wholesaler that's always interested in adding to its inventory." The man scrutinized Luke, seeming to size him up. "How much you want for it?"

"How much are you offering?"

****

"Twenty thousand dollars!" Sitting in the privacy of the truck an hour later, I turned to Luke. "Well done!"

"I know nothing about coins…" He studied the cashier's check before meeting my gaze. "But I know horse trading. Next stop, the bank…*but* we split this fifty-fifty."

"Nope." Lips pursed, I shook my head. "A deal's a deal, *but* I will hold you to the winery investment." Despite the mental image of my totaled car, I forced a smile.

"Don't pretend you can't use the money." He spoke softly. "I've been thinking. I need help pruning the vineyards, but I can't afford to hire anyone—"

"Now you can."

"No." He shook his head. "This windfall *almost* covers the patio bar's expenses—*if* I do the work myself—but that brings us back to the winter pruning. I

117

need help, but I can't afford to pay wages, so maybe you—"

"I'm just passing through." Closed to any ideas, I crossed and waved my hands.

"Let me finish…You could work for room and board."

"What?" Squinting, I tilted my head. *What's he proposing?*

"You could stay in the cabin. No one's using it, and we could share meals." His brow creased.

"Your idea makes sense…dollars and cents, but…" I wrinkled my nose, skeptical of his neatly wrapped package. *Just sounds a little too cozy.*

"Think about it. With no expenses, you'd save what you'd otherwise spend on hotels and restaurants, and in a few months, you'd have the down payment for a car…plus you'll have a ten-thousand-dollar interest in the winery." His eyes shining, he took a deep breath. "What do you say?"

I shook my head. "I don't think so…"

"Why not?" He sat back as if I'd slapped him.

"For one thing, we'd be in each other's hair day after day." *Night after night.* A vague uneasiness settled over me. "It wouldn't work."

"Why not?"

Half laughing, half sighing, I shook my head. "It just wouldn't."

"Give me one reason."

"What would your neighbors say?"

"You mean Bea." He took a sharp breath. "We had a little chat."

"What about your aunt? What'll she think?"

"It doesn't matter what anyone else thinks. You and

I know this is a practical solution to both our problems."
He shot me a bright smile. "Come on. What do you say?"

It's appealing, but... "We run the risk of too much
'togetherness.' " I grimaced as I met his gaze. "Do I have
to spell it out for you?"

"Oh." He scratched the back of his neck. "Look,
this'd be a business relationship—"

"Relationship?" Skepticism rising, I arched my
brow.

"Partnership...strictly a business arrangement."

I studied him for clues. *His idea sounds reasonable,
but can I trust him? Or for that matter, trust me?*

"Scout's honor." He held up three fingers as his face
warmed into a boyish grin. "Deal?"

Still undecided, I hesitated, but when no better
alternative came to mind, I offered my hand. "Deal."

He grasped it with both hands. "After we cash this
check, how 'bout an early dinner?"

"I'm starving, but if this is truly a partnership, it's
my turn to pay." *And then some.*

"That's fair but starting tomorrow." He grinned.
"Tonight's on me, but first...you like roadrunners,
right?"

Five minutes later, he parked across from an
enormous roadrunner. "This is Paisano Pete, Fort
Stockton's mascot."

I gave a low whistle. "How big is he?"

"Twenty-two feet long and eleven feet tall. He *was*
the world's largest until Las Cruces, New Mexico, built
a statue forty feet long and twenty feet tall." Gesturing
toward the busy intersection, he grinned. "But he's still
a traffic stopper. Want to see him up close?"

"Sure." I jumped down from the truck.

My hands brushing his as we crossed the highway, we climbed the steps to the statue.

"What the...?" Luke scooped a dime from the sidewalk. "Would you look at this?"

My jaw dropped as a smile came to my lips. "Is it rare?"

He shook his head. "Just an ordinary dime, but it *is* rare because this one and the one yesterday are the only coins I've *ever* found. What are the odds?"

****

A half hour later, we sat across from each other in a tufted booth. Exposed bricks lined the walls of the country steakhouse, where an enormous sign read steak smoked on-site daily, and tantalizing aromas wafted from the grill. My stomach growling, I ordered a sirloin and baked potato.

He ordered brisket and sweet potato fries. Then he raised his beer stein. "To finding dimes."

I drank to it, then fondling the brooch at my neck, toasted again. "To solving mysteries."

His slow smile deepened as he clinked glasses. "Upping the ante, are you?"

I undid the brooch and held it near the table's candle for better light. "The lever and hinge are so tiny, they blend into the setting." I touched the button, and the back sprang open, displaying the hair's intricate weave. "I wonder whose lock this was."

He leaned across the table. "Could I see?"

"Sure." I handed him the locket. "Last night, I dreamt about a young girl and a woman with an upswept hairdo. Think this baby-fine hair belonged to either one?"

****

On the drive back, Luke gestured toward the moon rising over the mountains. "What a great full moon."

"Nope." I thought of the recent string of events. "What a grateful moon."

"You're right." Nodding, he kept his eyes on the road. "Things seem to be falling into place."

"Which reminds me." Glad for the anonymity of the dark, I spoke to his profile. "Were you serious about me moving into the cabin?"

"Definitely." He side-glanced. "What do you say?"

"I'm debating whether to extend my stay at the hotel or…"

"Why don't you check out in the morning?" His voice softened. "What time should I pick you up?"

****

I watched the news before turning in. The top story featured an aquarium that collected fifteen years' worth of coins from its wishing well to fund marine conservation.

That night, I dreamt of a fish tank filled with dimes. A voice said I could keep all the coins I could carry, and I grabbed as many as my hands would hold.

But when the alarm went off and I opened my eyes, my clenched fists were empty. Chuckling to myself, I swung out of bed and stepped on a cold, thin disk.

Another dime? That wasn't there last night. I studied the silver coin in the moonlight. *Is this a "souvenir" from my dream or a message?*

A half hour later, as Luke helped carry my bags to the truck, I showed him. "Looks like you're not the only one finding dimes."

"We should start a collection." He broke a smile.

"Think they mean anything?"

****

Luke punched in the cabin keypad's keys, then opened the door. "The code's nineteen, nineteen."

"The same year as the Mercury dime." She flashed a grin. "Did you program that number?"

"That's the preset code, but I can change it if you like."

"Nope. This one, I can't forget."

"Good point." He studied her in the cabin's surroundings. *Seems right.* "Want to get settled or have breakfast first?"

"This is a working partnership, right?" Her eyes twinkling, she dimpled. "I can unpack later. Why don't we eat and then start pruning?"

"I like your work ethic." A coin gleamed from beneath the table, and he stooped to retrieve it. "Another dime…"

"This isn't random."

"One is an accident, two a coincidence, and three a pattern, but counting yours, four dimes are proof."

"Someone *is* trying to tell us something, but what?" She caught his gaze.

"And who?"

Chapter 8

When we broke for lunch, I followed him into his kitchen, glancing at the faux-brick backsplash and track-lit granite countertops.

"Are frozen burgers okay?" His head in the mini fridge's freezer section, he spoke over his shoulder.

"Absolutely, can I help?"

"Nope, I'll just nuke 'em."

I pulled up a stool at the breakfast bar.

"Want the radio on?"

"It's up to you." Feeling like a visitor, I shrugged, unwilling to express a preference.

He pushed the button, and a country song twanged on the radio.

"A two-step." His face lit up. "*And* you'll be in town Friday. Interested in kicking up your heels?"

"I don't know." I wrinkled my nose. "I never really learned how to dance."

"I'd be happy to teach you." His dark eyes flickering, he held my gaze a beat too long.

I bet you would. A hot flash made me shrug off my sweater. "Thanks, but we're keeping this arrangement strictly business, right?"

As he sliced the tomatoes, a slow smile warmed his face. "True, but nothing says business associates can't socialize."

I focused on his full lips, remembering how they

felt, and his tantalizing grin melted my reserve.

The microwave beeped.

Attention refocused, I jumped from my seat. "Where do you keep your plates?"

"The second cupboard on the left, over the sink."

Standing on tiptoe, I stretched to reach the dishes, and felt his gaze burn into my back. Turning, I lurched beneath his stare's intensity.

The air was so electrically charged, I could barely catch my breath. Gathering my composure, I set the table and sat at the far end of the breakfast bar.

"Want anything to drink?" His voice was thick.

"Water's good." I tried to sound nonchalant despite my racing pulse.

He handed me a chilled bottle, set out the condiments and buns, brought the burgers to the bar, and took a seat.

Only the radio's background music broke the silence.

After several uncomfortable minutes, I side-glanced. "Good burgers."

"Thanks." He dipped his head in a nod.

Then a country-western ballad about a cheating heart came on the radio.

Cody came to mind. *Was he cheating? Did he find someone else? Is that why he broke our engagement?* Reemerging, I shook off the resentment. "What's on the agenda for this afternoon?"

"More of the same—pruning vines."

Nodding, I collected the plates, then washed them under running water. "Since you cooked, I'll do the dishes, and if we're going to share the labor, it's my turn to make dinner tonight."

"Works for me."

"Nothing fancy, but my cooking hasn't poisoned anyone yet." I set the plates in the dish rack to drain.

He chuckled deep in his throat.

Pushing aside thoughts of Cody, I wiped down the bar and counters, staying busy. "Did you hear about the Italian chef who died from food poisoning? He pasta way."

"Ba-doomch." Luke pantomimed tapping a snare drum. Then his slow smile returned. "Ready to trim vines?"

****

After dinner, I stretched, rotating my neck and shoulders. "I didn't realize how much work was involved with vineyards."

He chuckled. "You've put in a long day. Why don't you relax, while I clean the kitchen?"

"Sounds good." I hid a yawn behind my hand. "I've still got to unpack, then shower and turn in. What time do you want to start tomorrow?"

"Come around seven for coffee and breakfast. We can go into the fields when we finish."

A yawn overtook me. "Sorry. See you in the morning." With a wave, I let myself out, too tired to worry about my new surroundings.

I punched the code in the cabin's keypad, pushed open the heavy wooden door and, as I entered my temporary quarters, again felt transported back in time. The viga beams' dark wood contrasted against the whitewashed tongue and groove ceiling, and the focal point—the kiva fireplace's hearth and mantle—seemed to smile, as if welcoming me home.

Then I noticed my bags waiting to be unpacked.

Crap, knew I forgot something. I hung up my clothes, found homes for my toiletries, turned down the bed, and took a long, hot shower in the Talavera-tiled bath.

Exhausted, I climbed under the covers. Then something tickled my neck. Wide awake, I leaped from bed and turned on the light.

A silvery white feather lay centered on my pillow as if hand-placed.

This wasn't here when I got in bed. Where did it come from?

I checked the door and windows—all bolted and locked. I glanced at the hearth's glass doors—closed. *Nothing could've flown in or blown in.*

Twirling the downy feather in my fingers, I glimpsed the viga beams overhead but saw no perch for birds. *Where did it come from? If not roosting birds, a pillow?* I slipped off the pillowcases to check the material—fiberfill, not feathers.

Again, I tested the door. *Luke wouldn't have slipped in, would he?* I shook my head. *That doesn't sound like him...yet he* does *have the keypad code...*I drew an uneasy breath as I placed the feather on the nightstand.

Then I dragged the cedar chest in front of the door and brushed off my hands. *Let's see if anyone can push past that—even if they know the code.*

****

The alarm woke me at 6:45 am. Yawning and stretching, I turned on the lamp and shrieked as I bolted from bed.

Another feather lay beside me on top of the duvet. Fluffy and silvery white, the feather resembled the first. *How did those feathers get in this room?*

Dressing quickly, I rushed to Luke's and banged on

his door.

"Good morn—"

"Did you leave these?" Outraged that he'd trespass while I showered or slept, I twirled the quills in his face.

He caught my hand as he eyed the feathers. "Where'd you find these?"

"On my bed…" I squinted, trying to see the situation more clearly. "Did you leave them?"

He shook his head. "Nope, but from the looks of them, they belong to long-tailed gray hawks. Maybe they have a nest nearby."

"But how did the feathers get *in* the cabin." Angry he had violated my privacy—my trust—I fumed.

"I don't know." He shrugged. "My best guess is the fireplace needs a chimney cap—"

"The hearth has glass doors."

"Those bi-fold doors don't have an air-tight seal. If birds were near the chimney or nesting on it, a change in air pressure could've sucked their feathers into the room."

"But *onto my bed*?"

"It's possible, though not likely…" He stared at nothing, then turned toward me. "Do you recall if an air vent's over the bed?"

"Yes, every time the heat comes on, it blows right on me."

"I bet that's it. Warm air vents are perfect for nesting birds this time of year."

"You think that's what happened?" Embarrassed by my snap judgment, I winced.

"But if you think I stole into—"

"Sorry, guess I jumped to conclusions."

"Guess you did." He spoke through gritted teeth.

"I'll check the air ducts after I put a deadbolt on the door."

"That won't be necessary. Don't know why I ever suspected…" I chewed my lip.

"What? That I'd sneak into your cabin?" His neck cording, he clenched his jaw. "If I had any ulterior motives, you'd have known the first night…"

Squirming as the heat crept from my neck to my cheeks, I recalled that night all too well. I'd lain awake, relieved he'd been a gentleman, yet oddly disappointed…

I swallowed the lump in my throat. *Why can't I trust people? Why am I so wary* all *the time?* Cody's betrayal came to mind. *Is he the reason, or is this just another side effect of PTSD?* "Sorry." My chin dipping, I mumbled into my chest. "Didn't mean to—"

****

"Hey, our emotions got the best of us…*both* of us." He placed a contrite hand on her shoulder.

Instead of flinching, she radiated a warmth through her shirt.

Encouraged by her body heat, he turned her toward him and inhaled her subtle lemony scent.

Her gaze connected with his as she leaned into him.

His libido rising, he lifted her chin until her parted lips were millimeters from his. What began as a consoling embrace, graduated to tentative exploration, and exploded in a melding of lips and tongues.

What am I doing? He pulled back his head, gasping for air. Staring into her dilated eyes, he blinked and loosened his grip. "Sorry…something came over me."

"Me, too…" She gave an edgy laugh. "I take it we're not mad at each other, anymore."

"That's a given. I…" His groin aching, he stepped back. "That won't happen again."

"It was mutual, so…" She took a deep breath. "Let's just try to forget it."

"Are you okay with pruning the vines on your own today?"

"Relatively. Why?"

Collecting his wits, he swiped his hand across his chin. "I'd better start pouring the slab—after I check the cabin's air ducts." *How can I work alongside her when I can't keep my hands off her?*

****

Just before noon, a high-pitched whine pierced the air.

Ears perking, I searched the grapevines. Nothing seemed out of the ordinary—just swaths of dried grass between rows of reedy vines. *Am I'm hearing things?*

Another sharp whine sliced the air. What looked like a small mound of hay slowly approached. Then yipping, a tawny fluffball of a puppy hunkered down as if wanting to play.

"Oh, you little cutie." I stooped to pet the fur baby, its curly coat matted with straw and caliche dust.

The puppy lifted its front paws, begging to be picked up.

Its coat was so puffy, I expected a heavy butterball, but it lifted effortlessly, and beneath the bushy fur was nothing but bones. "You're all fluff. You can't weigh more than a few ounces." Cuddling the pup, I glanced about for its owner or mother, but nothing else moved among the vines.

The puppy wriggled, tickling my ears with his velvety tongue.

I laughed as goosebumps broke out on my neck. "I'd better get you scanned for a microchip. In the meantime, let's get some meat on those bones." Nuzzling the pup, I whispered in its floppy ears as I walked back for lunch. "You can stay with me until we find your owner. Just need to check."

"Where'd you find him?" Trowel in hand, Luke straightened his back.

"He found me." Avoiding the wet cement, I stepped closer. "Want to hold him?"

"Sure, let me wipe off my hands first. Just finished floating this concrete." A moment later, he reached for the puppy.

As I leaned toward him in the exchange, his fingertips accidentally grazed my breast. My nipples stiffened, and I stepped back. Then avoiding his gaze, I pretended not to notice. "He's a sweetie, isn't he?"

"And cuddly as a teddy bear." The puppy licked his ears, and he laughed aloud. "What are you going to call him?"

"How 'bout Teddy for teddy bear." I smiled at the idea. "I'll try to find his owner—make signs to place around town—but in the meantime, do you mind if I keep him in the cabin?"

"Not a problem." He laughed as the pup reached for his ears. "No, you don't, you little stinker." Then he turned toward me. "I'm going to town this afternoon. Want to come along?"

****

During the short drive, the puppy found the rubber ball in the cupholder and happily teethed it while I cuddled him.

In town, the veterinarian scanned Teddy but found

no microchip. "Sorry."

"No collar, no tags, no chip." I grimaced. "The only thing left is to put up signs. Okay to leave one here?" I carried the puppy inside my jacket as I distributed the other signs until I met Luke at the grocery store. "I'd better pick up a dog bed and a bag of puppy chow."

Back at Luke's, the puppy entertained himself by bringing us the ball, then stretching out his front paws and whining until we threw it again.

"Doesn't he ever get tired of playing fetch?" Luke grinned as he tossed the ball.

"I don't know, but he's wearing me out." I hid a yawn. "I'm going to hit the hay." I whistled. "Want to try out your new bed, Teddy?"

****

Inside the cabin, the puppy continued his game until I tucked the ball on the cedar chest, out of his reach. "Sorry, kiddo, but I'm going to shower, and then we're both going to sleep."

I relaxed in the steamy shower until the THUMP…Thump…thump of the ball bouncing into the room sent chills down my spine. *Déjà vu.*

Then Teddy bounded in after it.

Chuckling with relief, I stepped from the shower. "How did you reach the chest, you naughty pup?"

He nosed the ball toward me, then bowed and whimpered, asking me to throw it.

"This is the last time." I tossed the ball and, after brushing my teeth, entered the main room.

Teddy crouched before the rocker, as if begging it to throw his ball.

"You silly pup." I set his toy on the hope chest and placed him in his dog bed. "Now, go to sleep." Yawning,

131

I climbed into bed and turned out the light.

Creak…creak…creak.

Just as I slipped off to sleep, a rhythmic squeaking woke me.

Creak…creak…creak.

What's making that sound? I turned on the light, squinting against its glare.

The chair rocked back and forth as if someone sat in it.

Again, the dog bowed, whimpered, and rolled his ball toward the chair.

Goosebumps rose on my arms, but I shrugged it off as an overactive imagination. *Teddy must've bumped the rocker.* Then I compared the pint-sized pup to the tall chest. "But how did you reach the ball?"

Cocking his ears as if listening, he brought me the ball.

I put it in the nightstand's upper drawer. "Let's see you get that ball now." Then I put him to bed, turned off the light, and lay awake, staring at the ceiling.

Creak…creak…creak.

I flipped on the light and screamed.

Again, the chair teetered back and forth as if someone sat in it, rocking.

The puppy was asleep, nowhere near the rocker.

Hopping from bed, I pushed the chair in the corner, confining it between the two walls. "Move now. I dare you!"

Again, I turned off the light, and lay awake, straining at every sound.

My eyes were still wide open when the alarm went off. I dressed quickly and peeked at the rocking chair. *Good, it hasn't moved.* The puppy in tow, I knocked on

Luke's door.

"Morning." He opened the door with a welcoming smile. Then one glance at my face, and his smile vanished. "Another rough night?"

I relayed the evening's events. "I can't explain them. Can you?"

"Maybe Teddy bumped the rocker."

"That's what I thought, but the chair just rocked on its own. Am I going crazy or being haunted?"

His forehead creased. "Did you find any feathers last night?"

"Nope. Bouncing balls and rocking chairs replaced them."

"I have a hunch…" He opened the door. "Want to come along?"

"Sure." With the puppy trotting after me, I followed Luke to the cabin.

He punched in the code, and as we entered, the furnace turned on. Then he pointed to the vent over the bed. "Yesterday, when I checked the air ducts and changed the filters, I closed this vent, so no feathers would blow onto the bed." He gestured toward the rocker in the corner. "I take it you moved it there."

"Yup. It was right—"

"Over here?" He moved it to the exact spot it had been.

"How'd you know?"

"Watch."

Within seconds, the chair teetered. Then it began creaking as it rocked back and forth.

"See what I mean!" I panicked as the chair gained momentum. "Am *I* being haunted, or is it this place?"

He chuckled as he motioned from one vent to

another. "When I closed the vent over the bed, the air pressure increased through the others. Plus, I redirected this vent to blow away from the bed."

I squinted. *What kind of nonsense is this?* "Your point?"

"The point is ghosts don't rock chairs. Air does."

"You're telling me the air pressure's strong enough to move this chair?"

"Have a seat." He gestured toward the rocker.

As soon as I sat, a draft from the vent whooshed against my chest. "You're right. That vent really forces the air." Then I remembered how the puppy had bowed and whimpered by the chair. "But why would Teddy try to give his ball to the chair?"

"Maybe because the chair moved, he assumed someone was sitting in it." He shrugged. "Who knows what dogs think?" He leaned over to pet the puppy.

"That might explain it…but another thing." I scratched my head. "How could Teddy reach the top of the cedar chest to get the ball. Even if he stands on his hind legs, he's too short."

"Can you show me?"

I took the ball from the nightstand and placed it on the chest.

Within seconds, air from the same vent rolled the ball over the side and onto the floor with the same THUMP…Thump…thump.

The heat rose from my neck to my face. Smothering a giggle, I retrieved the ball, too embarrassed to meet his gaze.

"Satisfied?"

"You must think I'm an idiot." I swallowed a sigh. "But the rocking chair, the dog staring at it, and the bouncing ball last night—on top of the feathers the night before—just unnerved me. Sorry. I don't normally get so spooked."

"No harm done." His smile was empathetic, then stiffening, he glanced at the door. "Want me to add a deadbolt?"

"No." I shook my head, sorry I'd distrusted him.

"In that case, let's get breakfast. I'd like to finish that patio floor this morning." He pushed open the door.

"Good morning, Lucas." Rosie stepped from her car, carrying a sack. "Oh, Maeve, I didn't know you were here…"

"Luke asked me to help with the pruning, so I'm bunking here." I squirmed like a kid caught with my hand in the cookie jar.

"Glad someone's using this cabin—so much history here." Rosie smiled as she handed him the bag. "Breakfast tacos with plenty of salsa."

"What for?"

"It's Taco Tuesday." Her smile maternal, she shrugged. "Besides, you're my favorite nephew."

The puppy yipped as he dropped the ball at Rosie's feet.

"Who's this *perrito*?" She leaned over to pet him.

"That's Teddy." I grinned as he rolled on his back, begging to be scratched. "He's a friendly little guy—just showed up yesterday." My smile sagged. "We've put signs around town, trying to find his owner. Do you recognize him?"

"No, I've never seen him before, but I'll be happy to hang a poster in the café."

"Great, I've got one left." I started for the antique chest.

"Oh, my heavens." Straightening her back, Rosie watched. "I remember this cedar chest."

"You do?" Luke's eyes lit up.

"And this rocking chair, too." Rosie crossed to the rocker and skimmed her fingers over its back, as if caressing it. "My father refinished it just after my sister—your mother—was born, though originally it belonged to your great-great-grandmother."

"If Mother told me their histories, I've forgotten."

"Really?" Rosie's eyes darkened. "These were Marianna's when she married Mateo just before the Spanish-American War—"

"Wait a minute." Luke held up his hand. "Who's Mateo?"

"Oh…" Rosie's eyes flashed. Then frowning, she chewed her lip. "You've never heard the story?"

"*What* story?" He gave a dry laugh. "This is the first I've heard of any Mateo."

Lowering her chin, Rosie made a humming sound in the back of her throat. "Ramon wasn't your great-great-grandmother's first husband. Mateo was."

"A love triangle." I handed Rosie the last found-dog flyer.

"Thanks, I'll hang it in the café." She scanned the poster before continuing. "Marianna was so in love with Mateo that, when he enlisted in the Rough Riders, she convinced Ramon to join, too."

"What's her love for Mateo got to do with Ramon's enlistment?" A deep V appeared between Luke's eyes.

"She asked him to watch Mateo's back."

"You mean the Buddy Program, where friends enlist, train, and sometimes serve together." I nodded, familiar with the idea. "Was Ramon Mateo's friend?"

"No, but he was devoted to Marianna."

"From her diary, we know she married him." Luke glanced at me. "What's the story?"

"Ramon was her second"—Rosie drew a deep breath—"or some speculate he was her first *legal* husband…" Tapping her nose with her finger, she gave a deep nod.

"You mean—"

"Rumors say she had Mateo's child out of wedlock."

"So maybe Ramon wasn't our great-great-grandfather." Tilting his head, he half shrugged. "Maybe Mateo was."

"No, after receiving word of his death, she went into labor. The baby was premature and lived only a few days. Back then, they had no neonatal wards. People just did the best they could." Her shoulders slumping, Rosie trailed her fingers over the rocker's decorative trim. "According to family stories, Marianna slept in this chair, rocking the baby night and day until he…expired."

"How sad." I bunched my lips. Then the words sank in. "Wait. *This* rocker?"

"This very one."

I sucked in my breath. *Air vent or no air vent, something's weird about this chair*.

"So, Marianna lost Mateo and then lost his baby?" Luke hooked his thumbs under his arms.

"I didn't say that." Rosie shook her head.

"But Mateo died, right?" Shrugging, he spread his arms. "Why else would she marry Ramon?"

"A few weeks before the Rough Riders disbanded, she received a letter of condolence, saying Mateo had died of typhoid fever. She took the news hard and refused to eat."

"Young, pregnant, and alone—the news must've been devastating." I sympathized across time.

"The details are lost to history"—Rosie pressed her lips together—"but Marianna married Ramon when he returned from the war."

"So, Marianna *did* lose Mateo." Frowning, Luke leaned against the desk.

"No." Rosie vehemently shook her head.

"But you just said—"

"She *received word* that he'd been killed. Then six weeks after she married Ramon, she got another letter…from Mateo. He'd been delirious from typhoid fever but had recovered and was coming home."

"Whoa!" Luke jerked back his head.

"Yeah." Rosie stifled a sigh. "Imagine Marianna's dilemma."

"What thoughts went through Ramon's head?" Luke stared at the chair. "Did he know Mateo was alive? Did he deliberately marry Marianna under false pretenses, or was he in the dark like everyone else?"

Shrugging, Rosie gazed at the rocker "If only this chair could talk…what would it say?"

"Keep your options open?" Luke chuckled as he echoed his aunt's earlier words.

"No, wise guy, think of the tales this chair could tell."

"And you said this was Marianna's hope chest?" I fingered its smooth wood.

"Yes. As I recall, your great-great-grandfather Ben made it." Rosie nodded, then glanced at her watch. "But I'm late for work." Starting for the door, she gestured to the sack. "Hope the tacos are still warm. If not, wrap them in a wet paper towel and reheat them for ten seconds in the microwave." She hugged Luke, then hugged me.

"Thank you for breakfast." I gave her a warm squeeze.

"And the family history." Luke grabbed the sack and opened the door.

I picked up the pup and waved goodbye as we walked to Luke's. "Your aunt's such a sweetie."

"She's been a second mother since my mom died."

"Sorry, I didn't know. When did she pass?"

"When I was away at school."

"That's something else we have in common. You're an orphan like me." My parents and grandmother sprinted through my memories. Then the rocking chair came to mind. "But even after people die, I believe traces of them linger."

"What do you mean?" As he pushed open the door, he caught my gaze.

"I think their personalities attach themselves to their personal effects…" Struggling to put my thoughts into words, I recalled items in my parents' home after their car accident—a cigarette waiting to be lit…a toothbrush waiting by the sink. "It's as if objects hang in suspended animation until their next use."

"Not following." Squinting, he shook his head.

"That's only part of it…" I pressed my knuckles to my lips, thinking. "I believe the more a person uses an object, the more that object *absorbs* their essence. Or maybe, the more a person uses an object, the more of themselves rubs off on it. I'm not sure which transmits or receives—the person or the object."

"Are you saying objects become more than *just* things?"

"Kind of…for instance, the scent of a person's cologne lingers on their clothes. Chair cushions and bed mattresses sag from their indentations. Carpets get threadbare. Shirt cuffs fray. You get the idea. Objects are affected by a person's use. But I'm not sure which is the actor, and which is acted upon. Does the cloth on a shirt cuff wear off, or does it fray from being worn?"

"Both. You wear it, and it wears out." He set Rosie's bag on the bar. "But let's continue this conversation over breakfast before the tacos get cold."

"Good idea." I set the puppy on the floor, poured two cups of coffee, and joined him at the counter.

He felt his bundled taco as he unwrapped it. "*Luke*warm." His eyes twinkled as he passed the sack of tacos, then opened the salsa.

"Rosie brought enough for four people." Grinning, I inhaled the spicy scents. "But I don't think we'll have any trouble finishing. I'm starved." I unwrapped a taco marked *Egg and Sausage* and bit into the tortilla's fluffy yellow filling with bits of chorizo. "Delicious."

"But what were you were saying before I interrupted you?" Slathering salsa on his taco, he nodded as if encouraging me to continue.

"We mentioned how objects are affected by *use*, but what about emotions?"

"What do you mean?"

I hesitated to share my ideas before thinking them through. "If materials can absorb scents like cologne or smoke, why can't they absorb emotions?"

"How?" His face widened in a cynical grin. "By osmosis?"

"I'm serious. What if strong emotions like fear or despair cling to objects?"

"Give me an example."

"The rocker, for instance. Marianna sat in that chair, rocking her baby every moment of its short life." I glanced at Teddy. "Like a dog shedding fur, what if she was so heartbroken when the baby died that she radiated that grief, and the rocker absorbed it? Then when something activated it, the chair discharged that energy…as vibrations."

"Are you suggesting the chair moved of its own volition?"

"Something triggered the movement, and I don't believe it was air flow."

"You watched the air currents set it in motion. You *felt* the force. It's simple physics." Shrugging, he lifted his palms in the air. "How can you say it's metaphysical?"

"I just told you." Frustrated at not making my point, I smothered a sigh.

"All right, for a moment, let's assume you're right— that the chair's haunted."

"I didn't say it was haunted."

"Okay, then let's assume it has paranormal properties. If that's the case, why didn't I notice anything strange when I stayed in the cabin? For that matter, why hasn't anyone else noticed anything odd in a hundred and twenty years?" Arms crossed, he sat back, challenging me.

"I don't know." At a loss for answers, I pulled my knees together, shrinking. "For some reason, maybe I'm sensitive to it."

"Have you ever experienced any paranormal activity before?"

The hotel incidents came to mind. "Only recently."

"What's different in your life?"

"What *isn't*?" I counted off on my fingers. "Got my Army discharge, totaled my car, met you, began working in the vineyard, staying in your cabin…the list of *firsts* goes on."

"Okay, but what prompted this unusual activity?" His gaze leveled with mine. "Think back."

"Well…" I chewed my lip. "It began after we found the dime and went to your aunt's for the barbecue—"

"Where she gave you the brooch. We've already established that the cameo was the trigger." His eyes wide, he arched his brow. "But instead of objects absorbing emotions, what if restless spirits *attach themselves* to objects?"

Recalling the image in the mirror and my dreams, I cocked my head. "Why would they?"

"To tie up loose ends, right some wrong…who knows?" He shrugged. "But without physical bodies, spirits can't directly communicate, so maybe they leave messages or signs."

"Like dimes and rocking chairs?"

Chapter 9

Friday, Luke finished framing the patio bar.

Luke—*Done yet?*—

Maeve—*Almost. Why?*—

Luke—*Come see ;)*—

He laid planks across the bar top, then carted out barstools, a bottle of wine, two of his finest crystal glasses, and a bowl of water for the pup.

With Teddy dogging her heels, she approached a few minutes later.

"Notice anything?"

Taking in the nearly completed bar, she gave a low whistle. "All you need is the granite top, and you're in business."

"Still have to finish a few things before we can open the tasting room, but the bulk of it is done." He set down Teddy's water bowl, then grinning, gestured to the barstool beside him. "How 'bout a glass of wine?"

"You read my mind." She climbed on with a sigh.

"Tired?" He poured her a glass.

"Just getting my second wind." She lifted the etched crystal glass and twirled it in the fading sunlight. "What's the occasion?"

"I thought we might celebrate."

"Celebrate what?" Tilting her head, she turned toward him. The sun accented her hair's red highlights and cheeks' rosy glow.

"Besides the almost-finished patio tasting room"—he raised his glass—"celebrate our one-week partnership."

Her green eyes flashing, she laughed as she clinked glasses. "To the weird circumstances that brought us together."

"May they continue." Giving himself a quick pep talk to bolster his courage, he caught her gaze. "I know a place with live country music. Want to kick up your heels tonight?"

She swirled the wine before answering. "I don't know how to two-step."

"I'd be happy to teach you."

"I wouldn't know what to wear." She shrugged.

"Now you're just making excuses. Come on. When I first asked, you weren't sure if you'd still be here." He chuckled. "You're here. You might as well go. It'd save you from my cooking tonight."

"I love your cooking." Her smile widened.

"Then I'll cook tomorrow—give you the night off. What do you say?"

****

"The tempo's quick, quick, slow...slow...Quick, quick, slow...slow...Basically, we just walk in a straight line. I start moving forward on my left foot. You follow by stepping back with your right." He caught her gaze. "Do you know why?"

She shook her head.

"Because ladies are always right."

A giggle escaping, she faced him.

"Same with your hands. Put your right hand in mine and your left hand here, on my shirtsleeve's seam." He tapped his shoulder. "Got it?"

Cringing, she groaned. "I'll look like an idiot on the dance floor."

"No, you won't because"—he winked as he placed his right hand on her shoulder blade—"I've got your back."

She gave a nervous laugh. "Why'd I let you talk me into this?"

"Relax. Just have fun. You'll like the two-step once you get the hang of it." He gave her hand a playful squeeze. "Remember, it's just like walking. Quick, quick, slow...slow..."

The music started.

"Ready?" Leading, he walked forward as he counted. "One, two, three...four..."

Moving counterclockwise, he kept them near the center of the floor with the slower dancers, leaving the outside for the more experienced couples.

"They're literally dancing circles around us." Watching the faster dancers, she winced.

"Gotta' walk before you can run." He chuckled. "Quick, quick, slow...slow...Quick, quick, slow...slow...Got it?

****

By the end of the evening, I was doing the sweetheart position, one-and-a-half turns, and free spins as we spun around the dancefloor.

"You're right." Breathless after a set, I turned toward him as we took our seats. "The two-step *is* fun."

"Glad you're enjoying yourself."

Even in the dimly lit bar, his eyes twinkled.

"Just hope your toes aren't too bruised tomorrow."

"I'll survive." He flashed white teeth as he leaned back his head and laughed.

The alternate band started the next set.

"Come on." I took a swig of beer, set down the bottle, and grabbed his hand, tugging. "They're playing our song."

"I need a breather." He shook his head. "Besides, we don't have a song."

"What's the name of this one?"

"Bubbles in the Bucket."

"That's our song." Laughing, I yanked with all my might and pulled him to his feet. "Come on!"

"Ma'am, you don't know your own strength." Chuckling, he put his arm around my back.

I placed my arm on his shoulder, then acting on impulse, lifted my chin and stood on tiptoe to give him a challenging kiss.

He tightened his grip, squeezing me tight while he pressed my body against his muscular frame and drew me into a deeper kiss.

The downy hairs on my neck stood on end, tingling, as goosebumps broke out along my arms and thighs. A bolt of energy shot down my spine, and a swarm of butterflies fluttered in my stomach. *What was that?* My lips responding, I reached my arms around his neck and returned his kiss.

Then like an air strike, Cody kamikazed through my mind. Shrinking back, I loosened my grasp and pushed away. "Think I'd better sit this one out, after all."

"Might be wise." He nodded.

My mouth burned from his whiskers' rasp, and I still tasted him on my lips, but I had to set the record straight—*now*. "Sorry, I shouldn't have started something I had no intention of finishing."

"We both got caught up in the moment." He ran his

hand over his chin, his five-o'clock shadow grating like sandpaper, even over the band's blare.

"Maybe this"—shrugging, I gestured toward the band and dancefloor—"wasn't the best idea." *Really?* I snickered at myself. "I mean—"

"I know what you mean—" He nodded. "Probably not the brightest move to ask you here in the first place."

"Tonight *was* fun—the dancing, I mean." Recalling the kiss, I squirmed. "Okay, it was all fun." Then I gave an uneasy giggle, crossing and waving my forearms, as if canceling my words. "*Sorry*, seriously, if we're going to maintain a business relationship, we've got to keep this relationship professional."

"Relationship?" His brows shot up.

"*Partnership*." I swallowed hard, helplessly out of my element. "You know what I mean."

"Do I?"

****

With his kiss still tingling on my lips, the strained silence during the ride home was deafening. I hugged the door as the specter of Cody wedged between us. *The less I say or do, the shallower the hole I'll have to dig out of...*

Luke turned on the radio, flipping through stations until he found country western music. A wistful song came on the air about a soldier being lonely and homesick.

Cody…Does he miss me…ever think of me? What am I doing here? Still no direction, a temporary job but no career plans and no place to call home. I'm just drifting. What would Grandma say? I sighed.

"Did you say something?"

"That song just reminds me. I don't *have* a home."

"Yes, you do"—he glanced from the road—"at least, through pruning season."

My snuffle passed for a laugh.

"Hasn't this past week worked out all right?"

"Until tonight." I pursed my lips.

"Hey, we make a good team." He side-glanced as he turned in the driveway. "You're a natural at pruning, and with you trimming the vines, I have time to build the patio bar. Our partnership's working, don't you think?"

"I had." Shrugging, I gestured to the cabin. "But don't forget. This arrangement's temporary."

"You're welcome to stay as long as you like." He parked and turned off the engine.

"Thanks." I gave him a wary smile, grateful for his hospitality, yet uncertain of my future.

"Come on." He opened his door. "I'll walk you home."

"All six feet?" Gesturing to the nearby cabin as I stepped from the truck, I snickered.

"I'll make sure the vents aren't fanning feathers or rocking chairs." He gave me a half-smile.

"Suit yourself." Shrugging, I pressed the keypad and opened the door.

The dog scrambled across the gray-slate floor, chasing the red ball. After retrieving it, he padded back to the rocking chair, dropped it, and woofed, as if urging an unseen person to toss it.

No one near the chair, it rocked back and forth: squeak…squeak…squeak…

"Is it my imagination, or did Teddy just *fetch* that ball?" Luke's back stiffened.

"That's how it looked…" Goosebumps broke out along my arms.

"No matter what's causing the chair to rock, I have to admit this is weird." He crossed to the rocker and stopped its movement. "Newton's first law of motion. An object at rest tends to remain at rest, but…" He glanced at the overhead vent. "How 'bout I take it to my place? Then we'll know for sure whether the forced air makes it rock."

Good riddance. I breathed a sigh of relief. "I'll get the door—got to let the pup out, anyway."

He hoisted the rocker and, as he passed, leaned toward me in a goodnight kiss.

I tucked in my chin. "Let's not start that again…"

"Right." He swallowed a sigh. "Night."

"See you in the morning." I lingered on the porch, musing as the dog finished his business. *Is that rocker haunted?* I recalled Luke's idea of restless spirits attaching themselves to objects.

After bolting the door, I searched online. *What makes inanimate objects move?* One article suggested telekinesis. I shook my head, dismissing that idea. *I don't have any psychic abilities.* Another article proposed poltergeists. *Farfetched, but now that the rocker's gone, will the incidents stop?*

"Hope so." I pet the puppy and set its ball on the chest, out of reach. "Time for you to sleep." Then I turned on the shower and undressed while the bathroom steamed.

Just as I was about to step in, a THUMP…Thump…thump sounded as the ball bounced into the room, followed by the puppy.

"You little stinker, how'd you reach this?" I put the dog in the main room, shut the bathroom door, and set the ball on the shelf.

Five minutes later, I stepped from the shower and yelped.

The puppy lay on the bathroom rug, asleep next to the ball.

That's weird. Maybe Teddy nosed the door open. I checked the door's latch. *Maybe I didn't close it completely. But what about the ball? Maybe it rolled off the shelf...* I took a deep breath to steady my nerves. *That's what I'll tell myself, anyway.*

"Come on, puppy. You can sleep with me tonight." I carried him to bed and turned off the lights. Then just as I began drifting off, a blast of frigid air coursed over my body.

The bathroom door slammed shut like a gun shot.

My pulse racing, I turned on the lights and bolted upright. "Who's there?"

****

The next morning, Luke opened his door before I knocked. "Saw you coming." He glanced at my face and took a deep breath. "Okay, what now?"

I recounted the gust of air, bathroom door, and rubber ball. "I'm beginning to think it wasn't the chair, but the cabin that's haunted."

"Listen to yourself." He cocked his head. "Blasts of air, doors shutting, and a ball rolling off...you're describing changes in air pressure. I bet you a dollar it's the air vents again."

"No, it's more unsettling than atmospheric pressure." I shook my head as I helped myself to coffee. "Why would the temperature be freezing with the furnace set to heat? If warm air blew out of the air ducts, you might convince me, but this draft was frigid."

"I'll check the heating system's vents today." He

shrugged. "Maybe it's as simple a fix as changing a setting."

"Would you mind checking now?" I gestured toward the cabin with my chin. "Sorry, I don't mean to nag, but with all these unexplained incidents, it's getting so I dread going in there."

"It bothers you that much?" A deep V showed between his brows.

Bunching my lips, I nodded.

"All right. Let's find the problem."

I punched in the cabin's key code, and as I entered, an icy chill made me shudder. "See what I mean?"

"Yeah." The corners of his mouth turned down. "Let me check the furnace. It's an old forced-air system. Sometimes the pilot light goes out." He ducked into the utility room off the bathroom and returned a minute later. "Got any matches?"

"Not unless you left some. Let me check the kitchenette's drawers."

"The first one on the right is the junk drawer. If matches are anywhere, they'd be there."

"Bingo." Grinning, I handed him the pack. "So, you're saying the icy gusts in here weren't ghosts, but—"

"A pilot light went out. That's all. The fan stayed on, even though the furnace turned off—nothing paranormal or even abnormal." He stifled a chuckle. "This cabin's old. Everything in it is old, and I keep meaning to research just *how* old. One of these days I'll get to the library."

"Maybe Rosie could tell you its history."

"Maybe." He shrugged. "She's the family historian, but I don't think she's as knowledgeable about the town's past."

"Didn't you tell me the hotel's clerk was the unofficial town historian?"

"That's right. Mamie would be the best resource. When she doesn't work at the hotel, she volunteers at the library."

"Maybe we could stop by—"

THUMP…Thump…thump. The ball rolled into the room.

"Okay, this is creepy." A cold shiver shot down my spine. "I put that ball on the shelf last night."

"Maybe I disturbed it when I turned on the pilot light. Come on…" He gave me a cajoling smile. "A bouncing ball is nothing to fret about."

"It is when it happens for the umpteenth time." *And I'm not six years old.* I growled in my throat. "Don't condescend! I'm telling you, something strange is going on here. These peculiarities all *seem* to have reasonable explanations, but they keep happening. Frankly, they're getting on my nerves. I…" At a loss for words, I stared.

"What?"

"There." I pointed at the chest. "The brooch…"

"What about it?"

I swallowed. "I *know* I left it inside the velveteen pouch *inside* the chest—*not* on top." I about faced. "Explain that, why don't you?"

"No clue." Shrugging, he lifted his palms.

"Now, do you believe me?"

****

"Got to agree, neither the air vents nor pilot light can explain that. Are you sure you—"

Her frown stopped him from finishing.

"Maybe the supernatural is at work." He took a deep

breath, accepting the possibility, no matter how remote. "And these events started after Aunt Rosie gave you the brooch?"

"Yes, it's the only common denominator."

"If that brooch is the link, who or what is trying to communicate?"

"And why?"

"All good questions." He picked up the cameo. Then turning it in his hand, he clicked the lever and stared at the delicate weave of hair. "Whose *was* this?"

"Rosie mentioned Marianna had a baby that didn't survive…"

"Are you thinking what I am?" He lightly ran his fingers over the baby-fine plait. "Could this hair belong to that child?"

"Maybe…Marianna cuddled it until the end, which reminds me. Did the chair rock on its own in your apartment?"

"Can't say I noticed, but if it's the brooch that's…what? Enchanted? Possessed? *Haunted*…" He rubbed his eyelid. "It sounds crazy, but maybe whatever's haunting it rocked the chair."

"It *is* crazy, but I'm starting to think it's true." She met his gaze, then glanced at the chest. "I still haven't organized Marianna's journals. I just stacked them in the chest—"

"*Her* hope chest." He narrowed his eyes, reflecting. "How strange that Marianna's belongings are together once again."

"I wonder if she used to keep her diaries in that chest."

"Possibly." He shook his head, rousing himself. "But you were saying…"

"Tonight, I'll arrange the journals according to dates, and we can read them in chronological order. Maybe Marianna mentioned whose hair is in the brooch."

"Good idea—maybe after dinner?" He glanced at the time. "Let's grab a bite before the morning's gone. I plan to finish the patio bar if you want to prune vines."

"Sure." She opened the door, and a clap of thunder sounded. "Then again…"

Drops of rain splattered the ground.

"Better make a run for it. I'll take Teddy. Here, boy." He picked up the puppy and held him close as he dashed toward his quarters.

"I'm right behind you."

Once inside, he set down the dog and took two bowls from the cupboard. "I made oatmeal."

"Hits the spot on a rainy morning." She glanced out the window. "How long is it supposed to rain?"

He pulled up the app on his phone. "Looks like all day. The patio's covered, so I can work, but you won't get much pruning done. The fields will be too muddy."

"Why don't I run into town to do some research at the library?" She caught his gaze. "Okay to borrow your truck?"

****

"Luke said you might be here." I recognized Mamie behind the library's information desk.

"Yes, I volunteer Tuesdays and Saturdays. What brings you in?"

"Research. Could you help me find information about the previous owners of Luke's property."

"Sure, let's start with the Appraisal District's online search. This way." Mamie led me to a computer and found the link. "Type in the address, then click the *search* button."

Three previous owners appeared, two in the nineteen-seventies and another in the fifties.

"We'd hoped to find more historical information, going back to the eighteen-hundreds." *This search might not be so easy...*

"Got it. " Mamie nodded. "You want the original land surveys and homestead records, right?"

"Exactly." Relieved to be in good hands, I took a deep breath.

"To give you a little background, Spain gave land grants from the 1700s to 1810, when Mexico declared its independence. Then Mexico offered colonization policies until 1836, when Texas declared independence, and settlers became eligible for first-class headrights."

"Which were—"

"Land grants given to the heads of families to encourage immigration. Based on the date they arrived, family men got a league and a labor of land, or roughly 4,000 acres, while single men got about 1,500 acres, and second-class headrights received 640 acres."

"That's a lot of land."

"It is today, but back then, land was dirt cheap." Mamie smiled over her shoulder as she typed in an address and ran a search. "A Peter Pearson sold 640 acres to Isaac Turner, and he sold the land to Mateo Ramirez."

"Mateo." Repeating the name under my breath, I recalled Rosie's story.

"You know the name?"

"I recognize it, but I doubt it's the same man. What year did Ramirez buy the land?"

"Eighteen-forty-five."

"No, the Mateo I'm thinking of wouldn't have been born until the late 1870s." Grimacing, I shook my head. "It couldn't be the same person."

"Possibly, it was the man's father or grandfather...?"

"Maybe." I brightened at the idea. "How long did the land stay in the Ramirez family?"

"Apparently it's still in the family, though they sold off or bequeathed small parcels. Let me check." Mamie scrolled through the pages. "Here's another Mateo Ramirez."

Could this be Marianna's first love? "What's the year?"

"Eighteen-ninety-eight."

"Really? That's the right timeframe." I moved closer to read over Mamie's shoulder. "Does it say anything else about him?"

"Only that he bought the land November first."

I recalled Rosie's timeline. "So, Marianna would've been married to Ramon."

"Who's Marianna?" Mamie half turned in her seat.

"Sorry...I was thinking aloud. She was Luke's great-great-grandmother." I glanced at the screen's charts and tables. "Too bad this site only records statistics."

"What do you mean?"

"Wish it showed family trees, as well—you know, who married who or when they were born or died."

"A genealogy." Mamie nodded as she opened another browser and typed in a link. "This site shows lineage-linked ancestor trees, so maybe you'll find what you need here."

A customer waved from the circulation desk.

"I have to check out his books." Mamie jumped to her feet. "Have a seat and take your time searching."

I typed in Mateo Ramirez, Marianna Rodriguez, Marianna Garcia, and Ramon Garcia but found no leads. *A dead end…*Giving up, I decided to search my family tree instead, starting with my grandmother, Milly Taylor.

The name showed up with a link.

Not believing my eyes, I reread it. *I was an only child, and so was my mother. I thought we had a family shrub instead of a tree*. Intrigued, I clicked the link. *Sure enough. There's my mother's name listed beneath Milly's.*

Not only did the tree show the next generation and several previous generations that led back to Cadence and Ben, but it linked Milly to a second family tree through her marriage to a man named Matthew Taylor.

I wonder why Grandma never talked about her husband… I followed the tree back a generation to Matthew's parents, Raymond Taylor and Sofia Ramirez. *Ramirez? Could Sofia be related to Mateo? No, Ramirez is a common name, but Sophia's name* is *highlighted.*

I clicked the link, leading to a third chart of the Perez family. Sofia Ramirez was the daughter of Valentina (Tina) Isabella Perez and Mateo Ramirez.

I caught my breath. *No. It can't be*. I retraced the lineages, reread the names, then double-checked the dates. Married 1899. Chills slid down my spine as I sat back, staring at the computer screen without seeing.

"Is anything wrong?" Mamie lightly touched my shoulder.

"No, I…" I took a deep breath, still struggling with the idea, then pointed to the screen. "According to these charts, I'm related to that same Mateo Ramirez we just researched."

"And you didn't know?" A smile spread over Mamie's face.

"I had no idea…" I blinked. "If you hadn't pointed me toward the right links, I might never have made the connection." *What are the odds?*

Chapter 10

"So, then Mamie checked the public records." I relayed the story as Luke helped me put away the groceries. "It turns out—about six title deeds ago—Mateo Ramirez owned this land."

"The vineyard?"

"Yup, *and* he's my great-great-grandfather through a woman named Valentina Isabella Perez—Tina for short."

"Mateo, the same Mateo that married Marianna?"

"One and the same." Groceries forgotten, I gave him a wry smile.

"You're kidding."

"Nope—and there's *more*."

"My head's spinning now." He shook his head as if to clear it.

"My grandmother married Mateo's grandson, Matthew."

"And you didn't know?"

"Nope—I knew nothing about Matthew Taylor or his side of the family. Grandma *never* mentioned him, other than to say he died just after my mother was born."

"So…?" Tilting his head, he paused, listening.

"So, it appears Matthew hadn't left her widowed. Instead, he just *left* her, remarried a woman named Luisa, and had a daughter Barbara, who married a John Perkins."

"Barbara Perkins…that name's familiar." Squinting, he stared at nothing.

"Think." I let him struggle a moment before relenting. "Who else do you know named Perkins?"

"Bea?" He caught his breath. "Barbara was Bea's mother, the one who left her the vineyard next door."

I nodded as part of the puzzle emerged. "Your property and hers must've been part of the original 640 acres."

"That's a whole lot of coincidences."

"No, sir, I do not believe in coincidences." I shook my head. "But how are these pieces tied together? What's the common denominator?"

"What do you mean?"

"Why are all these flukes located here—between us, surrounding us?" I frowned, straining for answers. "Why are we seeing these parallels between timelines, people, and places? There's got to be a reason—a message—*something*. What do we share in common?"

"I think better on paper." He grabbed a pad and pen, then sat at the breakfast bar. "Let's make a table of the three families: Cadence and Ben's, Marianna's, and Mateo's. Right now, the connections are too hazy to see any pattern. Once we diagram the bloodlines, generation by generation, maybe we'll see the link."

"Good idea." I pulled up a stool beside him. "Only instead of three families, chart four."

"Who'd be the fourth?"

"Bea's because she's linked through my grandfather." I smacked my head with my palm. "Oh my gosh…"

"What?"

"If Bea and I share the same grandfather, we're

cousins." I smacked my head. "Which is why Aunt Rosie includes Bea at family suppers."

"And you thought you didn't have any family."

"What a tangled web our ancestors wove." As the family connections became clear, I grabbed his arm. "Luke."

"What?"

"You're descended from Marianna, right?"

"We knew that." He gave me a puzzled smile. "So…?"

"So, I'm descended from Mateo." I waited for the connection to click.

"What's your point?"

"Four generations later, Marianna and Mateo are together…again…" I gazed into his eyes, not seeing the man before me, but what he represented—the love of Marianna's life. *Wow*. "Do you think…" I broke off, too embarrassed by my thoughts to continue.

"What?" The corners of his eyes creased in a suspicious smile. "After learning all we did today, you might as well drop another bombshell on me."

"No." Shaking my head, I glanced away. "The idea's too far-fetched."

"Try me." He gently turned me toward him.

"Do you think there's any connection between the dime, the ball, the slamming doors"—as I spoke, more incidents came to mind—"the dreams, the face in the mirror, and the feathers…?" I peeked through my lashes, watching his response.

"Obviously, *you* do." His slow smile lit up his face, and a curl dangled onto his forehead.

As if a cue, an overpowering urge seized me. I stared at the ringlet, wanting to brush it back before running my fingers through his hair, slipping my arms around his neck, pulling him close, and kissing his full lips.

Then, Cody's face flashed before me, counteracting the heat flushing through my body. I straightened my spine. "I…uhm…I can't help but believe Marianna is *somehow* linked to these events."

"Why?" He blinked.

"Why would she be linked, or why would *I think* she is?" *How long* are *his eyelashes?*

"Why would you think so?"

"What if she wants to recreate her love with Mateo…through us?" Inexplicably drawn to his expressive eyes, I leaned toward him. His lips so close, I felt his breath. A chill passed through me, and I shuddered as a fluttering tickled the pit of my stomach. *What is* wrong *with me?*

With a dismissive laugh, I squared my shoulders and tilted away. "I told you the idea was ridiculous." *Why this attraction?* My mind moved in one direction, while my body moved in the other. Gripped by an overwhelming desire to feel those persuasive lips on mine, I drifted toward him, aching for his touch. With a rush of adrenaline, my pulse spiked, and my breathing became jagged. I discreetly dried my moist palms on my thighs as I imagined his arms embracing me.

My mind in a fog, a dim thought took shape. *Is this love or lust? Or is this urge something less corporeal?* "I…uhm…I'd better take the puppy out." Swallowing hard, I jumped off the stool and gave a sharp whistle. "Come on, Teddy."

Luke's jaw hung loose, as if my hasty exit surprised him. "What about dinner?"

****

Alone in my cabin, I reran the recent events while I organized the journals chronologically.

Why am I so physically attracted to Luke? Recalling the butterflies and heart palpitations, I snickered. *The sensations are real, but the urges are so sporadic and impulsive, it's as if they're external. Am I somehow being manipulated? And if so, by whom?*

The more I sorted through my thoughts, the more questions surfaced. *We're moving so quickly...too quickly. We met just weeks ago, yet we spend every waking moment together.* I took a deep breath. *Maybe that's the problem. Maybe it's time to get a car and move to El Paso...put enough distance between us to know what's real and what isn't.*

As I reordered the journals, a yellowed envelope fell out, and I caught my breath. *Grandma's handwriting.* Addressed to Mr. Matthew Taylor, it was unopened and marked *Return to Sender*. I traced the 1966 postmark with my finger, then carefully opened the envelope.

Dear Matt,

Two years ago, I married you for better or worse—for love—forever. Recently, you've become someone I don't know—someone I glimpse between business trips. Your job requires travel. I understand that, but you're home less and less, and when you're here, you're so uncommunicative, I barely recognize the man I married.

Today, I learned why. I saw an old friend at a birthday party, who introduced me to her neighbor, Luisa Taylor. I asked if we were related. Imagine my surprise when she showed me her wedding picture with you.

Who's your legal wife, and who's your common-law wife?

Milly

I reread the letter, not believing my eyes. *Did he leave Grandma or divorce her?* I glanced at the *Return to Sender* handstamp. *Or did he ignore her like he disregarded her letter? Which woman was his common-law wife?*

****

Was it something I said? As Luke finished putting away the dry goods, he replayed their conversation. *Why did she take off like a shot?*

A knock at the door interrupted his thoughts. "Forget something, Maeve?"

"Is that any way to welcome an old friend?"

"Bea?" He about turned at her voice. "What're you doing here?"

"Again, I ask, is that any way to greet an old friend?" Standing tall, chest thrust out, she gave him a shrewd smile. "Good to see you alone for a change."

"Maeve just left." He sniffed as he closed the cupboard door.

"So I gather." Her voice like plush velvet, she gave him a knowing grin. "Mind if I sit?"

"Why?" He leaned against the counter.

"Might make this call less awkward." Her smile hardened. Then instead of sitting, she rested her elbows on the breakfast bar, arching her back to show off her ample bosom, and lightly trailed her fingertips along the polished granite surface.

"We've got nothing to say." He turned his back as he put the canned goods in the cupboard. "If you'll excuse me, I'm busy."

"Then how about a friendly glass of wine?"

"What do you want?" He about faced.

"Nothing." She tossed her hair, permeating the apartment with its strong cinnamon smell. "Other than to catch up with an old friend." She caught his gaze. "Now, how about that drink before I leave…?"

Would a drink get rid of her? Breathing shallowly, he debated. "One quick glass, then I have to get back to work."

"What're you working on?" Moving toward him, she led with her chest.

"The patio bar—"

"I thought you didn't have the financing." Her eyes narrowed.

Shrugging, he poured two taster-sized glasses of wine and handed her one. "Cheers."

Her hand brushed his as she took the mini glass. "Oh, come on. You can do better than that…" She grinned as she held up her glass. "Okay, I'll start. Time to uncork and unwind."

Rolling his eyes, he sniffed at her persistence and half-heartedly clinked glasses.

"Don't be a party-pooper, Luke. Drink with me." She smiled coquettishly over the rim of her glass. Then, her eyes dancing as she met his gaze, she raised her glass and clinked his. "Let's try this again. Take life one sip at a time."

His lips barely touched the merlot, but he toasted.

She wore a satisfied, twisted smile.

"Don't get any ideas." Duty done, he set down his glass. "I'm busy, and it's time for you to leave."

"I know it's over between us." Her lipstick leaving a red print on the rim, she set her tiny glass on the counter. "But I want us to be friends." With a dejected sigh, she pouted.

Head back and eyes narrowed, he appraised her. "What fiendish scheme are you plotting now?"

"Nothing." She shook her head as she stepped toward him. "I just want us to end on a high note. We've had our lovers quarrels—"

"A *lot* more than quarrels."

"But we've had our good times, too, and I'd like to remember those."

"Are you serious?" He squinted, trying to read her face.

"Yes." She shrugged. "Why else would I come here on a rainy afternoon?"

"I don't know…" He made a dubious growling sound deep in his throat.

"Come on." She held out her arms.

For an instant, he glimpsed the woman she had been.

"One hug before I go?"

****

"Knock, knock." As I rapped on Luke's front door, the dog nosed it open, and I followed him inside.

Bea's red talons gripping Luke's back, she opened heavily mascaraed eyes to meet my stare before she nuzzled his neck. "Remember, I'm just next door if you need me."

I knew it. The journal fell from my hands, making a loud plop as it connected with the cement.

Teddy barked.

"Maeve." Luke turned as he broke away. "Bea was just leaving."

"So nice to see you again, Maeve…" Her voice like whipped honey-butter on a warm biscuit, Bea gathered her purse, then gave Luke a smoldering glance over her shoulder as she sauntered out the door. " 'Til next time."

Is history repeating itself? I retrieved the journal, fingering my grandmother's letter as I studied Bea's retreating form. *Like grandmother, like granddaughter?*

Or am I the "second wife," horning in? Bea was *here first.*

Or does Luke want his cake and eat it, too?

I'm not sure what's real and what isn't. Drawing a deep breath, I made up my mind. *It's time to move to El Paso…put some distance between Luke and me.*

"Bea just—"

"You don't have to explain yourself." I snapped my mouth shut before I said more.

"But it isn't the way it looked—"

"This is your house. Do what you want." Mad at him, Bea, myself—the entire situation—I heaved a sigh. "Besides, it's time I moved on—"

"At the top of the news, the El Paso County Commissioners Court may implement a ban on fireworks' sales this summer." The television blared to life. "But vendors are asking for leeway."

"What? How'd that turn on?" He turned off the TV.

The television blasted on at full volume. "Fernie Samaniego, who owns several fireworks bus—"

Again, he switched off the set. "What the—"

"Vendors are requesting the county to allow the sale of fireworks between June 28 and July 4—."

He turned off the TV.

It boomed to life. "Even with a ban on missiles and rockets—"

Luke pulled the plug. "What is going on?"

I half expected the TV to turn itself on despite being disconnected. When it remained silent, I gave an uneasy laugh as I caught Luke's gaze. "That's…weird."

"To put it mildly."

"Has it ever done that before?"

"Nope." He shook his head.

Then a faint creak drew my attention. I turned toward the nearby rocker, gently swaying back and forth, as if someone were rocking. "Do you see that?"

"Yup."

With each rock, the squeak became louder and more insistent.

The dog began barking.

"Now do you believe me?"

Nodding, Luke caught the chair's top rail to stop its movement. Then he let go.

Again, the chair started teetering back and forth, creaking.

"Okay, rain or no rain, that's it. *Out*." He pushed open the door and shoved the rocker onto the patio.

I blinked, unsure which issues to focus on first: the chair and TV or Luke and Bea. *Even if this place isn't haunted, I won't stay where I'm not welcome.* My shoulders sagged. *But what choice do I have? Where could I go?*

Luke slammed inside and brushed off his hands. "That should end these strange happenings."

"Excuse me." I tried to squeeze past.

"Where are you going?" His jaw fell open.

"Ho…uhm…" I shook my head, angry at my slipup. "Away."

"Why? What's wrong?" His eyes bunched.

"What isn't?" *Is this guy for real?* I scowled.

"Can't we talk?" He gestured toward the rocker on the patio. "I got rid of the problem."

"That isn't the problem…okay, part of it…but you

obviously have feelings for Bea, so I won't stay—"

"Whoa, whoa!" He shook his head. "I don't have any 'feelings' for Bea. She was saying goodbye."

"She's leaving?"

"No, she just accepted that whatever we had is over, and she wants to be friends." He shrugged.

"And you believe her?" Snickering, I cocked an eyebrow.

"Yeah."

"Don't you see what's going on?"

"Nothing's going on." He spread his arms wide, palms up. "I told you what happened. That's all there is to it."

"Maybe *you* think so, but she's got other plans. Trust me." Straightening my spine, I made a snap decision. "Now, if you'll excuse me…I've got to pack."

"Pack?" His head jerked back. "Why?"

"Because I'm doing what I should've done in the first place. Leaving."

"Where would you go?" He scratched his head. "For that matter, how would you get there?"

"I don't know. I'll call a cab…stay at the hotel until I can buy or rent a car." *Why didn't I think this through?* Frustrated with myself, I heaved a sigh. "I'll think of something, but I won't stay where I'm not welcome."

"Who said you're not welcome? I want you here." He ran a hand through his hair. "At the very least, until after the pruning season ends." His shoulders drooping, his brown eyes appealed.

"You do?" Relenting, I took a step toward him. Then recalling him in Bea's arms, I wagged my finger. "Oh, no, you don't. You just want your cake and eat it, too."

"What?" He groaned. "I don't get you. A couple of

hours ago, you lit out of here like a dog from a bath. Then you walked in on me, making accusations, and now you're leaving. What's going on?"

"When you phrase it that way, I do sound…erratic." Emotionally exhausted, I dropped my arms to my sides. "Where do I start?"

"At the beginning." His smile gentle, he raised his brow.

"You'll think I've gone off the deep end."

"Try me."

"You'll think I'm crazy."

"*Nothing* can top what I've just seen and heard." He nodded toward the TV. "So why did you rush out of here before?"

"I was"—wincing, I squinted—"confused."

"About what?"

"I *suddenly* felt so inexplicably attracted…" I swallowed my words.

"Did you just say you're attracted to me?" Grinning like a caricature of a leading man, he spoke with an affected French accent. "But *oui*, of course—how could you resist *moi*?"

His comic relief broke the tension, and I smiled despite myself. "Seriously, something came over me *quickly* as if I'd been slipped a club drug or love potion."

"What do you mean?"

"From out of nowhere, I felt an overwhelming urge to touch you…hold you…*be* held." I wriggled as the heat crept up my cheeks.

"Normally, I'd be flattered, but it doesn't take a genius to see you're upset—and *not* coming on."

At a loss for words, I nodded as I tried to unsee the image of Bea in his arms.

"I'd bet good money that hormonal rush, the rocking chair, and the electrical issues"—he gestured toward the TV with his chin—"are all somehow connected."

"Through the brooch?" *It'd be nice to think the cause was external.*

"Maybe."

"But if so, *why?*"

"Maybe someone *or something* is trying to communicate."

I exhaled my frustration, then held up the diary. "I finished organizing the journals in chronological order, and this is the next one. Want to read it—maybe find a clue?"

"Why not?" With a shrug, he pulled out a barstool. "Might as well sit down and be comfortable."

I opened the diary to a vintage baby portrait mounted on cardstock. "Wonder whose picture?" I handed Luke the stained photo.

The scrawled date on the back read November 19, 1900. "Ramona? She was born in October that year."

"Maybe the journal mentions it." As I scanned the handwriting, I caught my breath. "Wow."

"What?"

"*December twenty-second, nineteen-twenty, the ranch. Today we buried our daughter Ramona. She just turned twenty.*

"Marianna outlived both her children." I grabbed my stomach, counteracting the sinking sensation.

"*December twenty-fifth, Christmas. I had no appetite to cook or bake. Instead, I sat in the rocker, thinking. After a premature birth, miscarriage, and the death of my only child, I'm not a mother. And if I'm not a mother, what am I?*

"January first, nineteen-twenty-one, New Year's Day. As I sat rocking with my locket in my hands, I fondled Kenneth's hair. If my babies are ghosts, does that make me a ghost mother?"

"Kenneth?" Glancing from the journal, I caught Luke's gaze. "Do you suppose…?"

"Marianna mentioned the rocker, locket, and hair in the same sentence." Lips pressed together, he nodded. "I'd bet Kenneth was the premature baby, and—"

"It's *his* hair in the locket!" Jumping to my feet, I closed the journal. "Are you thinking what I am?"

"Let's go see." He opened the door.

"Come on, Teddy." I whistled, and the puppy bounded ahead.

Outside, the sun was slipping behind the violet-blue mountains. The sky was a rich twilight blue—deepening yet crystal clear, as if clarifying the situation.

Bluing. I recalled my grandmother adding bluing to laundry to whiten the wash. *What made me think of that?* I shook off the memory with a laugh. "Didn't realize the time."

The vineyard reflected the rusty-red tones of the late winter sunset.

Dusk. I held back a sigh as I glimpsed the winery and cozy cabin. Heartrending in its homey beauty, the scene tugged at my earliest recollections.

The child of vagabond parents, I was often on the road at dusk, just as the lights began coming on in the houses we passed. Growing up without a permanent address, I fantasized about living in one of those comfortable homes instead of viewing them through the car window.

"Gets dark early in the mountains." He caught my

gaze, did a double take, then stared.

"Is something wrong?"

"Your hair…"

"Is something on it?" I swiped at my head.

"No." He chuckled. "The sunset captures your hair's highlights—gives it a reddish glow."

"Oh." Pleasantly surprised, I gave a nervous laugh as the heat crept to my cheeks. "Thanks."

He reached out his hand and hesitated. "May I?"

"Sure." Wondering what he was doing, I quivered as his hand swept my hair behind my ear. As arousing as a caress, the gesture sent a shockwave through my body.

Then his hand molded itself just above my neck, gently supporting my head as he leaned toward me.

Without warning, I ached to feel his mouth on mine. He leaned closer.

His warm breath tickling, I met him in a rush of hormones and adrenalin. Then lifting my lips, I closed my eyes, reveling in the give and take of his kiss.

Only Teddy's insistent bark woke me from the daze.

Then, like a fly buzzing at the window, a high-pitched sound droned—squeak…squeak…squeak—as the chair rocked back and forth on the patio.

In the fading twilight, a nearly transparent silhouette emerged.

I pulled away with a scream, and the image vanished.

"What?" He followed my stare.

"I saw a woman…cradling a baby…" I spoke without turning toward him, watching as the chair gradually slowed its rocking, then came to a standstill. "What's going on?"

****

"I don't know, but I'll bet *somehow* the rocker, the TV, and our attraction are all tied to the locket." After punching in the code, he opened the cabin door. "Let's take a look."

Maeve removed the cameo from the velveteen pouch and handed it over. "At the library, I read mourning jewelry was popular before photography became affordable. People kept the hair of deceased loved ones as touchstones to remember them."

"Makes sense." He opened the tiny hinge. "In some ways, this remembrance is better than a picture. It's *part* of the person."

"A bridge between the quick and the dead…" She nodded. "In fact, the word *locket* comes from the practice of keeping a lock of hair in a pendant."

"Didn't know that." As he fingered the woven, baby-fine hair, he recalled the silky texture of her hair. He glimpsed her lips, still red and swollen from his kiss. *Get a grip.* He tore his gaze from her and glanced at the double bed that filled the small cabin's main room.

As his loins responded, he struggled to take his mind off her receptive lips and sinuous body. *She moves like wine swirled in a glass. And the legs*…Initially thinking of the streaks on a glass after swirling wine, he glanced at her legs and stiffened.

He abruptly sat on the cedar chest, crossed his legs, and began calculating mathematical equations to distract his thoughts. *Two squared is four, squared is sixteen, squared is two hundred-fifty-six, squared is sixty-five thousand and…can't think straight.* He shook his head and concentrated. *Two doubled is four, doubled is eight, doubled is sixteen, doubled is thirty-two, doubled is sixty-four, doubled is a hundred-twenty-eight…no, a hundred-thirty-six—*

"Are you all right?" Wearing a bewildered expression, she stared.

"I…uhm…just remembered something…" Turning at an oblique angle, he set the locket on the chest and edged sideways toward the door. "Why don't you stop by in an hour? Pizza okay?"

****

As I got into bed that night, I fondled the locket's downy strands. *Threads weaving the past into the present. Did this hair belong to Marianna and Mateo's baby?*

I turned off the light and began dozing when a baby's faint cry woke me.

Teddy? I flipped on the light, but the puppy was asleep.

Barely audible, the muffled cry seemed to originate outside.

Is a cat in heat? I cracked the door.

Leaves rustled and the wind howled as wisps of mist began swirling before me.

With a yelp, I slammed the door and peeked through the window. *Full moon.*

The eddying fog gathered slender tendrils of moonlight, as if twisting optical fibers until the vapor became a luminous, rotating spiral over a long, flat rock.

I blinked, and when I opened my eyes, the whirling light was gone. All was dark outside except for the stars and moon. *Was I sleepwalking?* I fixed a cup of chamomile tea, then read in bed until I fell into a troubled sleep.

The next morning, I dismissed the memory as a weird dream.

But after breakfast, as Luke and I crossed the courtyard, a sweet, heady fragrance stopped me. Following the scent, I drew closer to a blooming tree to inhale the perfume of its delicate, white blossoms. "What's this?"

"A loquat tree. Won't be long until these buds develop into fruit."

Something about the tree sparked a memory, and I stooped to examine the smooth rock beneath it.

"Anything wrong?"

"I dreamt about this stone last night." Brushing away dead leaves, I leaned closer. "The shape looks almost like a fallen tombstone."

"Now that you mention it, it does. It's flaggy limestone from McKittrick Canyon."

"Which means…?"

"Flagstone's flat surface would be perfect for etching an epitaph." He stared at the rock, seeming to peer inward. "And if I recall, the realtor told my grandfather this *was* an old gravesite."

"Whose?"

"He didn't know." He shook his head as he studied the thin slab. "No one remembers."

A chill ran up my spine. "If this *is* a grave, would it have any connection to the odd occurrences lately?"

"Anything's possible." He shrugged as he stood and entered the shed. "See you at lunch."

Still thinking about the stone as I sauntered into the vineyard, I froze. *Something's off-kilter. What's wrong?* Then it registered.

Instead of the neat lines of staked vines, one row lay partially toppled.

My blood ran cold. *Did I prune the vines wrong?*

Accidentally slice them? No...I haven't started that row yet, so what happened? My heart thumping, I ran to the collapsed vines and saw the slashed roots. *Who chopped the vines?*

Chapter 11

An hour later, Luke and I walked the police officer into the vineyard. Shaking his head, the man stooped in front of the first severed vine and took the two pieces in his hands. "Think it's kids? A prank?"

"No, sir." Luke's chest rose in a silent sigh. "Whoever did this knew exactly where to cut to do the most damage." His voice sounded hollow as if he'd had the wind knocked out of him.

I dreaded hearing the answer but had to ask. "Will it kill the vines?"

"No, but it'll take years until they produce again." His shoulders drooped. "That translates to lost time and lost income."

I knew his shoestring budget. Grimacing, I caught his gaze.

"Vandalism in Fort Lincoln. Who'd have thought?" The officer took snapshots of the lopped-off pieces, then began jotting notes. "Any idea who did this?"

His eyes narrowing to slits, Luke glared across the creek. Then he shook his head. "Nope."

After a few more questions, the officer put away his pad and left.

As soon as he was out of hearing, I pounced on Luke. "You *really* don't have any idea who did this?"

"I have an idea"—his eyes hard, he regarded the neighboring property—"but no proof."

I followed his stare. "Bea?"

****

That night, a crying baby woke me again. I flipped on the light and strained to hear the muffled sound.

After circling the main room's perimeter, I stepped into the bathroom, but the farther I ventured from the cabin's center, the fainter the cries. Backtracking, I slowly moved between the pieces of furniture, listening.

The sound seemed to come from the hope chest. I pressed my ear against the wooden trunk. Though marginally louder, the cries were still indistinct.

Is that crying, sobbing, or chirping? I recalled a similar sound once, when I left a smoke detector in the garage, and the temperature dropped below freezing. Its insistent tweets didn't stop until I brought it inside and changed its battery.

But what's making this *sound?* I unpacked the diaries, careful to keep them in chronological order.

Though still faint, the intermittent cries were louder.

The chest's empty. Where's the sound coming from? I put my ear to the cedar frame. *And is it crying or rustling like cellophane?*

Unable to think of other options, I loosened a corner of the lining's ancient stitching, and a mound of sand emptied into the chest.

What the…? I fingered the fine, beige powder. It felt coarse but not gritty. *That's not sand. That's sawdust.*

I ripped out the lining, and a horde of black carpenter ants swarmed from their hollowed-out excavations. Behind the fabric, the antique, wooden chest was riddled with tunnels where the ants had laid their eggs.

I was about to slam down the top, when I noticed

several yellowed, crumbling documents tied together with a faded pink ribbon. Only partly visible, the bundle was wedged in the corner behind the torn lining.

What's this?

****

I showed Luke the letters, clippings, and yellowish-brown pages at breakfast.

"Have you read them?"

"Not yet but look at the page numbers—these are the first sixteen pages of Marianna's diary."

His eyes widened.

"Exactly." I smiled as I sipped my coffee. "Want to read a page or two before we head out to the vineyard?"

"Sure." Taking plates from the cupboard, he gestured toward the crumbling, dog-eared pages with his head. "Why don't you read, while I dish up the bacon and eggs? You make Marianna's words come alive." He set two steaming breakfast plates before us, then sat close, peering over my shoulder."

I fingered the pages' straight-edged stubs. "We guessed right. Someone used a ruler to tear these off. Look at the neatly sliced borders.

"*December twenty-fifth, eighteen-ninety-six. Today was our first Christmas in the new house. Cadence gave me this notebook for a diary, and Ben made me a cedar hope chest.*

"*January first, eighteen-ninety-seven. Today I met Mateo Ramirez. He doesn't know it yet, but one day, I'll marry him.*"

I skimmed the entries, reading only phrases aloud in between bites of toast. "*Spoke at the general store…met Mateo's family…exchanged Christmas gifts…stole a kiss under the mistletoe…*" Chuckling, I held up the page.

"Notice the handwriting?"

"What about it?"

"See how flowery and ornate it looks compared to the first entries?"

He grinned. "Our Marianna's growing up."

I skimmed the entries as I turned the crumbling pages. "Ah, now we're getting to her story.

"*Sunday, March sixth, eighteen-ninety-eight. Our wedding day.*

"*March seventh. We moved into the cabin Mateo built on his family's property. As a wedding gift, his parents deeded us the forty acres.*"

"A deed?" Luke raised his brows. "Did she say what kind of deed?"

"Unh-uh." My mouth full as I sampled the scrambled eggs, I shook my head. Then swallowing, I continued reading.

"*May first. Mateo left today to enlist in the Rough Riders. I begged Ramon to join him. He didn't want to enlist, but he agreed.*

"*May twenty-ninth. Mateo's battalion is training while waiting for orders.*

"*June fifth. Too soon to tell, but I think I'm pregnant.*" I shared a look with Luke while I sipped my coffee.

"*June fifteenth. Received Mateo's letter. He and Ramon were ordered to Jacksonville, Florida, before sailing to Cuba.*

"*July first. Received Mateo's note. They were in a train accident. Five of his troop were killed, and fifteen were wounded, but he's safe.*

"*July tenth. Received Mateo's letter. They arrived in Jacksonville.*

"*July thirtieth. It's true. I'm pregnant, but I want to surprise Mateo when he comes home.*

"*August ninth. Received Mateo's letter. Fifty men of their unit died from typhoid while waiting to ship out. I pray Mateo's safe and comes home soon.*

"Look at this." I nibbled at my bacon before unfolding a yellowed newspaper clipping dated August thirteenth. "*Hostilities Have Been Suspended. After three months and twenty-two days, the war that raged between Spain and the United States was quietly terminated.*"

Then I opened a letter from the War Department dated August eighteenth. "*It is with profound sorrow that the United States government regrets to announce that Mateo Ramirez, Jr. has gallantly sacrificed his life in the line of duty.*"

I glanced up from reading. "That poor girl.

"*August thirtieth. I don't believe Mateo's dead, but I'm sick with worry. I can't keep food down, and I can't sleep. Instead, I doze in the rocking chair.*

"*September fourteenth. Ramon returned home today. I begged him for news of Mateo, but he said they were separated several weeks ago, and he knew nothing.*

"*September fifteenth. Cadence visited. When I told her about Mateo and the baby, she invited me to live with her and Ben, but I said no. This is Mateo's and my home, and I want to be here* WHEN *he returns.*

"*September sixteenth. Ramon proposed.*"

****

"Marianna, be reasonable. You're a widow with a baby on the way." Hat still in hand, Ramon twisted the rim between his fingers.

"I'm not Mateo's widow." Refusing to listen, she tossed her chin. "I'm his wife."

He spoke gently, as if to a child. "After a month, it's time to let go false hopes." He clenched and unclenched his hat as he curled its rim first one way and then the other. "I've loved you since the day we met. Marry me"—he swallowed—"if for no other reason than to give your baby a father."

****

"*September seventeenth. Mateo's brothers ordered me to leave.*"

****

"Get out." Mateo's brothers surrounded her on the front portico.

"No." Marianna stopped sweeping, straightened her back, and stood her ground. "Your parents deeded this land to Mateo and me as a wedding gif—"

"Mateo's dead. The land returns to the family." Mateo's oldest brother Fernando pressed closer. "And you're not family, so leave."

"Mateo's not dead." Her senses reeling, she retreated to the door's threshold. "Even if he were, as his wife, this land belongs to me."

"Our parents deeded this land to Mateo—not you." Fernando pointed at her belly. "Despite your trying to pass off that bastard as our brother's, he never married you, you *puta*."

"Get out!" Broom in hand, she swung at them, slammed the door, and collapsed on the rocking chair.

****

"*September eighteenth. The birth pains began just after midnight. Too late to go for help, I delivered the baby myself. He's a beautiful baby boy but so very tiny.*

"*September nineteenth. I baptized the baby and named him Kenneth. He eats, but his breathing is so shallow, he pants. Rocking him seems to comfort him, but his little heart beats faster than a bird's.*

"September twentieth. Kenneth drew his last breath today just before dawn. I bathed him and wrapped him in the quilt I made. Ramon stopped by for my answer and, when he saw the bundle, wept before he grabbed a shovel, dug the grave, and etched the tombstone. I held Kenneth until the last moment, kissed him one last time, and lay him to rest.

"Are you thinking what I am?" I glanced at Luke as I stood.

Moments later, Luke prized the flat rock from the ground, flipped it over, and brushed away the loose soil from its sides. "Do you see any etching?"

"No."

"Maybe this isn't the same stone."

"Or maybe the etching is so worn, we can't read it." I held up my index finger. "Back in a minute." I returned with a roll of aluminum foil. "Wrap a sheet of foil around the stone, while I get a dry paintbrush from the shed."

When I returned, I knelt in front of the foil-covered stone and lightly drew the brush back and forth across the surface, then up and down.

Nothing appeared.

Disappointed, I shook my head. "Help me flip it over?" Again, using light strokes, I brushed the foil against the stone's coarse but featureless surface, and a date emerged—9.20.1898.

"Kenneth's grave." Standing, I brushed off my knees. "To think this baby was the only person ever related to *both* you and me."

Luke stared at the grave, then smiled through his wince. "The product of your great-great-grandfather's and my great-great-grandmother's love."

"The *fruit* of their love." I wrinkled my nose. "What a shame they were married such a brief time."

"Wonder what thoughts went through their minds after Mateo returned?" Gazing at nothing, he shook his head.

"Want to read more of the journal and find out?"

"How 'bout after dinner? I've got to varnish the patio bar and cabinets before it rains." He squinted at the clouds before glancing at her paintbrush. "Though, if you'd lend a hand, we'd finish in half the time…"

"And *when* would I prune the vines?"

"Your choice." He shrugged, but his eyebrows puckered in a silent plea.

"Of course, I'll help." Hearing myself, I went slack-jawed. *When did I start putting his needs ahead of mine? Have we become a team?*

From the corner of my eye, I caught movement in the tall grass. *What's that?* My military training kicked in along with adrenalin. My heart rate increasing, I broke into a cold sweat.

Then I shifted mental gears, recalling my cognitive behavioral therapy for PTSD, and took slow, deep breaths. *I'm a civilian now,* not *a sentry, watching for enemy infiltrators. This is Texas, not Afghanistan.*

Flashes of white and yellow swiveled and twisted, entwining, interlacing, and undulating in seemingly endless motion.

As curiosity overcame anxiety, I edged closer.

Two intertwined lengths coiled and corkscrewed, never pausing. Instead, they glided, twisted, slid, and spiraled against each other, slithering in a sensual dance.

I stared, too mesmerized to move. *What* is *that?*

Then it registered. *Mating snakes!* Fascinated by their carnal undulation, I couldn't look away. *I'm a voyeur charmed by snakes.*

Looping and twisting around each other like a two-strand French braid, the snakes simultaneously slid down a previously undetected hole, and the sensuous gymnastics ended as abruptly as they began.

Wow. Physically aroused, I side-glanced at Luke.

He gave a faint chuckle. "I've never seen anything quite like that."

"Me, neither." Reluctant to meet his gaze, I replayed the image of the snakes' entwined bodies, rippling and rolling. I closed my eyes, visualizing Luke's naked, muscular body pressed against mine, then turned away to dispel the sudden, overwhelming desire. "Maybe I'd…uhm…better trim the vines, after all."

****

"Do you want me to read, or do you want to do the honors?" After dinner, I gathered the diary's cropped pages.

"I can, if you like."

Still unable to look him in the eye, I focused on the loose sheets of paper, arranging them before handing them off. His fingers grazed mine, sparking a jolt of electricity up my arm.

He cleared his throat. "*October first. This morning, Ramon helped me move the rocking chair and hope chest. Mateo's brothers watched us like hawks, but I took only what I brought to the marriage.*

"*October second. I married Ramon in a simple ceremony. After losing Mateo, his baby, and our home, I was empty, but for Ramon's sake, I hid my tears.*"

"How sad." My own petty discomfort eclipsed, I

stared without seeing.

"Want me to stop?"

"No, keep reading." I ventured a glance. "Let's see if these pages hold any answers."

"*November twenty-first. I think I'm pregnant. Though only six weeks after our wedding, I* FEEL *pregnant.*

"*November twenty-second. Received Mateo's letter. He's alive. What do I do?*"

"What thoughts must've gone through her mind?" I slumped in my chair. Then remembering a loose envelope, I fingered through the other documents. "Here it is!"

"What is it?"

"This might be the letter Rosie mentioned. Look at the name and scratched-out address: Mrs. Mateo Ramirez, Ramirez Ranch, Fort Lincoln, Texas." Maeve pointed to a rubber-stamped *Forward* with another address. "This must've been her and Ramon's address—Rural Route 2."

"And notice the return address: Fever Ward, Division Hospital, Jacksonville, Florida." Luke opened the envelope and unfolded the crumbling stationery.

My darling Marianna,

This is my first opportunity to write to you. I was delirious from typhoid, but I'm on the mend. The hospital is releasing me, and I'll be home in another week or two.

I miss you terribly and can't wait to hold you again.

Yours,

Mateo

"What date was the letter postmarked?"

"November eighth." Luke checked the envelope.

"Two weeks before she received the letter." I jerked

back my head. "Marianna must've gotten that letter right before he returned. Can you imagine?"

"Here, your turn to read." He handed me the diary's loose pages, then settled in beside me. "I want to hear how this dilemma plays out."

His shoulders touching mine, I tried to focus.

"*November twenty-third. When I showed Ramon the letter, he asked if I wanted a divorce. Though Mateo will always be the love of my life, Ramon's my husband. I told him about our baby, and unable to hold back his tears, he took me in his arms.*

"*November twenty-fourth, Thanksgiving. Mateo returned.*"

****

To keep her mind off Mateo's imminent visit, Marianna busied herself with Thanksgiving dinner. Stirring and shaking the parched corn, she plated the roast turkey, stuffing, mashed potatoes, and cranberry sauce for her new in-laws.

Other than Ramon, no one knew of Mateo's return from the dead, but nagging thoughts crept in during dinner, and she fingered the letter in her apron's pocket. *What if he shows up while they're here? What if he makes a scene?*

The meal went smoothly until she served the coffee and pumpkin pie.

Then a knock at the door suspended all conversation.

Her mother-in-law scowled. "Who could that be?"

Marianna exchanged a look with Ramon.

He nodded and, shoulders sagging, answered the door. "Mateo, welcome back." He spoke as if by rote.

"Hello." Mateo's voice was monotone.

"Come in. We're just having dessert." Ramon opened the door.

Separated only by the doorsill, the two husbands regarded each other.

Gazing at Mateo for the first time since he enlisted in May, she swallowed hard, bracing herself.

He shook his head. "No thanks. I've come to see my…" His voice faltered. "Is Marianna here?"

"Yes, come inside." Though the color drained from his face, Ramon swung the door wider.

"I'd rather not." Hat in hand, Mateo fingered the rim.

Her heart skipping a beat, Marianna ignored her in-laws' stares, grabbed a wrap, and stepped out on the porch.

Mateo came to attention as his gaze connected with hers. "Can we speak privately?"

Her pulse racing, she glanced at Ramon.

He gave a brief nod, then winced before averting his eyes.

She turned toward Mateo. *Am I doing the right thing?* Butterflies in her belly as she faced the love of her life, she recalled the nights in his arms.

"Can we talk"—using his hat, he pointed to a motte of live oaks—"over there?"

Welcoming the privacy, she silently led the way, but Ramon's wounded gaze as he closed the door troubled her. *What do I do? What do I say?* She swallowed the lump in her throat as she turned toward Mateo. "Have you recovered from typhoid?"

He nodded. "Just too late…" Then as he studied her, his flat tone insinuated. "Why'd you leave?"

"I didn't leave." Anger replacing sorrow, she tossed

her chin. "Your brothers forced me out."

"That's not how they tell it." His steady gaze accused. Then breaking the stare, he hung his head. "I never knew about the baby"—he fingered his hat's rim—"until too late."

The memories rushed in like a squall line. A sob escaped, and she pressed her fingers to her lips.

Mateo reached out to her.

Trusting neither him, nor herself, she shrank away, binding herself in her shawl, and stared at the ground as she recounted the details of their son's short life.

"If I'd only known." His hands clenching into fists, he mangled his hat's rim. "If I could've been there…"

The anguish in his voice intensified her loss, and the tears streamed down her cheeks unchecked. She ached to slip her arms around him—ease his pain and hers—but instead, she dug her fingernails into her arms as she wrapped her shawl about her like a shield.

"Marianna, we can try again. It's not too late." He stepped forward, as if to take her in his arms.

She backed away. "It *is* too late. I'm married to Ramon."

"But you're my wife." Palms up, he appealed.

Recalling Ramon's moist, red eyes, she shook her head. "Not anymore."

"Come back with me. We can start again." He caught the tips of her fingers. "I've missed you."

Lightheaded from his touch, she gasped.

He tugged at her hand. "I've never stopped loving you."

Despite her tingling skin, she pulled away.

"You love me, too. I know you do."

"I did…until you were pronounced dead." She

clenched her fists so tightly, her nails cut into her hands. "Ramon's my husband now"—tears welling up, she swallowed—"and I'm pregnant with his child."

****

"*November twenty-fifth. This morning, I woke spotting, cramping, and crying. I'm afraid I've lost the baby.*

"*November twenty-sixth. Spotting stopped.*

"*November twenty-seventh. No spotting. Praying the baby is safe.*

"*December fifth. I signed the divorce papers. Still waiting for Mateo's signature.*

I skimmed the entries, gently turning the crumbling pages as I mumbled phrases. "*December twelfth…baked Christmas cookies…fifteenth…saw…*Ah, now we're getting somewhere.

"*December twenty-fourth. I saw Mateo at the feedstore and asked about the divorce papers. He said he wouldn't sign, that his brothers had told him a different tale. Instead of them forcing me from our home, they said Ramon and I had disgraced the family name. "If that's what you believe, divorce me." But Mateo shook his head. "Never."*

"How can people be so mean-spirited?" I glanced from the papers.

"Human nature." Luke shrugged. "Some people will say or do anything to defend their actions…or their family."

"It all boils down to greed or pride."

"Sounds like that's the case for Mateo's brothers, but from the diary, we can't know whether Mateo thought like them, or they blinded him to the truth."

Agreeing, I turned back to the journal.

"December twenty-seventh. Mateo cornered me at the general store, saying he wanted me back, no matter what I'd done. I told him I'd done nothing wrong. Life had played him a terrible trick, but when he was declared dead, I'd acted in good faith. Now the honorable thing for him was to sign the divorce papers.

"He left the store, but I found a wrapped gift in the wagon. Inside the box was a dainty woman's watch with a note in his handwriting: 'until doomsday.' I went cold, then rewrapped the box, took it to the post office, and mailed it back. Why won't Mateo let me go?"

"Some people can't take a hint." Luke grunted as he exhaled.

"But Mateo's tone is *dark*." A shudder slid down my spine.

"December twenty-eighth. As I left the butcher shop, Mateo entered, and I told him to stop following me. He said he wasn't, that this was a small town, and I couldn't avoid him. I told him I wanted to divorce him, not avoid him. Then I tried to pass him in the doorway, but he stepped in front of me. I lost my balance and fell down the steps, twisting my ankle.

"When I told Ramon, he grabbed his rifle. I've never seen him so angry, but I begged him to let it go.

"December twenty-ninth. This morning, when I woke, I was bleeding. I'm afraid I'll lose the baby. First Mateo's baby and now Ramon's—and I blame Mateo.

"December thirtieth. The baby's dead. Nothing can bring him back. Mateo was once the love of my life, but the shock of his death, then his reappearance, his stalking me, and now my miscarriage have changed that. Ramon's my husband, and I'm learning to love him. If Mateo won't accept Ramon's and my marriage, we have

to move away.

"*January first, New Year's Day. Stayed up all night packing. Early this morning, Ramon's father and Ben rode with us to the town line. Mateo and his brothers stopped us, but I reminded him that the War Department had declared him dead. With or without him signing the divorce papers, Ramon and I were legally wed. I spurred my horse and never looked back.*

"*January third, eighteen-ninety-nine. Arrived at the homestead.*"

I turned to page sixteen. Except for the ink stamp, it was blank. "That's all she wrote."

"Nothing in these pages was incriminating. Why did she hide them?"

"I can understand her keeping her early feelings from Ramon." I grimaced. "But those were traumatic times. She lost her first husband, lost his baby, and was forced from her home. Then after she remarried, her first husband reappeared, accused her of adultery, and prompted her miscarriage." I winced. "Would you want any reminders?"

Chapter 12

The next morning just before dawn, a tap on my shoulder woke me. On high alert, I jumped from bed. "Who's there?"

I switched on the bed lamp, saw the chaos, and screamed.

The furniture was clustered in the center of the room. The desk stood at the foot of the bed, which was wedged between the hope chest and table, with the chairs stacked on top.

Who or what moved everything?

Teddy barked as a shadowy figure crossed the room and floated through the fireplace.

I ran to the window, searching the dark for the shadow.

Only the moon peered back like a giant eye.

Hyperventilating, I called Luke's cell phone as I glanced at the time—nearly six.

He answered with a sleepy grunt.

"Can you come over?" I scanned the room, still not believing the mayhem.

Five minutes later, he knocked on the door, yawning. "What's the matter?"

"Tell me what you think of the décor." I gestured to the furnishings as I closed the door.

A scowl settled on his face. "Is this your idea of a joke?"

"Nope." I shook my head. "Someone or some*thing* made this mess."

"Any idea what?"

"No clue." I gave him a twisted smile. "Just don't tell me air vents caused it."

"Forced air can blow feathers or rock chairs—but rearrange furniture?" Scowling, he shook his head. "This morning's incidents are outside the laws of physics." He started moving the chest. "Let's put the furniture back, while we decide what to do."

"I'll tell you one thing." I lifted a stacked chair off the desk. "I don't want stay in this cabin."

"I don't blame you." He picked up the heavy end of the desk, while he waited for me to lift the other. "We have two choices. You can either stay with me, or I can bunk here."

The heat rose to my cheeks. "You mean—"

"That came out wrong. You could sleep in my bed, while I camp out in a sleeping bag, or I could sleep on the floor here…" He worked his jaw, as if thinking over the options. "Or if it's only for a night or two, I could bring the rocker back and sleep in that."

"None of your ideas sounds that comfortable but sitting up all night sounds the worst." The idea of Luke being nearby calmed my fears, but recalling a cramped, red-eye flight, I shook my head at his sleeping in the chair.

"According to her diary, Marianna slept in it." He met my gaze. "Besides, I've napped in it, and it's not bad."

"Maybe it didn't bother you for an hour or two, but all night? Your back would kill you the next morning."

"Maybe." He shrugged. "Maybe not. What do you

say we try this arrangement tonight and see?"

****

"Until now, everything that's happened could be explained by natural causes, but the rearranged furniture's different." I poured an after-dinner cup of coffee. "Let's call a spade a spade—a ghost a ghost." I grimaced. "We're being haunted, but by whom?"

"Marianna would be my guess, but why?" His forehead wrinkling, he stirred his coffee. "What does she—or whoever it is—want?"

After we put away the dishes, Luke hauled the rocker to my cabin.

"You're really going to sleep there tonight?" I unlocked the door as goosebumps broke out on my arms. The image of a woman rocking a baby in that chair still haunted me.

"I'll try, but I've got my sleeping bag just in case." He set the chair near the fireplace.

As if hypnotized, the dog sat in front of the rocker, cocking his head with his right ear raised. Then he tilted his head the other way, raising his left ear.

"I hate to say this—"

"Then don't." He set down his duffle bag.

"Teddy seems to be listening to someone." A shudder slid down my spine. "It's creepy."

"He hasn't seen the chair lately. He's probably refamiliarizing himself." Luke's face warmed in a slow grin as he reached into his bag. "Hey, I brought a bottle of tempranillo. Want a glass?"

"Great idea." I eyed the chair. "Might help me relax. I'll get the glasses and a bottle opener."

"I also brought a deck of cards. Do you play canasta?"

Several hands later, the lights flickered.

I flinched. "Power outage?"

"I hope not." He ran a hand across his brow.

My cell phone rang and buzzed simultaneously. Caller ID read *Unknown*, and I pressed the *decline* button. Immediately, the phone rang again. "Same caller." I silenced the ringer, but the vibration continued.

After the third consecutive call, Luke glanced from his cards. "Maybe it's important…"

"Probably a telemarketer." But I answered on the fourth call. "Hello."

Dead air.

"Hello…?"

Silence. Then from across the room came a faint squeak…squeak…squeak, followed by Teddy's whine.

Though the air vents were closed, and the dog was nowhere near it, the chair teetered back and forth, squeaking as it rocked.

"Do you see that?" My gaze riveted on the chair, I tucked my phone in its holster.

"Yup."

"Good, I'm not crazy." I gave a nervous laugh.

The air shimmered like a 3D projection as a hologram appeared in a burst of light.

Dressed in a soldier's uniform, the translucent figure wore a blue campaign shirt, bandanna, double-loop ammo belt, and rusty-brown trousers with suspenders.

I recognized the uniform from the library's photos of Rough-Riders. Then I remembered the blur from my first visit. *I didn't imagine it!*

The figure was so transparent, the hearth showed behind it. It stared as if transfixed, its penetrating eyes seeming to bore through my flesh and into my genes.

In a blinding flash and deafening explosion, it disappeared in the fireplace.

Instinctively, I grabbed the puppy, closed my eyes, and took cover, shielding the pup with my body. My ears still ringing from the blast, I peeked.

The wooden mantle's veneer dangled from the masonry.

I drew a ragged breath as I turned to Luke. "Did you see *that*?"

"The flash...the explosion? Yeah." Busy inspecting the damage, Luke spoke over his shoulder. "What was it? Ball lightning?"

"No, the gho..." Weaving on my feet, I grabbed his arm to steady myself. I moved my lips, but my words couldn't keep up with my thoughts. "I...I think I saw a ghost..."

"You're pale enough to have seen one."

I attempted a smile. "For a split second, an image appeared in a Rough-Rider's uniform. Who'd have worn that outfit?"

"Both Ramon and Mateo fought in the Spanish-American War, but since Mateo once owned this cabin, I'd guess—"

"Mateo, my thoughts exactly." I reached for Luke's hand. "Now what?"

"Beats me. Your vision, the flash, the explosion—none of it makes sense, but whatever it was, it exposed a concealed compartment." His hand shaky, he pointed to the fireplace.

"What?" Still cuddling the pup against my chest, I examined the partitioned shelf. "I thought that thin strip was part of the mantle, not a wall safe."

"It's such a tight fit, a master craftsman must've

made it." He fingered the hinge and shallow drawer. "I had no idea this mantle hid a false bottom."

"Think anything's inside?" My imagination grappling with the possibilities, I peeked inside the narrow slot. "I see papers and a small box. Sorry, Teddy, but I need both hands." I set him on the floor and removed the safe's contents.

"Let's examine this under a better light." He strode toward the counter's track lighting.

Carrying the cache, I couldn't hold back a giggle. "I feel like a kid on Christmas morning."

He grinned. "Open it."

I held my breath as I lifted the cover off the tiny cardboard box, yellowed with age. Inside was a delicate ladies' watch with a folded note. "*…until doomsday.*" With a gasp, I unfolded the paper to read the other side. "*I'll love you for all time, from now*"—catching Luke's gaze, I flipped over the note—"*until doomsday.*"

"Marianna read only one side."

"This note wasn't a threat. Mateo loved her."

"But she never knew." He bit his lip. "What a shame."

"I wonder if she misinterpreted his other actions. We've read Marianna's side." As the implications sank in, I grabbed his arm. "Do you think—"

"Mateo's giving us his side of the story." Luke echoed my earlier words as his slow smile spread across his face. "My thoughts exactly."

"Finishing each other's sentences, we sound like an old, married couple." I chuckled as I returned his smile. Then without warning, a physical sensation gripped me—a visceral ache to mold my body to his, sternum to sternum, heartbeat to heartbeat.

The physical pull from my solar plexus to his was so compelling, it seemed magnetic. With the electrical energy surging through my body, I was an open circuit impatient to complete the loop.

Get a grip. I breathed slowly, catching my breath. *This is the second time I've felt this way...why? What's causing it?* I eyed the watch and note, afraid to raise my gaze to his. *If he feels the same way...*I swallowed, refusing to finish the thought. Instead, I opened the tri-fold documents, fingering the embossed seal on the first page as if it were Braille.

"Is that a deed?"

His words jolted me from my reverie, and I read the print aloud. *General Warranty Deed. The State of Texas. County of Abe Lincoln. January 7, 1899. Know all men by these presents...*

"Read that paragraph." He pointed to the words.

*"To have and to hold..." From this day forward...*I squirmed at the familiar phrasing. "*...the property belonging unto the said Mateo Ramirez. Grantor does hereby bind itself, its successors and assigns the said premises unto the aforementioned Marianna Rodriguez Ramirez and her successors...*"

"Do you realize what this is?"

Too agitated to grasp the significance, I shook my head.

"It's the deed to the Ramirez ranch. Look at the address." He ran his finger beneath the property description and embossed notary stamp. "Mateo deeded it to Marianna, and he had his signature notarized. I wonder if he recorded the deed with the county clerk."

"What difference would it make?"

"Recording it would make it public. Look at the

date. My guess is this document precedes any later transfers or sales of the property." He pointed out the words *Grant, Bargain, Sell, Assign, or Convey.* "Without this deed, would the Ramirez family have owned the land, let alone have had any right to sell it?"

"So what? The point's moot." I shrugged. "Even though you'd inherit the land as Marianna's descendant, you already own it."

"Not quite." As he unfolded the second page, he shook his head. "From the legal description, I believe the Ramirez ranch included twice as much land as this vineyard. Look at this drawing."

"A vintage map..." My mind raced. "Can you tell the modern boundaries from these landmarks?"

"This looks like Dry Gulch Creek, that intermittent stream at the edge of the vineyard." He drew his finger along a squiggly line, then laughed as he pointed out three small circles. "Yes! These must be those three cottonwoods."

"You're right." I glanced at the three rings, recalling our hike around the vineyard's perimeter. "But the map shows the creek flowing through the *center* of the ranch, not along the edge."

"Exactly." The corners of his eyes creased in a smile.

Squinting, I wracked my brain. "What am I missing?"

"This deed to the Ramirez ranch includes not only this vineyard, but Bea's, as well."

"Ah, now I see the legal repercussions." As I grasped the document's scope, Bea came to mind. "This outcome should prove interesting."

"Even *if* I'm reading this legalese right and *if* Mateo

recorded the deed, I wouldn't follow through on it." He shook his head. "I'd just like to satisfy my curiosity."

"Where would you start?"

****

"The county clerk's office might be a good place." He crossed to the fireplace's yawning compartment and jiggled the drawer. "For now, I'm more interested in how this safe works." He closed the drawer, then pressed, pulled, and pushed every inch of the mantle. Finally, he tugged at the corner's barely noticeable rise, and the drawer fell open. "How 'bout that?" Shaking his head, he chuckled. "That safe's been Mateo's secret for over a hundred and twenty years."

"What did you touch?" Maeve moved closer. "I don't see any difference between that corner and the rest of the mantle."

"Place your finger here." He patted the cedar beam.

"Where?" Her green eyes searched the mantlepiece.

"Here." Taking her hand in his, he gently rubbed her finger over the wood's bulge. "Feel that slight swelling?"

"*That's* the lever? I thought it was just the wood's grain." Her hand still in his, she turned toward him. "Clever to hide it in full view."

"Ingenious." He turned her hand, so their palms touched. Then interlocking his fingers with hers, he rubbed his thumb across her palm in a circular motion, pulling her closer until the swell of her breasts pressed against his chest. His heart rate increasing, he gazed into her dilated pupils. *Does she feel the same way?*

Her breath hitched as her lips parted.

His groin aching as his jeans tightened, he wanted her. No longer able to block the impulse, he wrapped one arm around her back as he cradled her head in his other hand.

Her eyelids fluttering, she threw her arms around his neck and, with a muffled moan, pressed closer.

Their bodies silently communing, he ran his lips over her throat, sucking at her supple skin and moving his lips along her collarbone.

Encouraged as she shuddered and tilted her hips against him, he nudged open her shirt's top button and nuzzled her breasts. Then he drew her to him in a deep kiss that left him wanting to slip off her clothes and feel her warm, soft skin against his. The urge to take her overpowering, he eyed the bed.

Whoa. What am I doing? As if shot with a water cannon, he pulled away, breathless.

She regarded him through wide, shellshocked eyes.

Like the lights coming up in the theater, the feverish mood broke. His arms fell to his sides as he stepped back. "Sorry, I—"

"No, I'm as much to blame—"

"I don't know what came over me." A nervous, self-conscious laugh escaped his lips.

"So suddenly, *right?*" Nodding, she met his gaze. "Like an outside force took over…" She swallowed, took a deep breath, and glanced away. "This isn't the first time I've felt this way."

"Me, neither." He gave a wry chuckle as he shook his head, trying to clear his thoughts. "And that blast in the fireplace should've scared me out of my wits, but I was too…distracted."

"It's been one thing after another: the flickering lights and phantom phone calls, the chair rocking, the ghost, and then the secret compartment opening." She gave a frustrated cry. "We didn't have *time* to get scared."

"But more than those bizarre events, what disturbed me the most were the"—he groaned—"physical urges."

"You, *too*?" Her pupils dilated. Her shoulders dropping, she leaned toward him and parted her lips. Then clearing her throat, she stepped back and pressed her hand to her chest as if to collect herself. Her fingers connected with her shirt's open button, and flinching, she fastened it.

"So, we were *each* attracted to the other…" *Good to know*.

"What if these feelings aren't our own? What if some external force is causing this sudden, mutual attraction?"

"Why do you ask?" He stared into her face, noting her shifting expressions.

"I've never experienced anything like this." Wincing, she hunched her shoulders. "We're moving so fast. We met just a few weeks ago, yet it seems I've known you forever…almost as if we'd loved each other before, and now we're back together again."

"You've heard of love at first sight." He tilted his head. "Maybe that's what this is."

"Maybe." She pursed her lips. "But I think it's more than just that."

"*Just* that?" He caught her gaze and grinned, remembering her responsive lips all too well.

"You know what I mean." She playfully punched his arm.

"The funny thing is, yes, I know exactly what you mean because I thought the same thing. Is *something* controlling us?"

****

The next morning, Luke visited the county clerk's office. Unfolding the document, he handed it to the clerk. "Can you check if this deed was ever recorded?"

"Of course, but the search may take a few minutes." The clerk called from the adjacent annex as he checked the file cabinets. "Unfortunately, our computerized records only go back to 1980."

"Take your time. That deed's been patiently waiting since 1899." Luke grinned. "And honestly, I'm not sure it matters whether the deed was recorded."

"Let me assure you it matters quite a bit." The clerk gave a deep nod as he fingered through the files, then glanced up from his search. "Texas is a 'notice' state, which means recording a document gives notice— legally notifies the public—of a property transfer."

"And that's important because…" Luke shrugged.

"Because it establishes priority. If an unscrupulous dealer ever tried to sell or convey the property twice *or* if anyone ever contested a recorded deed with an unrecorded document, he wouldn't have a legal leg to stand on."

Luke recalled Marianna's diary entry about her in-laws forcing her from the cabin. *What roles did Bea's ancestors play in their claim to the land? And how important is that ownership to Mateo's peace of mind?*

"I'm no lawyer, but I'll tell you this. Nothing establishes ownership in a chain of title like a recorded deed. In court, it's irrefutable proof of proprietorship." The clerk closed the file drawer, opened the one below, and arched his brow. "But this is the last drawer. If the deed's not here, it was never recorded."

Despite his earlier nonchalance, Luke held his breath as the man searched through the folders, their brittle papers crinkling.

Finally in the hush of the empty building, the metal file drawer squeaked close.

"Here it is." Returning to the lobby, the clerk showed him the record.

"So, the deed's valid?"

"Absolutely. A warranty deed guarantees the owner holds title to the property."

"Good." Luke breathed a sigh of relief.

"But only to the date listed." The clerk bunched his lips. "In a hundred and twenty years, the property must've changed hands several times, so if a more current warranty deed is found, that would take precedence."

Luke digested that information. "But what if the later owners never had clear title? What if they kept the property 'in the family'?"

"You're talking about a quitclaim deed that's used to transfer property informally among family members."

"What's the difference?" Luke tilted his head. "Is one better than the other?"

"In lieu of a warranty deed, a quitclaim deed legally transfers the property, but it doesn't guarantee title or ownership."

"I don't follow."

"Let me put it this way." The clerk looked into space, seeming to gather his thoughts. "A warranty deed says, 'I guarantee that I own this property, and the title is intact,' while a quitclaim deed says, 'I give you whatever interest I have in this property, but I make no promises. My title might or *might not* be good, and someone else may even own the property, but whatever I have is now yours.' "

"So, in case of a challenge…"

"The warranty deed wins in court."

"Thank you." Luke shook his hand. "You've been a wealth of information."

"My pleasure." The clerk's eyes twinkled. "But listening between the lines, I suggest you get an attorney."

"Why?"

"In Texas, squatters have rights." The clerk gave a wry laugh. "If a person's lived on the property in question for at least ten years, he could gain legal ownership through a process called adverse possession."

"Which is what?" *This deed is a can of worms.* Luke smothered a sigh.

"The short answer is if he meets five requirements— hostile claim, actual possession, is open and notorious, exclusive, and continuous—the property's his in the eyes of the law."

"What's hostile—"

"Interpreting these legalities is beyond my paygrade and best settled in court." The clerk held up both hands as if warding off more questions. "Do yourself a favor. Hire a lawyer."

****

Waving goodbye as Luke left, I glanced at the drizzly sky, then checked the weather app on my phone. With an eighty-three percent chance of rain for the next two hours, I decided to wait before pruning vines.

"It's a sleepy morning, anyway, Teddy." Yawning as I pet the dog, I eyed the rocker. *Luke said he slept all right. Wonder if it's comfortable.*

I eased onto the cushioned seat, rested my elbows on the chair's arms, leaned back, and gently pushed off with my feet. My eyelids closed as I rocked, and within minutes, I slipped into a deep sleep.

Chapter 13

Marianna held her baby close, stroking his fine hair as she breastfed. *Rocking relaxes Kenneth*. She smiled at the tiny bundle in her arms while she rhythmically rocked the chair with her foot.

When he whimpered, she moved him to her other nipple and caressed his smooth, soft back.

But as he fussed, he began coughing, then gasping for breath.

Marianna gently patted his back as he rested against her shoulder. Then she shushed him and sang Hush-A-Bye Baby.

The dream setting changed. Tears running down her cheeks as she cradled the motionless bundle, Marianna watched from the cabin's doorway. Ramon jabbed the crusty soil, straining to break through the hardpan. His shovel gave a metallic ring each time it hit a rock, but he wiped his brow, stabbing again and again.

Marianna held the wrapped baby until the last moment. With a parting kiss, she tucked a small container inside his patchwork quilt, and lay her son to sleep for the last time.

His face stoic, Ramon covered the grave and stood the etched flagstone in the ground.

Again, the dream transformed. The setting remained the same—Marianna stood by the grave, tears running down her cheeks—but the timeline changed. The toppled stone had darkened with age.

Still dreaming, I saw myself standing beside the grave. A silent spectator, I recognized the loquat tree, but the blossoms had grown into juicy clusters of fruit.

Kneeling, Marianna turned red eyes toward me and raised her hands, imploring.

A crash of lightning and a peal of thunder, followed by the puppy's frantic barking woke me.

"Teddy! Calm down. That's just thunder. Come here." As I called, I patted my thigh, which usually brought him running.

Instead, he paced the cabin like a caged coyote.

"Teddy, come here, boy."

He cowered at the other side of the room, his hackles raised, and his tail tucked between his legs.

"It's all right." I stood and approached him, speaking in a soft, soothing voice. "It's just thunder and lightning." Picking him up, I carried him to the window and peered through the downpour. "See, the storm can't hurt you."

As the rain washed away the tree's snowy petals, pale yellow fruit emerged.

Are those loquats? Staring at the tree, I recalled my dream. *Or was it a visitation?*

Then a convertible sluiced through the driveway's puddles, splattering mud in its wake.

Bea jumped out, ran through the rain with a soggy paper in hand, and rapped on Luke's door. When no one answered, she strode to the cabin and hammered on my door.

What does she *want?* I cracked it open as Teddy jumped down. "Yes?"

"You have my dog." Bea handed me the

waterlogged poster as she pushed past.

The puppy cowered in the far corner.

"Teddy's *your* dog?" I blinked. "Why didn't you claim him when I posted the signs? Why'd you wait a month?"

"Just saw the poster today." Bea's eyes narrowed. "Give me my dog." She gave a shrill whistle.

Teddy started trembling.

Something's not right…"What's his name?"

"Spot." Bea all but sneered. "Here, Spot."

Tail between his legs, the dog crept behind the bed.

"Either Teddy doesn't recognize you, or he's afraid of you."

"First, you horned in on Luke." Legs planted wide, Bea plunked her fists on her hips. "Now, you're stealing my dog."

"Nobody's horning in or stealing anything." I silently counted to five. "I just want to be sure Teddy belongs to you."

Bea pulled out her cell phone and punched 911. Her index finger poised to connect, she scowled. "Give me my dog…or do I have to bring the sheriff in on this?"

****

"Bea took Teddy."

"*What*?" Pinching the bridge of his nose, Luke groaned as he shut the door.

I relayed the conversation.

"If Teddy was her dog—which I doubt—why'd she wait a month to claim him?" Shaking his head, he spoke under his breath. "Bea for bitch. Well, she just made up my mind."

"About what?"

He shared the county clerk's advice. "I hadn't

planned to pursue any legal action, let alone hire an attorney, but Bea's changed my mind."

"What about legal backlash?"

"We'll cross that bridge *if* we come to it."

I recalled the woman's threat to call the sheriff. "Could you face any court fees?"

"Don't borrow trouble." He rested a hand on my shoulder as he glanced at the rocker. "Worry's like a rocking chair. It gives you something to do but doesn't get you anywhere."

I chuckled at the image until I recalled my catnap. "But does a rocker *take you places*?"

He squinted.

I described the visions. "Were those dreams, or did Marianna pay me a visit?"

"Who knows? Maybe a spark of energy lasts after death—like starlight. The twinkle we see as stars is really the afterglow of suns, millions of lightyears away."

"You're comparing starlight to a person's spirit." Seeing his point, I nodded. "But why would Marianna show me the grave—both during the burial and *now?*"

"What do you mean, *now?*"

"I dreamt the loquat tree had fruit, yet before this morning's rain, I'd seen only its blossoms. Marianna appeared when the fruit was ripe…in other words, *now.*" I squinted, trying to make sense of the dreams. "Do you think she wants us to find something…*do* something?"

"You mean, *uncover* something?" Rubbing his chin, he turned toward the tree. "After the rain, that hardpan would be soft—easier to shovel. If we ever thought of exhuming her baby, now would be the time."

"But digging up a baby's bones would be grisly." I shook off a chill. "Even if our guess is right, why would

Marianna want us to unearth her and Mateo's only child?"

"For one thing, he's related to us both, so we'd be her likely choices. For another, Kenneth's grave was makeshift, at best." Luke gestured with his chin. "Maybe she wants us to give her baby a proper burial."

"And funeral." I glimpsed the tree through the window. "But Marianna could've made her wishes known anytime during the past weeks. Why show herself today—just as the loquats ripen?"

"What's happened recently?"

"Where do I start?" Counting off on my fingers, I reviewed the past 72 hours' events. "We found the diary's lost pages, learned of the baby's grave, and discovered Mateo's secret compartment. Then Bea made a play for you—"

"Said goodbye—"

"Besides brainwashing you and essentially stealing Teddy"—I glanced through the window at the vineyard—"maybe she chopped the vines."

"That thought occurred to me, too, but without evidence, it's guesswork." He raked his hand through his hair. "Though, she did grow up around vines—"

"So, she'd have known where to cut them." I wrinkled my nose. *Bea for bitch.*

"After her performance with Teddy this morning, I wouldn't put it past her, but we can't jump to conclusions." He took a deep breath and blew it out. "Let's go back to your question. Why would Marianna appear *today*?"

"And just as the loquats ripen…" I bit the inside of my cheek. "Last night, Mateo shared his side of the story, when he revealed not only his love for Marianna, but the deed."

"Which will be a legal challenge before it...*bears fruit*." His cheek dimpled.

I chuckled despite the topic, then wriggled, remembering our sudden attraction. "And who could forget last night's kiss?"

"I can't." A glimmer lit his eyes.

"I mean..." I forced myself to look away. "You're Marianna's great-great-grandson, and I'm Mateo's great-great-granddaughter. We're the *fruit* of their love, and as far as I know, their first descendants to have—"

"An emotional connection?" He stepped toward me.

"A rapport." I took a step back. "Could Marianna and Mateo somehow want to relive their love through us, their offspring?"

"Vicariously?" He shook his head. "I'm not sure I believe in ghosts, let alone buy that idea."

"Then let the proof be in the pudding."

"What do you mean?"

"We've both admitted to sudden...inclinations."

"Hormones and pheromones could account for those." Grinning, he leaned closer. "Not to mention living and working in close quarters these past weeks."

"It's more than that, and you know it." My pulse fluttered.

"Even if that's so, how would last night's apparition fit into your idea that Marianna and Mateo could or *would want* to relive their lives through us?" He raised his chin.

"Your guess is as good as mine." Shrugging, I held up my palms. "But we know their time together was cut short—first by the war, then by Mateo's misreported death. They didn't finish what they started. Maybe they want us to tie up their loose ends."

"That's just more speculation."

"True." I nodded. "But last night, we both saw Mateo."

"*You* saw the apparition, not me."

"We agree we saw *something*. We can't be sure what or who, but that entity led us to the watch and deed, which proves Mateo's love for Marianna."

"That's true…" He rubbed his brow. "Until last night, she didn't know he loved her, did she?"

"So, through dreams"—I glanced at the rocker—"Marianna showed us what may be the baby's grave. Maybe she wants him exhumed."

"We're back to *why*?"

"I can only guess, but maybe she regrets the baby's hasty burial. Maybe she wants their child's memory to live on. You said even your grandfather's realtor didn't know whose gravesite it was." I mentally replayed the past weeks' sequence of events. "So far, these odd happenings have benefitted us."

"What odd happenings?" He caught my gaze.

"Besides discovering the deed last night, we found the dime last month."

"And these have helped us *how?*"

"The sale of that antique dime not only paid for the outdoor tasting room but was the reason I stayed. Even my car accident—"

"Now you're adding your accident to the list of 'odd happenings'?"

"Maybe…" I tilted my head, thinking. "It sounds weird, but we wouldn't have met otherwise."

"These incidents are just coincidences."

"I don't believe in coincidences, remember?" I

tossed my chin. "But from the recent events, I think Marianna and Mateo are reaching out to us. We just don't know what they want."

"Or *why* they'd want to interact."

"Maybe it's to gain our trust." I shrugged. "Or maybe it's to gain our support."

"I'm sorry." Swallowing a smile, he shook his head. "I can't take those assumptions seriously."

"Why not? You know their information's reliable—the deed proves it." I took a deep breath. "Marianna and Mateo have earned my trust, and I think they're entitled to our help."

"For the sake of argument, why would Mateo want our help?"

"Unfinished business. Think of it from his perspective. Through no fault of his own, the War Department declared him dead. As a result, he lost his child because of complications brought on by his reported death, and he lost his wife to another man. Then, because of a misunderstanding, Marianna turned against him."

"True…" He rubbed his chin.

"They both have unfinished business—but they're dead. Who better to turn to than their descendants?"

Groaning, Luke ran his hand through his still-damp hair.

"After all they've been through, they deserve our help." I appealed with a smile. "Besides, who knows where the venture will lead?"

He sighed. "So, which 'loose end' do we tie up first?"

****

After the rain stopped, Luke and I got shovels from

the shed, moved the headstone aside, and began digging.

At roughly four feet, my shovel caught on a decomposed cotton remnant. "This might be part of the quilt Marianna used to wrap Kenneth." I rubbed the muddy, threadbare scrap between my fingers, trying to sense its history.

"If we've already dug to the burial depth, this soil could be the baby's decomposed body. Notice the darker color?"

"Hallowed ground." Speaking in a whisper, I replaced the decayed cloth scrap. "We should keep it intact. Be right back." Minutes later, I returned with a plastic storage container. "How's this?"

"For now, it's perfect." After several minutes of shoveling the wet soil, Luke unearthed a rusted tin can. "Will you look at this?"

Only the word *tobacco* was legible.

He caught my gaze. "What's a tobacco can doing in a baby's burial?"

"Open it and find out."

He undid its disintegrating metal hinge, tipped its contents into his hand, then unfolded the damp paper.

"*This certifies that Mr. Mateo Ramirez and Miss Marianna Rodriguez were united in holy matrimony according to the ordinance of God and the laws of Texas.*"

"The date's right." I pointed to the words. "March 6, 1898, but why would she bury their wedding certificate along with their baby?"

"She believed her husband had been killed in the war. Then her premature baby died. Maybe she wanted to bury that entire chapter of her life."

"That would make sense since she married Ramon

two weeks later." I scratched my head. "But finding this wedding certificate the day after Mateo revealed the deed is too coincidental to be a coincidence."

"Maybe your dream *was* a visitation."

I stared at the yellowed paper, trying to fit it into the puzzle. "Marianna's in-laws stole her inheritance, and this document may play a role in restoring it. Let's not rebury it."

"Good idea." He refolded the paper and tucked it in his pocket, but he added the can to the container.

"That soil's all that's left of Marianna's baby. I can't imagine her grief." I blinked away unexpected tears. "I know we're doing the right thing."

****

The next morning, I compared notes with Luke on our ride back from town. "The funeral director recommends a green reburial with a graveside service." The desert marigolds sprouting along the road brightened my spirits. *Spring. Life.* "He also suggests drawing a map of the property to show the burial site, then filing it with the property deed, so Kenneth's grave won't be forgotten."

"I think Marianna would like that." Luke side-glanced as he drove.

"How'd it go with the lawyer?"

"Sounds like we have a good case. The deed map clearly includes Bea's property, and the deed was recorded, so its authenticity is rock solid."

"What's next?" I glanced at the stream paralleling the road. Early catkins dangled from the cottonwoods.

"The lawyer's going to check Bea's deed. If it's quitclaim, as he suspects, he'll challenge it—and he's prepared to go to court."

"That ought to go over well." My jaw tightened. "One thing bothers me, though. Why did Mateo bring the title to light?"

"Apparently, he wants the land to go to Marianna's descendants."

"Yes, but why?"

"Maybe to clear his name"—he shrugged—"right any wrongs or resolve any misunderstandings. Maybe this is his way of finding peace."

"Until he showed us that deed and note, we'd read only Marianna's story." I leaned back against the headrest. "Think he needs closure?"

****

Three days later, Bea's convertible roared into the caliche driveway spewing dust and pebbles behind it.

Bea jumped out before the vehicle rocked to a standstill, then hammered on Luke's door.

"What brings you—"

"How dare you sue me!"

Responding to the shouts, I strolled over from the cabin.

Bea about faced and pointed. "*She's* the reason you've turned on me, isn't she? Admit it!"

"Maeve's got nothing to do with this legal inquiry—"

"I knew you were trouble the moment I caught Luke sneaking from your hotel room." Bea glared. "Now what are you trying to do—steal my land like you stole my dog?"

"Steal—interesting choice of words." Ignoring her barb about Teddy, I focused on the past's injustices. "If your title's solid, you have nothing to worry ab—"

"Of course, it is." Bea's eyes shot daggers.

"But if you *can't* prove ownership, the courts will show your family stole Luke's land."

"What are you babbling about?"

"Luke has the deed to the Ramirez ranch that Mateo gave Mari—"

"I grew up hearing that story about the tramp that tried to pass off her bastard as his." Bea curled her lip.

Bastard? My chest heaving, I glanced at the upturned soil that had been their baby's grave. "It's time the land is returned to its rightful owner."

"That land's been in my family for over six generations, and that's where it stays. See you in court." Bea turned on her heel, slammed into her car, and roared off in a shower of dust and gravel.

"How to make friends and influence people"—he grimaced—"sue them."

"You can't blame her for putting up a fight, but that land belonged to Marianna…and would've been Kenneth's." I caught Luke's gaze. "If Bea's family won't recognize Marianna and Mateo's marriage, it's lucky we found their wedding certificate."

"Even with that document, it'll be a court battle." His jaw tightened.

"What's the saying? Possession is nine-tenths of the law. If her family's lived on that land for six generations—"

"*And* paid taxes and made improvements on it…" He held up his index finger, emphasizing his points.

"Bea has a good case, but if her family grabbed that land from Marianna—"

"Against Mateo's wishes—"

"She'd only reap what her family sowed." I crossed my arms, still chafing about Teddy and the cut vines.

"Ready for some more 'good' news." His tone tongue-in-cheek, he wrinkled his nose.

"Now what?" I took a deep breath, bracing myself.

"The supplier texted that the countertop is delayed."

"So…?"

"So much for completing the tasting room early." His mouth twisted. "If we don't have a bar, why bother opening an outdoor tasting room?"

Like a tire deflating, my disappointment rushed out with a sigh. "All your work to finish the patio early. I'm sorry about the timing, but this is a temporary setback, just until the countertop's delivered." I shook his shoulder, then forced a smile. "In the meantime, *we* can enjoy it—maybe have our meals there. In fact, I picked the first loquats for tonight's dinner."

"The first fruits." His lips twitched in a wry smile.

As I recalled our kiss, a shudder slid down my spine. *We're the* fruit *of Marianna and Mateo's love*…I took a deep breath, refocusing. "Since it's my turn to cook, I thought we could eat *al fresca* and celebrate spring with a chicken with honey-loquat glaze."

"It's a date."

Is it?

****

That evening, as we finished dinner on the new patio, a high-pitched whine broke the stillness.

My ears perking, I scanned the vineyard.

A small mound of dried grass and burrs barked.

"Teddy?" I ran to meet him.

A chewed-through rope hung from his bleeding neck, so tight, it had rubbed off his fur and chafed his skin raw.

"Teddy, what did she do to you?" As I picked him

up, he fell against my chest, exhausted.

"If I had any qualms about suing Bea before, I don't anymore." Luke shook his head as he tried to loosen the rope. "I'll need scissors to cut through."

"Let's take him to the cabin. His food and water bowls are there."

Five minutes later, Luke cut off the rope as I placed his water bowl near him.

Not stopping to breathe, the dog drank it dry.

"He's dehydrated." *Bea for bitch.* I refilled the bowl, set it down, and opened a can of dog food. "Teddy, how could she do this to you?"

****

The phone's bleat jarred me from a sound sleep, and I glimpsed Caller ID through a fuzzy haze. *Cody?* My eyes snapped open as past emotions wrestled with common sense. On the fourth ring, curiosity prevailed. "Hey."

"Was hoping you'd pick up."

His voice brought back warm memories, quickly followed by resentment. "I thought you were in Afghanistan."

"I was…"

"And…"

"My division was part of the troop withdrawal."

The irony. I curled my lip. "Being deployed was your excuse to break up. Now you're back."

"You make it sound like I *wanted* to—"

"Didn't you?" Old wounds reopening, I fingered the disconnect button.

"You know tours last six to twelve months." He groaned. "You were mustering out. I didn't want to hold you back."

The lump in my throat prevented any accusations. I swallowed hard.

"I broke our engagement for you!"

"Like hell you did!" *You broke my heart*. I squeezed my eyes shut. *I will not cry*.

"Maeve…" His voice caught. "I've missed you."

I swiped at the tears.

"Could we meet for coffee?"

"You want to just pick up where we left off?" My sniff was sarcastic. "It's not that simple."

"Why?"

"Because when you broke up, you set other events in motion." Like a spring breeze, thoughts of Luke blew across my mind. "Life is a chain reaction of *choices…*"

"So, you've met someone else."

"Let's just say I've moved on."

"I see." He drew a hoarse breath.

I shouldn't have answered the phone. I fiddled with the disconnect button, debating whether to hang up.

As the seconds ticked by, Teddy woofed and brought me the ball.

"Well, could I write you—put on paper what I have trouble saying?"

Seven hundred miles is a safe buffer. "I suppose." Despite the warning flags, I gave him my address. "Where are you being redeployed?"

"I'm not. Instead, I'll help develop plans of actions and milestones."

"POAM." I nodded, familiar with the commissioning program. "Where are you stationed?"

"Fort Bliss."

The name hung in the air as I did the math. *Instead of a ten-hour drive, El Paso is only three*. The diaries came to mind. *Is this how Marianna felt when Mateo returned?*

Chapter 14

The next morning, I answered the knock at the door. "C'mon in, Luke. I was—"

"Hello, Maeve."

I stiffened at the baritone voice. "Cody…" My pulse racing, I took a step backward. "I thought you were going to write."

"I was. I *tried*, but then I thought I could explain better in person." As he handed me a half-finished letter, a stainless-steel watch flashed at his wrist.

I recognized the bezel. "You're wearing your Christmas present."

"Haven't taken it off"—grinning, he flexed his wrist—"not even to shower."

I remembered agonizing over which timepiece to buy—the gadget watch with the fish finder, pathfinder, altimeter, barometer, transponder, or sleep tracker—but since he liked scuba diving, I'd selected a dive watch. "It's waterproof as I recall."

His grin faded as he pulled at the expansion band. "Do you want it back?"

"Keep it." I glanced at the paper—*Maeve, I've been meaning to write, but*—then handed it back. "In fact, keep this, too." *No more reminders. No more tears.*

Shoulders drooping, he accepted the letter like a warrant for his arrest. "I just want you to understand why…" He stifled a sigh and started over. "Could we go somewhere for coffee?"

Lips pressed together, I shook my head.

He glanced at the time. "Just coffee—not a champagne brunch." A corner of his lips rose in a tentative smile. "Look, I'd appreciate getting something off my chest." He half-lifted the letter. "Like I said, I tried to write, but—"

"Cody, *you* broke up"—I pointed at him, then jerked my thumb at myself—"with *me*, remember? Not the other way around. So don't expect me to come running back. You can't have it both ways. Life doesn't work that way."

"Everything all right?" Luke's voice boomed from the doorway.

I took a deep breath, glad for the reinforcements.

"I'm Cody Winters." He stepped forward to shake hands.

"I'm talking to Maeve." His eyes flinty, Luke turned toward me. "Everything okay in here?"

"Yeah." My mouth dry, I swallowed. "Cody served with me at Fort Carson. Cody, this is Luke Kaylor, the owner."

Luke's eyes narrowed as his head dipped in a cool nod.

What do I do? Uncomfortable as I eyed the two men, a montage of the weeks with Luke flashed through my mind, while two years of memories with Cody reran like a bittersweet video. He was a ghost from the past that I didn't want to resurrect. *But this might be the only chance to learn why he broke our engagement.*

"Cody wants to catch up over a quick cup of coffee. Mind if I start pruning a little late this morning?" Lifting my brows, I silently appealed.

With the same wounded trust in his eyes as in Teddy's the night before, Luke held my gaze. "Do what you want." Then the color draining from his face, he turned and strode out.

"All right, Cody, one hour, then I've got to get back." I stared after Luke. *Is this a mistake?*

****

Arms crossed, I hugged the car door on the drive to town.

"There's a taqueria." Pointing, Cody slowed the car. "Looks like a good place for coffee."

Rosie's café. "No!"

"Why?" His head spun toward me. "What's wrong with it?"

"Too noisy for conversation." I took an uneasy breath, amazed at how easily I lied. "The drugstore in town has quiet booths in the back."

"Okay."

Five minutes later, we slipped into a booth made from recycled wood.

"Coffee?" The question rhetorical, the waitress set two mugs and a coffee urn on our table. "Want menus?"

"No, thanks." I shook my head as I glanced at the time, then turned toward Luke. "I've only got a few minutes, then I've got to get back."

"Why? Are you on the clock?" Cody's smile hinted at a joke.

"Actually, yes. I'm helping Luke prune vines."

"In exchange for what…?" His lip curling, he implied more.

"None of your business." *Coffee was a mistake*. I straightened my shoulders. "Say what you've got to say."

"Spit it out? State my case?" His narrowed eyes

challenged.

"No, I said…" *Oh, no, you don't.* I pressed my lips together, catching myself before he baited me into losing my temper. "What do you want?"

"I want *us*." He leaned across the table. "I want us to be the way we were."

"You can never go home." Shaking my head, I muted a sigh.

"Maeve, I was wrong to break up. When you mustered out, I didn't want to hold you back." His voice monotone, he stared into his coffee. Then he raised his gaze, imploring. "I convinced myself I was being noble, but I made a terrible mistake, and I'd love a second chance."

"It's too late. I'm in a new relationsh…*partner*ship."

"Which is it, a relationship or a partnership?" His face reddening, an angry V showed between his brows.

"A little of both." Pleased at the team Luke and I made, I raised my chin.

He reached for his phone, showing me its wallpaper—our photo with dozens of hot-air balloons rising in the background. "Remember?"

"Albuquerque." I nodded. "Good times."

"We had a lot of good times." His eyes snapped. "Hey, Albuquerque's only a four-hour drive from El Paso—or we could take that kayak trip we always talked about through Big Bend's Boquillas Canyon." His face brightened. "What do you say?"

Big Bend. The name conjured images of the getaway with Luke, as well as Marianna and Ramon's old homestead.

"I'll take that smile as a yes." Sitting back, he sipped his coffee.

I squinted. "What are you talking about?"

"You grinned when I mentioned that river trip, so I thought—"

"No, not at all." I stifled a sigh. "You misread me." *Again.*

His forehead wrinkled into a puzzled scowl, reminding me of the day I mustered out. *He looks the way I felt—adrift, lost.* Empathy softened my bitterness. "Cody, I don't think you want to get back together as much as you want to find a familiar face." I shrugged. "It's easier than starting a new relationship—takes less energy."

"No, I want to right a wrong. I screwed up what we had, and I'd like to make amends…start over."

"That's the second time this morning you've apologized." I scratched my head. "Maybe you're just looking for forgiveness…closure."

"I thought splitting up was the right thing…for *you*. I just want you to understand *why* I broke up and know I'd never make that mistake again." Reaching for my hand, he tugged my fingertips. "I never wanted to let you go, and I promise things will be different this time."

My hand lay limp in his.

"What do you say?"

"*You* thought splitting up was the right thing…for *me*." I parodied his words. "If you'd honestly been concerned about my welfare, you'd have discussed it with me, not broken our engagement."

"I made a mistake."

"Yeah, you did, a big mistake—"

"Maeve, you always gave without taking. This time, *take me back*." He pulled my hand to his chest.

Taut muscles stretched his shirt as his torso rose and

fell with each breath.

Synchronizing my breathing with his, I gazed into his blue eyes and saw the love I remembered. *How could I forget?*

****

Coffee turned into breakfast, then a tour around town.

"How did you end up in Fort Lincoln?" His shoulder brushed against mine as we walked.

"Long story." I smiled, enjoying catching up with an old friend. "After we broke up and you were deployed, I was at loose ends. Then days before I mustered out, my grandmother passed away. I had no one and nowhere to go, and when I totaled my car—"

"How did you meet Luke?" His jawline hardened.

"He helped me after the accident." Still amazed by the fluke of fate, I turned toward him. "Tuns out, we're distant cousins."

"Cousins?" He cracked a smile. "And you're working at his vineyard?"

"Luke needed help. I needed a job." I glossed over the physical attraction. "In the military, I had a routine— orders and schedules. After my discharge, I had no direction. Working at the vineyard gave me a sense of purpose." I studied Cody's body language, assessing him. "I'd had big expectations about civilian life…fantasizing about us and marriage…but they didn't pan out."

His chin dropping to his chest, he stared at the sidewalk.

"Loneliness is a powerful motivator. I'd understand if companionship were the only reason you contacted me, but I have to know. *Why* do you want to get back together?"

"I couldn't get you off my mind in Afghanistan or Fort Carson, and now I can't stop thinking of you in El Paso." Meeting my gaze, he tucked a windblown strand of hair behind my ear. "I miss you. I miss *us*."

His touch sent my pulse racing. Then the ache of separation slashed through the nostalgia like clippers lopping off vines. *I can't go through another breakup. I can't take the chance.* "Why do you miss me?"

"I just do." He shrugged. "Who can say why?"

"Give me one reason."

"I miss having you around. I miss *us* being a couple."

"Specifically, what do you miss? The convenience? A ready-made plus one?" I shook my head. "No, I think you're just lonely. Why don't you adopt a dog or subscribe to a dating site?"

"Maeve, I miss *you.*" Wearing a wistful, half smile, he stared into the distance. "I miss the smell of your hair, the way your eyes would light up when you'd see me." Then his Adam's apple bobbing as he swallowed, he turned toward me. "I've been thinking about the future, and I don't see one without you. Can't we patch things up…start over?"

Yes teetered on my tongue, but I shook my head. "You run hot and cold. How do I know you wouldn't change your mind again?"

"Because I love you. I've always—"

"Then why did you break up with me?" I tilted my head, challenging him.

"Circumstances." His voice cracked. "I was deployed and had no choice."

"Circumstances didn't call it quits. You did."

"I didn't want to stand in your way—"

"Are you sure it wasn't the other way around…?" I tightened my eyes. "You didn't want me standing in your way?"

"Look, Maeve, I was wrong." He rubbed his neck. "I made the biggest mistake of my life, and I'd do anything to get you back."

Despite his past performance, a part of me believed him…*wanted* to believe him…but his track record stopped me. "This is all too sudden."

"What's too—"

"You calling me last night, then showing up this morning." Flashbacks of the breakup whizzed through my mind. "I'd resigned myself to never seeing you again. Now you're here, professing your love."

"If I didn't realize it at the time, I do now. I love you."

"Too little, too late." I slumped, exhausted from sparring.

"What else can I *do*?"

"Take me home." I spoke in a monotone, then sniffed. *Home…do I even have one?*

****

Refusing to meet Cody's eyes, I stared out the window during the short drive, watching as the vineyard came into view.

Luke was in the fields, pruning the staked vines.

When the car turned onto the drive, he dropped his shears, straightened his spine, and started back toward the cabin.

At the door, Cody cut the engine. "Can I see you again?"

"That's a bad idea."`

"Then I'll call. Maybe we—"

"No." I shook my head.

"Can I write?"

"I don't know. Can you?" Struggling to lighten the moment, I gave a wry laugh. But the significance of the conversation sobered me. "That's the reason you gave for showing up this morning. You thought you could explain better in person."

"Just let me write." His Adam's apple bobbing, he swallowed hard. "I don't want to lose touch."

"Isn't it a little late for that?" *You didn't want me before. Now you do. Decide already.*

Luke crossed the caliche drive, scowling as he approached.

"Take care, Cody." Avoiding a confrontation, I hopped out of the car.

"I'll write—"

"Don't." I slammed the door and waved.

As Luke joined me, Cody revved the engine and pulled away in a haze of dust.

"Your 'friend' seems in a hurry." A vein pulsed at Luke's neck as he eyed me. "Are you all right?"

"Yeah." I had trouble meeting his gaze. "I'm fine."

"Then why are you trembling?"

I looked at my shaking hands. "Just chilly, I guess." Chafing my arms, I started for the cabin. "Let me get a jacket. I'll be right back."

"Just a minute." He caught me by my shoulders and spun me toward him. "What's Cody to you?"

I grimaced, both at the memories and the turns of events. "Until a few months ago, he was my fiancé."

"And now?" His grip hardened.

"Nothing but an old friend."

His hands dropped from my shoulders and hung limply at his sides. "You sure?"

****

Three weeks later, the attorney called.

Luke turned toward me as he hung up. "Bea's requested a settlement conference."

"Does that mean you have to go to court?"

"No." He shook his head. "At least, not yet. This is a pretrial conference, just the lawyers meeting with the judge, *but* my attorney said Bea's not able to establish the chain of title."

"Because of her quitclaim deed?"

"Exactly. Marianna's warranty deed proves legal ownership, and her wedding certificate establishes her as Mateo's lawfully wedded wife."

"Hopefully, this ends the rumor that Marianna had the baby out of wedlock."

"One more thing, when Bea's attorney submitted Mateo and Tina's January 1899 wedding certificate, he couldn't furnish any divorce-related document for his first marriage."

"So *technically*, Mateo was a bigamist." My brow shot up. "How will that stand up in court?"

"According to my attorney, bigamy invalidates the second marriage. In the eyes of Texas, Marianna was Mateo's wife, while Tina was just his mistress with no property rights." His smile was grim.

"Sounds like Bea doesn't have a legal leg to stand on." I sniffed.

"True, as Mateo's wife *and* the surviving joint owner, Marianna would've inherited the property after his death. But since Mateo went one step further and deeded the property to her, the ownership is airtight."

"So, you have nothing to worry about."

"Not quite." Luke took a deep breath. "I keep thinking about the county clerk's warning. If Bea's lived on the property for ten years, she could claim squatters' rights."

"And her family's lived there over a century, right?"

Lips pressed together in a thin line, he nodded. "This pretrial conference could go either way."

"Wouldn't you like to be a fly on the wall?"

****

The next afternoon, Luke replaced the receiver, scowling.

"Uh, oh. I know that expression." I took a deep breath, bracing myself. "What did your attorney say?"

"The county clerk was spot on. Bea claimed squatters' rights."

"So, despite the fact that she can't prove ownership, she could win, anyway?"

"Because her family's made improvements and planted a vineyard—even though Bea's let it go to weeds—the court could rule in her favor." He growled in his throat.

"What happens now?

"The attorney said Bea has to meet five requirements to win." He counted off on his fingers. "Hostile claim, actual possess—"

"Can you summarize?" I wrinkled my nose.

"Sure." His eyelids creased in a smile. "Bea meets the first three conditions, but the case hinges on whether her occupation was continuous and exclusive for the past ten years."

"Wasn't it?"

"Not exactly." He grimaced. "She attended school

for five of those and *technically* didn't inherit the property until four years ago, when her mother passed."

I chewed my lips. "So, her entire defense rests on timing…"

****

His nostrils flaring as he returned from the mailbox, Luke brandished the envelope.

I guessed the letter's author from his expression. "I'll read it later."

"Don't let me stop you." A vein twitching at his neck, he turned and strode away.

I glanced at Cody's handwriting. Crumpling the letter, I was about to toss it in the garbage, unread, until a morbid fascination overtook me.

Maeve, I've tried, but I can't get you off my mind. You know the old saying—time heals all wounds. Not true, nothing heals the hurt. I can't forget you, and I can't replace you.

I regret my decisions and wish I could undo them. Won't you please reconsider us—our life together? Call me when you get the chance. I really need to hear your voice.

Yours always,
Cody

My pulse raced until I relived the breakup. *Why don't his words mesh with my memories?*

****

Two nights later, as I slipped into bed, my phone buzzed.

Cody—*I understand if you need time to think things over, but I can't imagine life without you. I was wrong to break up, and you didn't deserve that treatment. Please give me a chance to start over.*—

Another text woke me the next morning.

Cody—*Remember that ramen shop in Fort Carson? I found a place in El Paso that makes Miso Ramen. How about lunch Saturday?*—

****

A call at 2:00 am set Teddy barking. After glancing at Caller ID, I turned off the ringer, let Cody's call go to voicemail, then listened as his words slurred against a noisy background.

"Maeve, don't hold a grudge. I can't imagine a future without you. I know you're there. Please pick up. I need to hear your voice."

****

On my way to the vineyard, my cell buzzed.

Cody—*Morning, Sunshine*—

A half hour later, another text.

Cody—*How about lunch Saturday?*—

An hour later, another.

Cody—*What's with the silent treatment? You still mad?*—

I deleted the messages. Then just before noon, my cell rang. I glimpsed Caller ID and let voicemail grab Cody's call.

While eating lunch on the patio, my phone rang again.

"Aren't you going to answer?" His eyes glassy, Luke set down his sandwich.

I shook my head as I silenced the ringer.

Seconds later, it buzzed.

"Trouble in paradise?" Despite his sarcastic tone, Luke's half-smile was empathetic.

I read his body language, debating whether to confide, then sighed. "I don't get it."

"Get what?"

"Cody broke off our engagement. Now, he not only wants me back, but he accuses me of holding a grudge."

"Are you holding a grudge"—his brow quirked—"or setting boundaries?"

Phrased that way, I smiled. "Sounds like you've been there."

Luke's laugh was a short snort. "You could say that, but before we get into that topic, I have to know. Are you over Cody?"

I swallowed hard. *Am I?*

****

Her phone buzzed again.

She flinched, then pressed the off button until the screen went dark. "Yes, I am."

Relieved, Luke took a deep breath. "I've always sensed a ghost between us."

"Marianna?"

"No, *your* past." Chuckling, he shook his head. "I just didn't know his name until recently."

She glanced at the phone.

"Yeah, I've also had experience with an ex, who wouldn't let go."

"Bea?"

"The barrage of regrets, promises, and accusations is upsetting"—he sighed—"especially in the beginning."

"What did you do?"

"I asked her to stop. When that failed, I told her to leave me alone in no uncertain terms."

"Did it work?"

"What do you think?" As he gathered their paper plates, he grimaced, recalling the circumstances. "That tack only made her confrontational."

"So, then what?"

"I blocked her phone number."

"But she lives next door." Maeve glanced across the vineyard.

"When Bea would 'drop by,' I'd tell her she wasn't welcome. Actually, 'Get out' were my words." He covered the container of potato salad, then pointed to the creek dividing the two vineyards. "Just like property boundaries, you've got to define your personal space."

"Put up proverbial fences."

He nodded. "Define what's acceptable and what isn't. If he annoys you, tell him. If that doesn't work, block his calls. Return his letters unopened."

****

"What if he shows up here again?" I chewed my lip. "What should I do?"

"Just whistle." Luke flashed a smile. "I'd be happy to send him packing." He met my gaze and held it a beat too long.

Speechless, I stared, unable to break the link. *Why couldn't I see what was right before my eyes? Maybe Marianna and Mateo weren't responsible for any physical attraction. Maybe the only ghost clouding my vision was Cody.*

****

Before going to bed that night, I turned on my phone to find twenty-four texts, six phone calls, and five voicemails.

I scrolled through the messages.—

Cody—*Are you there? Call me*—

Cody—*Hey! I miss your smile*—

Cody—*Text me, will you?*—

Cody—*I messed up. Can we talk?*—

Cody—*I can't sleep. Nightmares keep me awake—*

Nightmares? Didn't he mention nightmares before he broke our engagement? Searching for an explanation, I skimmed the other texts, but none shed light. Then as I read the last text, I drew a sharp breath.

Cody—*I never stopped loving you—*

How dare he use that word? Love is working together toward shared goals…caring for someone more than yourself. Luke came to mind.

Cody's clinging emptiness left me cold. When the phone buzzed in my hands, I knew what I had to do. "Yes."

"Hey, it's good to hear your voice."

"Cody, this calling and texting has got to sto—"

"Come on, Maeve. Be reasonable."

"I *am* being reasonable." As my blood pressure rose, so did my voice. "You broke up with me, and there's no going back."

"I've told you how much I regret that. I swear it'll never happen again."

"No, it's too late. Once and for all, it's over. *We're* over."

"You don't mean that. You're just upset."

"I *do* mean it. Don't call or text anymore."

"Take as much time as you need. Tell you what. I'll call you in the morn—"

"Are you listening?" I paused, counting to five. "Call or text me again, and I'll block your number." My fingers shaking, I hit disconnect.

The phone rang. *Cody* displayed on Caller ID.

Two clicks, and it was done. Then breathing deeply, I leaned back against the headboard.

The phone rang once. Caller ID displayed *Blocked*

and disconnected.

After seven repeats, I powered off my phone. *Is that it?*

Chapter 15

Pounding on the door at 3:00 am woke me.

His hackles up, Teddy began barking.

"Maeve, open up. We gotta talk."

Cody?

"I just wanna talk." His words slurring, he rattled the doorknob. "Come on. Open up."

"Cody, you're drunk. Go away!"

"I just wan—"

"Leave or I'll call the police." Hoping scare tactics would gain time, I pressed the phone's power button, trying to turn it on.

"Maeve…marry me." He called through the door. "New Mexico has no waiting period. We can drive to Las Cruses—"

"Cody, get out of here. I don't want to see you. I'm not going anywhere with you, and I certainly don't want to marry you. Now, leave!" Finally, the phone activated, and I dialed Luke.

He croaked, "Hello," then cleared his throat.

"Luke, Cody's at the door. Can you—"

"Be right there."

Seconds later, voices outside made me peek through the window.

"You're trespassing." Wearing only jeans and huaraches, Luke pointed to Cody's car. "Get out!"

"Butt out!" Cody took a swing, missed, and

stumbled to the ground, moaning.

Luke turned Cody on his back and began dragging him to his car.

I pulled on a pair of slippers, ran out, and grabbed Cody's feet as I helped load him into his car. Dead weight, he sagged between us. *Did he pass out?*

"If I ever catch you here again, I'll press charges." Luke slammed the door. "Now get out of here."

Mumbling, Cody fumbled with the car keys before the engine roared to life. "You ain't seen the last of me." The car lurched forward, snaking down the drive. When he reached the road, he overshot the curve and landed in the ditch.

"He's in no condition to drive." I stifled a groan. "He'll kill himself."

"Or someone else…"

The sounds of Cody revving his engine and spinning wheels resonated from the road.

"He's not going anywhere." Luke shook his head. "Just digging himself in deeper."

Then Cody began rocking his car. By switching back and forth between reverse and drive, the car's mass gained momentum.

"Don't be too sure…" I recalled M2 Bradley training.

As the tires grabbed onto the sides of the ditch, Cody stepped on the gas.

The car burned rubber crossing the road, knocked down a mailbox, and slammed into a boulder.

"I'd better see if he's hurt." Luke raced down the drive.

"I'll call 911." I punched in the numbers and reported the accident as I sprinted toward the scene in slippers and pajamas.

Slumped over the steering wheel, Cody snored in a dazed stupor. A half hour later, the police had trouble rousing him.

I waited on the caliche roadside until they finished the breathalyzer test. "What'll happen to him?"

The officer checked his notes. "His BAC is 0.28%."

I shared a blank stare with Luke before turning back. "What does that mean?"

"A blood alcohol content of 0.0% is sober. A BAC level of 0.08% is intoxicated, while .35% can be lethal."

I gave a low whistle as the tow-truck operator winched Cody's car on a dolly trailer.

"Because he had a moving violation, he's charged with a DWI, and his driver's license is revoked." He glimpsed the mangled mailbox. "Though he damaged property, the good news is he didn't harm anyone, *but* this is his second drunk-driving offense in two weeks."

Stunned, I glanced at Cody, snoring in the squad car's back seat.

"If convicted, he faces a minimum of two years in jail, though the court can sentence him to as long as ten, with an additional fine of up to $10,000."

"Wow…" I said a silent prayer, reflecting on the might-have-beens. "Thank you, officer."

Nodding, he climbed into the squad car, turned off its flashing lights, and pulled onto the road.

As the wrecker towed Cody's car, Luke reached for my hand. "How 'bout a cup of coffee?"

"I could use one." Linking fingers, I sighed as we walked up the drive, hand in hand. "What a night."

"I've had better." Though his eyes glimmered in the moonlight, any hint of a smile faded. "Let's get Teddy and go to my place. I know your friend's sleeping it off in jail, but I'd feel better if you weren't alone."

"So would I." The words came out before I thought. Then with an uncomfortable laugh, I glanced down. "Forgot I was still in pajamas and slippers. Give me a second to change."

"Sure, it's almost time to get up, anyway." He nodded at the morning glow behind the mountains. "Did Cody always act this way?"

"No, I don't recognize this behavior." I slipped on a t-shirt as I reran the events prior to the breakup. "Cody always seemed so solid…at least, he did until he received orders for his last deployment…"

Luke waited on the porch while I dressed. "Why, how did he act then?"

"Detached…numb…exhausted…" I zippered and belted my jeans, then slapped my palm against my head as the memory returned. "I'd forgotten, but he mentioned having trouble sleeping *then*, that he was having flashbacks from his previous deployment, when he was exposed to an IED blast." I stepped onto the porch.

"A what?"

"An improvised explosive device." As I locked the cabin door, I reviewed Cody's symptoms. *Alcohol abuse, flashbacks, sleep disorders, relational issues…* "I didn't put two and two together until now, but he's showing symptoms of PTSD. After the breakup, I was too numb to notice." Upset with myself, I turned toward Luke. "Why didn't I see that sooner?"

"As I recall, you had your own troubles."

"What do you mean?"

"When we met, you were leaving a job, moving, and ending a relationship." Luke's smile was empathetic in the pale light of the sunrise. "Don't worry, Cody's cry for help won't go unanswered." He pushed open his apartment door.

"Now he has a police record, no car—"

The puppy dashed ahead, nearly tripping me.

"Slow down, Teddy!" I grabbed Luke's arm to regain my balance.

Steadying me, he placed his hands on my shoulders and stared into my eyes. "Don't beat yourself up for others' actions. Things don't always happen for the reasons you think, but they always happen for the better."

"Do you believe that?" Closing the distance between us, I clasped his waist, hooking my thumb in his belt loop.

"Yeah, I do." He placed his arm around my shoulders. "Even if things don't work out the way you'd thought or hoped, they work out the way they're supposed to." His smile was lopsided. "You think you're the only one to get dumped?"

I grimaced. "Bea?"

"Bingo."

"You came through all right." *Even if Bea didn't…* "How'd you manage that?"

"Focus on the lesson—not the hurt. Once you see things for what they are, the drama's easier to let go."

My shoulders sagged. "If I'd just handled things differently…"

"What could you have done differently? Cody was the actor. You simply *reacted* to his performance."

"He wasn't always this way." Recalling the person he had been, I stared blankly into the past.

"I can't imagine dealing with combat-related

trauma, and I'm not saying emotional pain is easily forgotten." He gave my shoulders a friendly shake.

Brought back to the moment, I caught his gaze. "Then what are you saying?"

"Healing takes time, but you have to stop re-reading the same paragraph if you want to turn the page. To move forward, you've got to let go." He chuckled.

"What's so funny?" After the evening's events, I grabbed at any humor.

"Just got a mental image of Tarzan swinging through the jungle. Before he can grab the next vine, he has to let go the last." Turning me toward him, he slid his arms around me. "Leaving the past behind is the only way to move forward."

Cody's my past. I peered into Luke's eyes. *Are you my future?*

****

"Come on, Teddy." After dinner the next night, I whistled. "Time to go, boy."

"I'll walk you home." Luke held the door as we stepped outside.

Fireflies chased each other in the humid darkness.

I followed their blinking routes as I breathed in the spring air.

"Look! A shooting star."

"Where?"

"There, near Vega." He stood behind me, leaned forward, and pointed, resting his arm alongside my shoulder. "See?"

My gaze followed his outstretched finger and tracked the star's arc. "Yes…" He stood so close, his breath tickled my neck. A shiver shook me, and with a gasp, I turned toward him.

As if cued by an unseen hand, he wrapped his arms around me and bent his head in a kiss.

Lost in his embrace, I parted my lips and responded with a muffled moan, digging my nails in his back. By the time Teddy's barking registered, the car's headlights blinded me, and I pulled away from Luke's grip. *Cody?* Shielding my eyes from the glare, I went cold.

Teddy bared his teeth, growling while the hackles rose on his neck.

As the phone began to ring inside the house, a convertible roared into the caliche driveway, strewing pebbles behind it.

Leaving the beams on high, Bea jumped from the vehicle before it rocked to a stop. "You just *had* to sue me, didn't you? You just *had* to dredge up the past."

The jangling phone punched through her tirade.

"Thought you'd bankrupt me, did you?" Bea spoke with her hands, using broad gestures. "Well, you thought wrong!"

Snarling as he showed his teeth, Teddy jumped between us as if protecting me.

"Get that mutt out of here!" Bea kicked at the dog but missed.

Teddy lunged at her foot, sinking his teeth into the heel of her shoe.

"Stop it, both of you! Teddy, come here." Still shielding my eyes from the glare, I whistled, the sound discordant against the phone's incessant ring.

Glaring at Bea, Luke pulled Teddy off. "You deserve a lot worse after what you did to this dog. Get out of here!"

"Not 'til I've had my say. You thought you could ruin me—you and your *money-grubbing whore*." Bea spat the words at me.

"Get off my property and stay off!" Handing me Teddy, he strode toward Bea.

"You may have had your day in court, but you didn't win." Bea stepped back. "No, *you* lost, and you lost *big*!"

The land line went silent, then immediately jangled back to life.

I groaned as I nestled the quivering pup against my chest. *Guess the land will never return to Marianna's family. Sorry, Mateo.* Mentally picturing him in his uniform, I sighed. *Luke tried.*

Inside the apartment, the phone was relentless.

Who keeps calling?

"Get out of here before I have you arrested for trespassing." Luke closed in on Bea.

Keeping a step ahead of him, she backed into her convertible. "You with your piddling lawsuit, did you really think a couple acres more or less would break me?" She sneered. "Just wait 'til I marry Neuman with his ten *thousand* acres."

"Lucky man." His tone flat, he wore a wry smile.

"Eat my dust." She revved the engine, fishtailing on the caliche drive as the tires spewed rocks and grit.

The land line stopped ringing.

Turning, Luke reached for my hand. "C'mon, I'll walk you home."

His cell phone rang.

"Who keeps calling?" After an aggravated sigh, he punched the connect button. "Yes."

I unlocked the cabin but paused before opening the door.

"Oh…hi."

His tone changed so abruptly, I mouthed, *Who is it?*

He covered the phone's receiver. "My lawyer."

More "good" news? I braced myself as I stroked Teddy.

"I see." Luke's brow wrinkled. "I'll stop by at ten. Thanks for calling." He hung up, then scrubbed a hand over his face while he stared blankly.

He lost. I pressed my lips together, as disappointed for him as I was furious with Bea for gloating. I waited several silent minutes, giving him space, until my patience waned. "Well? What'd he say?"

His shoulders drooping, he spoke in a monotone. "I won."

"I'm so sorry…you *what?*" Prepared to console him, I laughed in disbelief. "You *won?*"

He dipped his head in a cheerless nod.

At a loss, I opened the door. "Why aren't you celebrating?"

"I never wanted a lawsuit, and despite Bea's actions"—he glanced at Teddy—"I hated suing her for her ancestor's mistakes…"

"Besides following Mateo's wishes, you righted a wrong. Don't forget, her family stole that land from Marianna."

"Yes, but is the hostility worth it?"

For a split second, the image of a uniformed Rough-Rider flashed before my eyes. Like before, the image was so transparent, the hearth behind it showed clearly.

Then the air exploded with light. With a deafening boom, the mantle compartment fell open.

"Now what?"

"Wild guess, but…" Weaving on my feet, I managed an unsteady smile. "I think Mateo approves."

"You saw another…?"

"Yeah."

He went white.

"Why don't you check the—"

"Yeah." He snapped his neck left, then right. As the vertebrae clicked into place, he took a deep breath and approached the open compartment.

"See anything?"

"Nothing inside, but…" He tugged at something. "A paper's wedged between the drawer and mantle." He half closed the drawer, releasing the tension, and a faded photo slid out.

"What is it?"

"Looks like a bride in a wedding gown." He handed over the vintage photo. "Think this is Marianna?"

Except for a water spot, the picture was well preserved. I recognized the familiar scrawl on the back: *March sixth, eighteen-ninety-eight*. "Must be—that's when she married Mateo."

"What a shame. It's water damaged."

"Or is that a teardrop?" I fingered the image, intuitively connecting. The face was ghostly pale, and the dark eyes, peering from beneath the wedding veil, seemed to pierce time. *I've seen this face, but where?*

The young woman in a *Gibson Girl* hairdo wore a lacy gown with puffy sleeves, a frilly bodice, a high collar, and…*my cameo*. I gasped.

"What?"

"That's the image I saw in the mirror and my dream the night Rosie gave me the brooch." I spun toward him. "And to answer your question, *yes*. It is."

He cocked his head. "What is…?"

"You wondered if the lawsuit's hostility was worth it. *It is*."

"How can you be sure?"

"Mateo revealed this picture right after you asked. This is his answer, proof he and Marianna appreciate you resolving what they couldn't."

****

Two weeks later, I walked back from the mailbox, fingering through the bills and junk mail, when Cody's handwriting jumped off an envelope. My first impulse was to trash the letter. Then curiosity prevailed.

Maeve, I want to apologize for being a jerk the other night. I wasn't myself. In fact, I haven't been myself for months—not since the IED blast killed two of my buddies.

The DWI was my wake-up call. Thanks to my commander's reprimand, I've started cognitive behavioral therapy for PTSD, and it's like I've opened Pandora's box. I realize now that I hurt you, and you deserve to know why. It wasn't you, and it wasn't us. It was entirely my fault. I tried so hard to avoid reliving the trauma that I pushed away all emotions, including my feelings for you.

I denied loving you until I drove you away, and for that, I can never forgive myself. I'm so sorry I broke our engagement and hope one day you'll forgive me.

Yours always,

Cody

Immersed in his words, I walked without looking. *Do I accept his apology? Yes, but...* "Can I forgive him?"

"Getting any good answers?"

"What?" Nearly stumbling into Luke, I blinked.

"You were talking to yourself." His smile was good-natured.

"Sorry, my mind was elsewhere." I held up the

letter.

His smile dimmed. "From Cody?"

I nodded. "He's started therapy. Sounds like he's coming to terms with his PTSD."

"For his sake, I'm glad." Luke met my gaze. "But does that change how you feel?"

****

The following week, a minister joined us to celebrate the graveside service.

Luke transferred the decomposed soil from its temporary container to a woven casket.

I removed the lock of hair from the brooch. Adding it to the humus, I caught Luke's gaze. "It's only right that *all* Kenneth's remains be buried."

Nodding, he sealed the casket for reburial and covered it with a spray of stargazer lilies, white roses, and irises. Then he set the basket beside the grave for the reinterment ceremony and joined me.

Rosie stood beside us with her hands folded.

The somber, gray-haired minister began the prayer. "This soil is hallowed ground. Bow your heads."

Vapors from a low-lying fog rose slowly beneath the loquat tree. The air shimmered and stirred within the mist.

Shapes seemed to materialize, but I dismissed the movement as warm ground air displacing cooler air above.

The minister raised his hands over the casket as he recited from Ecclesiastes. "A time for everything, and a season for every activity under the heavens: A time to be born and a time to die. A time to plant and a time to uproot. A time to tear down and a time to build…"

The wind rustled, and wisps of mist swirled above

the grave. The eddying haze gathered slender tendrils of fog, twisting them like silk fibers, until the vapor became a rotating spiral.

I blinked, and when I opened my eyes, three translucent forms emerged: Mateo in his uniform; Marianna in her bridal gown; and their bundled baby in her arms. Recognizing the quilt from the threadbare remnant, I pressed a hand to my heart.

Then Marianna met my gaze and smiled. Clasping the baby, she leaned against her husband as he placed a protective arm about her shoulders.

His eyes tightly shut, the minister continued to intone. "We can't see on the other side, but we believe the eternal light penetrates the darkness. Neither do we know what this spirit's afterlife will be, but we have perfect trust that You will welcome home the soul of Kenneth Ramirez."

An intense light shattered the air like sunshine ricocheting off mirror splinters.

When I opened my eyes, only our small group gathered about the grave.

Luke lowered the small, flower strewn casket into the earth, then handed Rosie and me each a pink rose.

Rosie released hers, then I let my rose fall on the woven coffin.

Luke turned a shovel of soil over the casket before handing the spade to Rosie first, then me.

The minister read from Genesis. "For dust you are and to dust you shall return."

After I scooped soil over the casket, Luke filled the grave and set the original stone upright.

"Now Kenneth can rest in peace." Rosie wiped her eyes.

Hope all three can. I fondled the brooch at my lapel.

Rosie hugged me before turning to Luke. "Thank you for letting me participate."

After seeing off the minister, I stared at the fresh grave. "Does this funeral mean Mateo and Marianna's spirits can finally be at peace?"

"Between their son's funeral and their land being restored, I hope so." Luke tugged my hand. "But you're asking if they still have unfinished business."

"I don't know." Distracted, I forced a smile. "I'm just trying to find a bright side to the baby's burial."

"Death is closure." He shrugged. "And closure is good…as are new beginnings."

"Maybe death is a new beginning…" The airy figures came to mind. *Were they a hallucination or a manifestation?* "Do you think Mateo and Marianna have moved on?"

"Not yet." His eyes twinkling, he shook his head. "They still have one loose end."

"What do you mean?"

"You're the one who brought up the idea of Marianna wanting to relive her love with Mateo, remember?"

Fidgeting, I recalled that conversation, along with its physical attraction: *Is this love or lust? Or something less corporeal…*

"Hey, I've started painting the patio." His smile was quixotic. "Want to see?"

"Now?" I did a double take at his *non sequitur,* glancing from the fresh grave to his beaming face.

"A time to be born and a time to die…a time to tear down and a time to build…" Taking my hand, he led me toward the warehouse. "Come on. Maybe you'll see the handwriting on the wall."

As I rounded the corner, I stopped so fast, my shoes slid on the crushed gravel.

Two-foot-tall, hand-painted letters filled the entire side of the building.

This wall isn't big enough to show my love.

Going down on one knee, Luke took a ring from its velvet box, and slipped it on my finger. "Be my partner…for life?"

****

The seconds ticked by like minutes. The longer he genuflected, the less confident he was.

"This is all so sudden, I…" She scratched her head, as if stalling until the answer came. "I wasn't prepared…" Blinking, she stared at nothing, seeming to search inwardly.

He tweaked her fingers. "Hey, this is me, your partner for the last three months, and I'd like to make this relationship permanent. What do you say?"

Her mouth moved wordlessly. Then she swallowed. "I'm speechless."

He wiped his brow with the back of his other hand. "One word will do…ye—" His voice cracked. "Yes or no?"

Chapter 16

A thousand thoughts converged as Cody's echoes competed with Luke's proposal, but I dismissed the memories, refusing to idealize. Instead, I recalled the day Luke and I met. *I had no family, no home, no job, no prospects, and after the accident, no car.* Then one by one, our shared trials and triumphs not only brought us closer but changed my life.

The sight of Luke on his knee banished any petty qualms. "Ye—"

"Because I can't keep kneel—"

"Yes!" I threw my arms around him. "I said *yes*."

"You did?" Scrambling to his feet, he kissed me, then paused, peering into my face. "You're sure?"

"Absolutely." Chuckling, I nodded. "Your proposal just took me by surprise."

"Then to answer your question."

"What question?" Immersed in the moment, I forgot all else.

"You asked if Mateo and Marianna have moved on." His grip tightened. "With us getting married, we're tying up the last of their loose ends. What else could keep them from moving on?"

I gazed into his face, seeing him through Marianna's eyes. "Four generations later, Marianna and Mateo are together again."

"History's repeating itself."

I breathed in the moment. Thrilled at the prospect of marrying him, I threw my arms around his neck and pulled him close. Then as a thought gripped me, I flinched.

"Uh-oh, I know that expression." Luke held me arm's length. "What's wrong?"

"What else *could* keep them from moving on?" I swallowed the sudden lump in my throat. "Their time together was short, and their love life was so convoluted." An earlier conversation came to mind. "As Marianna's great-great-grandson, and Mateo's great-great-granddaughter, we're their first descendants to be attracted…"

"We've already established that…" His eyes narrowed.

"Their *first* descendants to be attracted?" I paused. "You were attracted to Bea, who's *also* Mateo's great-great-granddaughter."

"The emphasis is on *were*."

"That didn't work out, so—"

"So don't borrow trouble." A deep V between his brows relaxed as he paraphrased Ecclesiastes. "This is a time to laugh…a time to dance."

"But what if history's repeating itself? Instead of tying up Marianna and Mateo's loose ends, what if we're only continuing their saga?"

****

The next morning, I stretched in bed and grinned at my engagement ring as memories of the proposal surged through my mind. I turned and twisted my hand, capturing the ring's sparkle in the morning light, while I tried on new names. "Mrs. Luke Kaylor."

Teddy cocked his head.

"Mrs. Lucas Kaylor."

He wagged his tail.

"Which name do you like, Teddy?" I scratched behind his ears. "What about Maeve Jackson-Kaylor?"

He woofed, then panted and pranced by the door, begging to go out.

Unlocking the door, I laughed. "Priorities…"

****

Ten minutes after Luke arrived for breakfast, a knock sounded at the cabin door.

I checked, but no one was there. "That's weird."

"Maybe it's the wind"—he shrugged—"a branch hitting the door."

"Probably…want more coffee?" I topped off our cups and was about to sit when the knocking sounded again. "Is someone playing a joke?"

"I'll get it." He flung open the door as if to catch a prankster. "No one." He stepped outside, looked left and right, and scratched his head. "That *is* strange."

The tapping sounded a third time.

Stiffening, I caught Luke's gaze. "You don't suppose Mateo or Marianna is back, do you?"

Again, the knocking sounded, but the noise seemed nearer.

I looked beneath the kitchen table.

Teddy was wagging his tail, banging it against the table legs.

"You kooky dog."

****

Later that night, a rapping at the door woke me.

"Teddy, cut that out." Half asleep, I rolled over.

The knocking got louder.

"Teddy, stop it!" I covered my ears with a pillow.

259

The knocking became a pounding.

Cody? I peeked out the window. *No one.*

As the thumping continued at the door, I flipped on the light, hoping Teddy was the unwitting offender.

But he huddled beneath the table, quaking.

The hammering became so incessant, it shook the door and rattled the threshold.

"Who's there?"

The noise stopped, but now too anxious to sleep, I lay awake, jumping at every sound.

The next morning, I told Luke.

"That's it." He wrapped his arms around me. "Either you move in with me, or I move in *permanently* with you."

"I agree." For the first time since the knocking began, I relaxed. "I'm happy either way."

"And since we haven't set a date for the wedding"—his dark eyes glimmered—"I suggest we make it as soon as possible—a week from now."

"A week! You're not serious, are you?" I broke away to see his expression. "What about the invitations, wedding dress, venue, flowers, cake—"

"All right, all right." Grinning, he held up his hands in mock surrender. "How 'bout two weeks?" Again, he slipped his arms around me, hugging me as he gently rocked me left and right. "What do you say? Two weeks from today?"

Weighing the preparations against the timeline, I took a deep breath. "Is that a challenge?"

"Maybe…" He tightened his grip.

"Then there's no time to lose." I pecked him on the lips, then poured a cup of coffee. "What about the colors?"

"That's your domain." He gave me a crooked smile. "I'm color blind."

"I was thinking dusty rose and golden taupe. Work for you?"

"Perfect."

"That was easy." Grinning, I set down my cup. "What about style?"

"I'm all for it. Style is definitely underrated."

I chuckled. "No, *which* style? Romantic, whimsical, vintage, modern, garden party—"

"What about holding our wedding here in the vineyard?"

"I love it." My jaw dropped as the idea took hold. "Maybe we could rent an arch."

"Or I could build one. We already have the arbor between the patio and the vineyard." His eyes lit up.

"Are you thinking what I am?"

"The winery could become a wedding destination."

"A sideline. Our wedding can set a precedent." Recalling the first time I'd seen the vineyard, I reached for his arm. "Remember our February picnic?"

"How could I forget?" He hugged me.

Another idea took hold. "And our wedding pictures can do double duty as publicity shots." I snuggled against his body. "With our winery-wedding theme, instead of dusty rose and golden taupe, what if our colors are Rosé and Champagne?"

"You're a born marketer." He leaned over in a kiss.

I met his lips, then pulled away. "But with only two weeks, what about invitations? How will we ever send them *and get responses* in time?"

"Emailed invites." He winked. "Quick, easy, and it takes only seconds to RSVP."

"Great idea." I nodded slowly, liking the plan. "Maybe tonight we can make up a guest list."

"Sure, most of my family"—he caught my gaze—"*and yours* are right here in Fort Lincoln."

"Do you want to tackle the invitations, while I start looking at wedding gowns? I recall a small bridal shop just past the hotel. After breakfast, I'll drive into town and maybe find a local florist and a caterer—"

"What about Aunt Rosie? Think she might be interested in a catering sideline?"

****

The mouthwatering aromas of cilantro, cumin, and chilies welcomed me into the taqueria along with Rosie's hug and cheery hello.

As I pulled away, she caught my left hand. "What's this?" Her eyes widening, she studied the ring. "When did this happen?"

"The night before last." I couldn't suppress the grin.

Rosie squeezed me in a bear hug. "When's the wedding?"

"Twelve days from toda—

"You're kidding, right?"

"Nope. Neither of us wants to wait, and we don't need anything extravagant—just a simple ceremony in the vineyard."

"How romantic." Rosie's face lit up, then she arched her brow. "And who's catering?"

"Well,"—I fidgeted—"that's something we want to discuss with you."

"I wouldn't hear of anyone else catering your wedding." Her cheeks beaming, Rosie lived up to her name. "Family is family."

"And something else we want to discuss. Have you

ever considered a catering sideline?"

"Why?"

"Because this wedding gave us an idea."

The taqueria's door opened, and a gust of wind fluttered the multicolored *papel picado* overhead.

I stepped aside for two customers to pass. "We're adding a wedding venue to Chateau Mont Bleu, and we need an in-house caterer. Are you interested?"

"You two *have* had your heads together." Rosie's eyes danced as she stared at the red-brick wall, seeming to look inward. Finally, she met my gaze. "For years, I've thought of expanding. Now may be the time."

"We hoped you'd say that."

"And speaking of time, do you two have your marriage license?"

"Not yet." I shook my head.

"With only twelve days until the wedding, you'd better hurry. Texas has a 72-hour waiting period, and have you found a minister yet?" Rapid-fire, Rose mentioned the key elements. "How about music? And flowers? And do you have your wedding gown?"

"No, no, no, and no." I blew air from my cheeks. "From here, I'm going into town to order flowers and begin looking for a dress. *Yikes!* Is a wedding in two weeks doable?"

****

Still hyperventilating, I stopped at the florist's.

"Can I help you?"

The saleswoman's tone cut through my mental fog.

"Yes." I didn't realize I was holding my breath until the word came out a sigh of relief. "We're getting married in twelve days. Is that enough time to place our order?"

"You're cutting it close, but we'll make it work." The woman gave me a reassuring smile. "What kind of flowers do you want?"

"I don't know." I felt the blood drain from my face. "I haven't had time to think about it."

"Let's start with your colors and go from there."

"Rosé and Champagne."

Nodding, the saleswoman opened the cooler behind her and took out a spray of roses. "A new variety just came in, Sensational Sonoran. Their blooms have soft pink centers with champagne outer petals and an overall garden rose look."

From a single stalk, the roses swelled into a compact cluster.

"One stem looks like a bridal bouquet." I stared in wonder. "And its colors are perfect."

"All right, we have the bouquet." The woman made notes on a pad, then looked up. "Now what about the boutonnieres, flower girl's petals, table centerpieces, altar arrangements, aisle decorations, and wedding arch?"

****

An hour later, I left the shop dazed by the details and variety of floral choices. Then mentally checking *flowers* off my list, I walked to the bridal salon with a bounce in my step.

The sumptuous window dressing lured me inside, but the interior was anticlimactic. Because the small shop had little space for dress racks, the styles were limited, and the selection was meager, at best. Despite the limited options, one dress caught my fancy, but the only sizes in stock were zero, two, sixteen, and eighteen.

"Try on the sixteen." The salesperson held the dress

against me as she spoke to our reflection in the mirror. "See how you like the style. We can always clip it, then have alterations take in the seams."

"Can't you order a size eight?"

"Not if you need it in twelve days." The woman's spine stiffened. "These dresses are made-to-order and typically take six-to-nine months to create." Her smile brightened. "But alterations can resize it."

"I can understand taking in a dress a size or two"—I cocked my head—"but cutting down a sixteen to an eight? I don't think so."

Now what? Order something online? I dragged my feet on the way back to the car. Then spotting a consignment shop, I stopped in on a whim. "Do you have any wedding gowns?"

"Not really." Tapping her chin, the saleswoman paused. "But we have a vintage dress that might work." She led me to a chipped mannequin sporting a light frock. "At the turn of the twentieth century, these outfits had several names: tea dresses, summer day dresses, lingerie dresses, lawn dresses, or simply whites."

The moment I saw the sheer dress, something clicked, and I lightly ran my fingers over the filigree fabric. "The material's so delicate, you can almost see through it."

"This is cotton batiste trimmed with yards and yards of Irish lace. Women wore these over full slips, but by changing the slip's colors, they expanded their wardrobe." The saleswoman smiled. "If you want to use it as a wedding gown, wear a white or ivory slip beneath. Would you like to try it on?"

As I slid the dress over my t-shirt and jeans, I pirouetted, admiring my reflection in the full-length mirror.

"Does it fit?"

"It'll be perfect over a slip instead of jeans." I grinned, excited at the find.

"Not sure if you need a bridal veil, but this antique, embroidered veil just came in yesterday. Judging from its wrinkles, it's been folded and stored for years, but a good steaming should take care of that." The saleswoman shook out the silk tulle.

A faint scent of mold wafted through the air.

"Look at all the scalloped lace." I fingered the circular veil's intricate needlework. "Was this a mantilla?"

"Possibly—this area has a rich Hispanic heritage."

"And what's this…a heart?" I traced the design surrounding a line of digits, then smoothed the lace to make the stitching more readable. "VIP01141899."

"Embroidered right into the tulle." The woman's mouth fell open. "It's so subtle, I thought it was part of the design."

"Maybe it was the manufacturer's product number." I swung out the veil, letting it fall over my hair to frame my face. Ignoring the musty scent, I studied myself in the mirror. "This look's perfect—just wish I knew the veil's story."

"Wouldn't that be lovely? But better than its history, you have a bona fide mystery." The saleswoman gave a wistful smile. "Take your time. When you're ready, I'll ring you up."

An intense hot flash seized me, suddenly drenching my face, neck, and chest with perspiration. I yanked off the mantilla and handed it over. "Please take this with you." Dizzy, I leaned against the cool wall as I wiped my brow.

"Are you all right?"

"Yes, thanks, I'm fine—just got overheated. I'll bring the dress up front in a minute."

"No rush." With a parting smile, the woman began folding the mantilla on her way to the cash register.

Still flushed, I took a deep breath to collect myself. *What brought that on?*

****

As I carried my shopping bags to the pickup, a fly buzzed me, then another and another. Kamikaze style, they dive bombed as I scurried to escape them and unlock the door.

One followed me inside the truck, biting the crown of my head. I slapped at it, finally killing it, but not before it drew blood.

By the time I started the engine and pulled into traffic, the flies were so thick outside, they swarmed the windshield. I turned on the wipers, but visibility was like driving through pelting, black rain. The flies massed about the windows, dodging the blades while they kept pace with the truck.

Not until I left town and began driving at highway speeds did I lose them.

****

After relating the incident, I turned to Luke. "What kind of blood-suckers are those?"

"Horse flies." He nodded, as if commiserating. "Only the females bite, but heaven help you if they swarm."

"On a happier note, look what I found." I shook out the tulle, releasing a faint musty scent. "Superstition says it's bad luck for the groom to see the dress, but I've got to show you this veil. The needlework's so fine, it looks hand-stitched even though it has a manufacturer's number embroidered inside a heart."

"Looks like a valentine."

Nodding, I traced VIP01141899 with my finger. "The number's so skillfully sewn into the design, it's hard to see."

"VIP…very important person." He grinned. "That's you, at least to me."

"More likely it's a product number or style code." I chuckled, then thumped my head with my hand. "Wait a minute. Instead of a number, what if these digits were a date? And what if VIP was someone's initials?" I traced the heart again. "You said valentine…"

"Yeah, so?"

"It can't be…can it?" I recalled the library research. "Didn't Mateo remarry a woman named Valentina Perez?" I caught his gaze. "And wasn't her middle name Isabella?"

"Now that you mention it, I think so. Why?"

"VIP…What if this were Valentina Isabella Perez's wedding veil?"

"That's a leap." His brow arched.

"Instead of 01141899…" I smoothed the lace to make the needlework more legible. "What if this reads 01-14-1899?"

"We know Mateo deeded this property to Marianna in January 1899 and remarried Valentina that same month." His eyes widened. "Are you thinking what I am?"

"If VIP were Valentina's initials, along with the date of their wedding, this veil might shed light on why Mateo made Marianna the beneficiary…"

"Guilt?" Half grinning and half grimacing, he shrugged. "The idea's tantalizing, but it's pure conjecture."

"You're right. My imagination's running away with me." I laughed as I glanced about the cabin. "Maybe it's these old walls. They've seen so much, it's easy to read more into things here than exists."

Staring at the room's white plaster with dark wood trim, he tilted his head at a philosophical angle. "If these walls are this cabin's 'bones,' could these echoes of the past be its 'soul'?"

****

After a candlelight dinner, I pulled a pen and paper from the desk. "Let's start our guest list."

"But first, a toast." He topped off our glasses.

I raised mine. "What to?"

"To these four walls once again witnessing love." He glanced about the cabin before gazing into my eyes. "Our love *and* Mateo and Marianna's."

As we clinked glasses, the lights flickered, and the wind howled through the chimney.

The front door banged open, and a gust of wind overturned the candles, setting fire to the paper.

"What the…?" I grabbed a damp dishtowel to smother the flames as Teddy cringed in the corner, barking.

Luke tried to shut the door, but gale-force winds pushed him back. Not until he threw his weight against the door could he finally latch and lock it. "That was no ordinary draft."

"Was it Marianna's doing?" I searched his face.

"Maybe Mateo's?"

I shook my head. "I don't think so…"

"Then who or what?"

"I wonder…" Lifting my head, I sniffed the air. "Do you smell that?"

He inhaled and wrinkled his nose. "Mildew or mold."

"I noticed it when the saleslady shook out the veil, then again when I showed you earlier." The embroidered heart came to mind. "No…it couldn't be, could it?"

"What are you thinking?"

"Could Valentina have caused that gust?"

****

As bedtime approached, Luke caught me in his arms. "It's less than two weeks until we're married." He nuzzled my neck as he drew me near. "Close enough."

I glanced from the rocker to the double bed. "Close"—his breath tickled, but I pulled away, stiffening—"but no cigar."

He nibbled my ear as he whispered. "No need to be *close*-minded."

"Uhn-uh, in these *close* quarters, you're already too *close* for comfort." Though smiling, I shook my head as I extricated myself from his grip. "Case *closed*."

"I had a feeling you were going to say that." He gave a rueful grin as he opened a box. "Which is why I bought this."

Inside the cardboard box was what appeared to be a roll of blue velour. "What is it?"

"An air mattress with a built-in pump. No more sleeping in that rocking chair. No, ma'am." He reached for my hand. "Of course, you're welcome to join me…take it for a test rest, you might say."

"Right…" I slipped my fingers from his grip. "Back in a minute with sheets and a pillow. Need a blanket?"

"You could warm me…" He dimpled.

"Hey, we've waited this long." More than tempted to yield, I cautioned myself as much as him. "We can wait a few more days." I nodded toward the dog, sleeping on a rag rug. "Maybe Teddy will join you."

"That's all right." Shrugging, he unrolled the mattress, then connected the pump. "I'd rather wait in hope."

I pulled the linens from the hope chest. "Need any help making the bed?"

His hands caressed mine as he took the sheets. "No, but you could help with other things."

"Never mind." Summoning my willpower, I pulled away. "So do you want to shower first or me?"

"You go—and don't worry about using the hot water. I'll need a cold shower, anyway."

Chuckling, I fired a parting shot before I closed the door. "This isn't easy for me, either, you know." Then setting my engagement ring on the sink's ledge, I undressed and stepped in the shower.

A few steamy minutes later, I cinched my robe and reached for my ring. The sink's cold porcelain taunted me as my fingers searched for it. *I* know *I put it here…didn't I?* My breathing ragged, I poked behind the faucet, got on my knees to search the floor tiles, and rummaged through the cabinet. *Where's my ring?*

"Luke!" I threw open the bathroom door and rushed out, along with the steam. "My ring's gone!"

"What happened?" Jumping from his chair, he raced into the room.

"I set it on the sink before I showered. Now it's gone." A tension headache starting, I pressed my fingers into my temples.

"It's got to be here." He dropped to his knees and explored every inch of the small bath's floor.

I ransacked the cabinet and double-checked the shower. "It isn't."

"The ring didn't just walk away." His eyes widened. "The drain!"

"I hope not." My heart sinking, I hunched my shoulders. "How could I be so careless?"

"Don't worry. We'll find it." Despite his consoling words, his face was ashen. "I'll be back a minute with a wrench. Get a bucket, lay some newspapers on the floor, and *don't* run any water!"

****

He took apart the drainpipe and emptied the trap. But two hours later, he shook his head as he reconnected the pipes. "It either washed away or never fell down the sink."

My guilt was so overpowering, my chest ached. "I know I had it before I showered."

"A ring is just a *thing*—"

"But it symbolizes our love."

"Our *love* is what's important." He took me in his arms. "Think positively. We'll look again in the morning light, but for now, let's try to get some rest."

Resigned, I nodded as I finished cleaning the watery mess. "When should I set the timer for coffee?"

"Six?"

I reached up to kiss him. "The shower's all yours. I'll program the brewer, then turn in. I'm bushed."

He gave me a reassuring squeeze. "Don't worry. The ring will turn up."

"From your lips to God's ears." Spouting Grandma's wisdom, I trudged into the kitchenette, set the delay-brew timer, and filled the coffee maker with water. *How could I be so stupid?* But when I scooped the grounds into the filter, something glimmered.

Towel-drying his hair a few minutes later, he paused when he saw my expression. "What's wrong?"

"I found the ring…"

"That's great!" He lowered his towel. "So why the long face?"

"In the coffee grounds…"

His Adam's apple bobbing, he swallowed. "Do we have another visitor?"

Chapter 17

About to dry the breakfast dishes the next morning, I reached for the dishtowel, but the towel ring was empty. "Weird...it was just here." I scanned the kitchenette before calling Luke. "Did you take the dishtowel?"

"Nope." He peeked around the corner from the utility room. "I'm troubleshooting the thermostat." He shook his head. "No matter what the temperature's set at, it stays 68 degrees."

"Not this again." The earlier cold drafts and more recent gust of wind came to mind. "Haven't Mateo and Marianna moved on?"

His mouth curving in a smile, he shook his head. "The heating system's old."

"Then explain that." I pointed at the missing dishtowel, hanging overhead from a viga beam.

****

At noon, Rosie delivered five to-go boxes.

I greeted her with a warm squeeze. "What're these?"

"Your wedding dinner entrées." Rosie beamed. "I want you and Lucas to choose your favorites."

"This is much too elaborate." Luke hugged her as he relieved her of the packages. "We don't need any food tasting. Anything you make is delicious. Besides, we're family."

"Exactly. You're *family*, so you deserve the best."

"Then join us for lunch." I opened the screen door

as Teddy bounced about our legs.

As she entered, Rosie cringed at the towel waving from the rafters. "Why's that hanging there?"

"Oh, I meant to take it down, but I got caught up in fixing the heater." Luke set the food on the table, climbed on a chair, and pulled the dishtowel from the beam.

Rosie crossed herself.

"This may be in left field…" I paused as I set another plate. "But did anything strange happen in this room?"

Rosie's nostrils flaring, she nodded. "Mateo's second wife hanged herself."

"Valentina?" I exchanged a look with Luke. "Where?"

Rosie lifted wide eyes toward the ceiling. "That same rafter." She swallowed. "According to rumors, she hanged herself with a dishtowel."

A shudder slid down my spine.

"This is the first I've heard of it." Luke tore off three paper towels for napkins, then pulled out Rosie's chair. "What happened?"

"The story's always been hush-hush, but from what I understand, Mateo never stopped loving his first wife. So much so, he often confused their names."

"I can't blame Valentina for being hurt, but to commit suicide over a slip of the tongue…?" I shook my head.

"Apparently, the last straw was a Freudian slip, when he called her Marianna in the"—she glanced at the bed—"boudoir…"

"Oh." Luke sank into his chair. "That's an indiscretion of a whole other magnitude."

"The scuttlebutt was that she left a suicide note

before hanging herself that night." Rosie winced. "Mateo found her the next morning."

I eyed the rafters from a different point of view. "No wonder Bea's family resented Marianna. The bitterness must've run deep."

"Deep enough to span four generations." Luke spoke under his breath.

"But enough talk of star-crossed marriages." Rosie began opening the to-go boxes. "Instead, let's plan a happy one, beginning with the entrées for your wedding reception, which, may I remind you, is eleven days away."

"Yikes. Knowing the timeframe is one thing but *hearing* it aloud is another." I took a deep breath to fortify myself.

Rosie's cheeks lifted in a smile as she described the contents of each to-go box. "This is gulf shrimp marinated in lime and cilantro. These are green chili and beef empanadas. This is grilled achiote chicken. These are three kinds of salsa with chips: black bean, green chili, and *pico de gallo*. And finally, *nopales* for any vegetarian guests." Palm up, she waved her hand across the food, inviting them to eat. "*Por favor come.*"

I sampled the dishes, savoring each taste and texture. "The jumbo shrimp are so plump and juicy, they *definitely* have to be one of the entrées. And the empanadas are so light yet crunchy." Groaning, I glanced at Luke. "We've *got* to include these, but I love the chicken's color and peppery flavor."

"A Mexican menu wouldn't be the same without chips and salsa. They're a necessity. And *nopales* are a traditional veggie." He shook his head. "I can't decide between these."

"Then let's not choose." I grinned at the thought. "Let's have a buffet."

"When in doubt, have them all." Rosie beamed. "A buffet it will be."

"That was easy." Pleased at how the wedding plans were shaping up, I returned her smile.

Then Rosie chewed her lip. "Did you have any luck in finding a dress?"

"I did, *and* I found the perfect veil." Jumping up, I rinsed my hands at the sink. "Want to see?"

"The veil, anyway…" Rosie glanced at Luke. "I wouldn't want the groom seeing the gown before the wedding."

"I can take a hint." He chuckled. "I'll be in the warehouse. Call me when you're finished."

"In that case, let me show you the whole outfit." I grabbed the dress and a slip from the closet and called from the bathroom. "It'll just take me a minute to change."

When I reappeared, Rosie's face lit up. "You look lovely."

"It's really a tea dress, but I think it'll do."

"It's perfect—just the right mix of conventional and unconventional." Rosie's eyes twinkled. "Now let me see the veil."

"I put it in the hope chest for safekeeping." I grinned.

"How appropriate."

As soon as the chest's heavy lid lifted, a swarm of flies divebombed my face, filled the cabin, and buzzed Rosie and Teddy.

The dog barked and snapped at the black flies.

I slammed the lid and thrashed my arms, fending off

the pests, but their sheer numbers were overwhelming.

They attacked in droves, dodging my flailing arms and biting my exposed face, neck, and arms.

I slapped them as they bit, and my hand came away bloody. "What the heck?" Whistling for the dog, I called over my shoulder as I scrambled out the door. "Run, Rosie!"

"What's all the commotion?" Luke sprinted from the warehouse.

"Flies." I caught my breath. "When I opened the chest, they swarmed us like *stuka* dive bombers. We had to run outside to escape them."

"They must've been breeding in the hope chest." Rosie swiped at her cheek and smeared blood from a bite. "They're like a biblical plague."

Luke handed her a tissue. "You two wait here. I'm going to spray those flies and end this 'plague.' "

I winced. "The insecticide won't hurt the veil, will it?"

"No, it's a non-staining formula. All it does is kill bugs." Grinning as he entered the cabin, he spoke over his shoulder. "By the way, I like the dress."

"Dang it, Luke!" Hands on hips, I huffed. "You weren't supposed to see it until the wedding."

Five minutes later, he emerged with the veil. "Here's the culprit."

I reached for it.

"Don't touch it." He pulled the tulle away. "It's covered in fly eggs and crawling with maggots. I'm going to fumigate it outside."

"I just bought it yesterday." My shoulders slumping, I turned toward Rosie, telling her about the manufacturer's number embroidered inside a heart, then turned back. "Can you show your aunt?"

As he searched the circular veil for the embroidery, maggots dropped to the ground.

"Gah." My skin crawled. "I modeled that veil."

"Here it is." Luke stretched the fabric taut, making the number more visible.

"VIP01141899." Rosie looked from one face to the other. "What's it mean?"

"What if VIP stands for Valentina Isabella Perez?" I pointed as I read. "And if you add dashes to read 01-14-1899, that number looks like a date stitched inside a heart."

Luke ran his finger across the digits. "Mateo married his second wife in January 1899."

"Could this be Valentina's wedding veil?" I searched Rosie's face for confirmation.

"The idea's far-fetched but not impossible." Rosie's reflective expression turned into a scowl. "But do you really want to wear this fly-infested rag at your wedding?"

I glanced at the veil alive with maggots. "No."

"Then how about shopping for a new one in El Paso tomorrow?"

****

Rosie knocked on the door at sunrise. "If we leave now, we'll be in El Paso when the store opens. Then we can stop for lunch, drive back, and be home by mid-afternoon."

"Perfect." As I poured coffee in the thermos, I shared the story about finding the engagement ring in the grounds.

"Maybe that *was* Valentina's veil." Rosie's eyes narrowed. "What did you do with it?"

"Luke got rid of it."

"Hope he burned it." She counted off on her fingers. "The ring, the dishtowel, and the flies yesterday…that all happened since you bought the veil?" At my nod, she grimaced. "That veil's spooky."

****

The three-hour drive flew by as we discussed wedding plans, and when Rosie parked at the bridal salon, I turned toward her. "Except for Luke, you're my closest friend. Would you be my Matron of Honor?"

"I'd be honored." Rosie leaned across the seat to hug me, then opened the car door. "Come on. Let's make this the best wedding ever!"

I tried on all lengths of veils, from twelve-inch blushers to knee-length mantillas. I weighed simple tulle against beaded lace, but finally settled on a waist-length, fifty-four-inch, sheer chiffon veil.

The saleswoman steered us toward a colorful array. "And your colors are…?"

"Rosé and Champagne."

"We have twenty off-white shades, from ghost white and white smoke to flax and vanilla. The hue differences are subtle, but ivory and ecru might be the closest matches to Champagne." The woman selected two from the assortment. "Which do you think would work better?"

"I had no idea off-white came in so many shades." I fingered the fabrics as I eyed the faint contrast of colors. "Ivory."

"Excellent choice. Now, how will you accessorize your veil?" The saleswoman stared at my head as if imagining the options. "Will you wear a glitzy hair comb, fresh flowers, a crown, or a bow?"

"I don't know." I blinked. "What do you recommend?"

"For this veil, I'd suggest a hair comb." The woman led us to a display case of chic bridal clips and combs.

I wrinkled my nose at the pearl and rhinestone confections. "These are too chichi—definitely not me. We're getting married in a vineyard."

"Vineyard…" The saleswoman nodded knowingly. "In that case, what about a transparent plastic comb but with a bridal hair vine?" She took out a wiry accessory, intwined with pearls, crystals, and silver leaves. "The beauty of these vines is their versatility. You can mold them around any hairstyle you choose."

"I love the leaf motif." I ran my fingertips over the spray of leaves. "Do the leaves come in other colors than silver?"

"Gold or rose gold."

I grinned. "Rosé gold!"

****

As she started the car, Rosie turned toward me. "My niece recommended a new restaurant nearby. Want to try it?"

"Sure." Ten minutes later, I followed her into a narrow noodle shop. A wooden counter stretched the length of the dining area and offered a clear view of the kitchen's open plan.

"Maeve?" An oddly familiar voice thundered from the back.

Cody? I tensed, recalling our last encounter.

He rose from his booth, his tall frame silhouetted against the restaurant's light.

I glanced at the door, then turned toward Rosie. "Maybe we should—"

"Maeve, how good to see you." As Cody strode toward me, he touched my arm, invading my personal space. "What are you doing in El Paso?"

His gaze never leaving my face, he reminded me of the dynamic man he had been once.

I swallowed, debating how to tactfully answer.

"We're shopping for her wedding veil." Rosie came to my rescue.

He blanched. "You're getting married?"

"Yes, the wedding's in how many days?" Rosie caught my gaze. "Ten?"

Cody's shoulders drooped as he congratulated me.

"Thanks." *Keep it short.* "Good to run into you, Cody." Uncomfortable, I whisked a smile. "But I hope you'll excuse us. Ros...*my Matron of Honor* and I have *wedding* details to discuss."

"Of course..." He stepped back as if I'd slapped him. "My AA sponsor is meeting me in a minute, anyway. Glad you found my favorite ramen shop. Be sure to try the Miso Ramen...and again, congratulations." His smile bleak, he gave a stiff nod to us both before heading back to his booth.

AA sponsor...? I returned a curt nod. *Of all the "gin joints" in town, why did Rosie pick this one?*

"Who was that?"

"An old friend." I shrugged.

"That's all?" Rosie stared after him. "He didn't seem overjoyed about your marriage."

"No." I gave an uneasy sigh. "Sorry I didn't introduce you, but..." I bit my lip.

Rosie's shrewd smile relayed her impression. "Because he's more than just an old friend?"

****

When Rosie dropped me off at the cabin, I gathered my packages. "Come in for a cup of coffee."

"Thanks, but I'd better get back to the café. Give Lucas my love." She drove off with a smile and a wave.

Unlocking the cabin door, I glanced about. "Luke? Are you here?" When no one answered, I peeked at the bags' contents and unwrapped the tulle from its layers of tissue paper. Then anchoring the veil's comb to my hair, I admired my reflection in the bathroom mirror.

The screen door flapped shut, and the dog's toenails pitter-pattered across the slate floors.

"Luke? Is that you?"

"Yeah."

Eager to show him, I sashayed into the living room and twirled around, letting the veil swing out. "What do you think?"

His eyes glassy, he muttered. "Nice."

"Nice?" I blinked. "That's it?"

"Sorry." His smile distracted, he seemed unfocused. "You'll make a lovely bride."

"Luke?" I reached my arms around him. "What's wrong?"

He pulled a crumpled grape leaf from his pocket. "Pierce's Disease."

Fingering the dried leaf's red edges, I recalled our first dinner conversation. "This was the bacteria that ruined your grandfather's vineyard, wasn't it?" I went cold. "Will we lose the vines?"

"Possibly...just like my grandfather." He ran his hand over his face. "I was so smug—thought I had all the answers."

"Can pesticides help?"

"California's been experimenting with a

neonicotinoid insecticide—"

"A what?"

"A nicotine-based pesticide."

Marianna's diary entry came to mind. "Didn't your great-great-grandmother use nicotine to treat chicken lice?"

"Nicotine-sulfate." He sniffed. "Maybe this insecticide isn't so new, after all."

"Nothing's new under the sun…" I flashed an encouraging smile. "But if it worked for her, it'll work for us."

"Hope you're right." His eyes bloodshot, he glanced outside at the swaying tree branches. "The problem is we have to spray as soon as possible—"

"So, what's stopping us?"

"The conditions have to be right—dry and still." He grimaced. "And the wind's picking up."

"If it doesn't work the first time, spray the vineyards again."

"The insecticide's not cheap." His shoulders slumped. "We can't afford to time it wrong…"

My chest squeezed tight. "So, you're saying we have one shot?"

****

While Luke drove to Fort Stockton for the insecticide, I snipped infested leaves from the vines, trying to slow the disease's spread.

An hour into the trimming, my phone rang. Though Caller ID displayed an unfamiliar number, I answered.

"Maeve."

The tenderness in Cody's voice stopped me cold. Despite the sun overhead, I shivered. "What do you want?"

"I want to apologize for the way I behaved the last time I visited you."

"Apology accepted." I was curt. "Now, if you'll excuse—"

"Please don't hang up." His tone implored. "I've joined Alcoholics Anonymous, and step eight of the Twelve Steps involves making amends to everyone I've ever hurt. You're the first on my list."

"I've already accepted your apology." My finger hovered over the disconnect button. "Now, if—"

"I wish you and Luke all the best."

"Thanks, best of luck to you, too." Ending the call, I debated whether to block his new number. *Is he sincere, or is this just another ploy?*

****

Luke returned four hours later. His face red as he climbed from his truck, he studied the gathering clouds overhead.

"What's wrong?"

"A storm's blowing in. We've got the pesticide, but we can't use it. Yet the longer we wait, the narrower the window to save the vines." His head hung low. "We could lose everything."

"No matter what happens to the vineyard, we won't lose *everything*." I wrapped my arms around him. "Not as long as we have each other."

The wind gusted through the vine rows in a mournful wail.

"Now what?" Looking at the darkening sky, Luke broke away.

A drop of rain splattered the driveway's caliche dust, then another and another. Within moments, biting pellets of rain assaulted us.

"That rain stings." Wincing, I rubbed my arm.

"That's not rain. That's hail." Luke opened the passenger door as he helped me inside. "Hop in." He crossed to the driver's side, slammed the door, and started the engine.

Little balls of ice collected on the windshield as he drove. Then larger hail pelted the metal roof, thundering inside the truck's cab.

By the time we reached the shed, hailstones the size of robin's eggs littered the ground.

Protected beneath the shed's roof, I opened the passenger door and stood on the running board to survey the truck's roof and hood. "Look at all the dents."

Luke groaned. "If Pierce's Disease doesn't destroy the vines, hail will."

Ten minutes later, the storm let up.

The ground was white with an inch of hailstones. Luke raced to the vineyard, slipping on the icy pellets.

I followed, a lump in my throat as I viewed the damaged vines and bruised, pea-size grapes. *All our work…*

His shoulders slumping, Luke bolted from vine to vine, row to row.

"I'm so sorry." I reached for his arm wanting to connect—ease his pain and mine.

"It's not your fault." Growling, he shrugged me off.

"I know, but this hail on top of Pierce's Disease is so…unfair…" My words trailing off, I spoke to the air as he dashed to the next vine. "Luke…?"

****

At dinner, he seemed in a fog.

"Want more Salisbury steak? Peas?"

Barely eating or speaking, he only nodded or

grunted.

****

The next morning, he stared blankly at his breakfast.

Caught between wanting to comfort him and give him space, I was stymied.

He got up from the table without a word.

"Aren't you going to finish your eggs? And you never touched your bacon." I forced a smile. "It's your favorite—hickory-smoked and uncured."

"Give it to the dog." He pushed open the door.

"Where are you going?"

"Where else? The vineyard. Try to salvage what I can."

I glanced at the window. "But it's raining."

"Then I'll fix the sprayer."

"You said the weather had to be perfect to spray the pesticide."

"I'm not spraying. I said I'll *fix* the sprayer!" He slammed out the door.

My chest tightening, I forced a deep breath.

****

Luke skipped lunch and tromped into the cabin at dusk, wearing mud-caked boots.

I set newspapers on the floor. "Why don't you leave your boots by the door?"

Apparently unaware of the mess, he glanced at his boots, then, grunting, unlaced them.

I stifled a sigh.

He trudged to the table in stockinged feet, plopped down, and rested his head on his hand.

I bit my lip, teetering between sympathy and aggravation.

His shoulders started shaking.

Is he crying? Moving closer to comfort him, I noticed his shirt was drenched. "No wonder you're shaking. You're soaked through."

"Huh?" He turned dazed eyes toward me.

"You're dripping wet. Why don't you change into dry clothes?"

"Why?" He shrugged. "I'll just get wet again."

"Luke…" *You're scaring me*, I wanted to say. Instead, I ladled a bowl of homemade chicken-noodle soup and set it before him. "Eat this. It'll warm you from the inside."

He dipped his spoon into the broth and began eating mechanically.

I dished a bowl for myself and sat across from him, trying to make eye contact.

But his glazed eyes stared without seeing.

Resigned, I gazed out the window, watching rivulets of rain flow down the pane. *His mood is as dark as the weather.* I changed the subject, trying to lighten the atmosphere. "Have you started building the wedding arch?"

"Don't you think I have better things to do?" He scowled.

Wincing, I tiptoed around the issue. "Well, maybe we can rent one." Then exasperated with his negativity—and myself for tolerating it—I confronted him. "Have you sent out the invitations yet?"

"Don't you get it? If we lose the crop, we lose the vineyard." His chair scraped as he stood. "I have too much at stake to waste time."

"In case you forgot, we're getting married in nine days." So tense that my muscles quivered, I jumped to my feet. "Of course, if you think the wedding is 'wasting time,' maybe we should postpone it."

His eyes flashed. "Maybe we should cancel it."

"Fine!"

"Fine!"

Not bothering to slip on his boots, he grabbed them and slammed out the door.

The wind knocked out of me, I sagged back into my chair.

The dog sidled alongside me, rubbing against my calves.

"Teddy, what've I done?"

The lights flickered.

"Great, now we're going to lose electricity?"

The lights flickered again, went off, came on, then dimmed.

"A brownout?" As I stepped toward the kitchen, the lights went out, and the refrigerator stopped humming.

A musty odor filled the air as I searched for the matches. *Mold? Mildew?*

Teddy sneezed twice.

The stench of rotting teeth and mothballs permeated the cabin. My eyes began to itch, and I coughed as my fingers found the matches.

Lightning splintered in a white-hot flash outside the window, momentarily lighting the kitchen.

A shadow stirred before the room went dark.

Did I imagine that? The frigid darkness enveloped me, and I struck a match. My numb fingertips fumbled from one drawer to the next until finally, I connected with a candle.

A low growl began in the back of Teddy's throat as a shadow crossed the room, and a freezing gust blew out the match.

Yelping, I tried to light another with trembling fingers. Despite my shaking hands, the flame finally took hold, and the candle's faint glow showed my breath's condensation.

A transparent silhouette emerged. Barely visible, it lifted a gauzy veil, revealing a scarred, wizened face, then glided across the cabin and through the bolted door.

Teddy lurched at the exit, barking and scratching.

Was that my imagination? No, Teddy saw it, too... My heart pounding, I tilted the candle over a saucer, then secured it in the melted wax. I searched the cabin in the scant light but found nothing odd, and embarrassed, I laughed at my fears. "Teddy, we're jumping at our own shadows."

The cell phone rang, and I flinched. *Luke!* "I'm so glad you called."

"You are?" The warmth came through Cody's voice. "Then I'm glad I followed my hunch."

"What?"

"Gut instinct...something told me to call you." His friendly tone changed to one of concern. "Are you all right?"

Though uncomfortable speaking with my ex, I was glad for the company. "It's storming here. The lights went out, and I'm just a little jumpy." I squinted. "But what do you mean 'something' told you to call me?"

"I don't know. Call it intuition...a sixth sense. Something made me pick up the phone."

After Luke's rejection, the idea of anyone caring enough to call eased the ache. I took a deep breath and let it out in a long sigh.

"Okay, spill it."

"What?"

"I recognize that groan. What's wrong?"

Where do I start? "To begin with, the vineyard's infested with leafhoppers, but because it's raining, we can't spray the pesticide. Worse, a hailstorm damaged the vines, which leaves them even more susceptible to Pierce's Disease. I'm worried the crop will fail." A lump caught in my throat.

"I'm sorry about the weather and hope the vines survive, *but* that's not what's troubling you, is it?"

Sitting at the table, I fought back tears. "Can't fool you, can I?"

"Hey, we've been through a lot together. I know when something's wrong." His smile came through the phone line. "What's really bothering you?"

It's true. He knows me better than anyone—even Luke. Lapsing into familiar patterns, I summarized the fight and cancelled wedding. "Then just before you called, the storm knocked out the electricity, and I saw...I *thought* I saw..." I shook my head. "My imagination took off." Talking about my fears lessened their grip, and I chuckled. "You probably think I'm crazy, but thanks for listening."

"Hey, I'm happy to be your sounding board—or shoulder to cry on—whatever you need."

I blinked. *Was he always this considerate? No...* "You've changed."

"I'm sober." His laugh was dry. "That's the difference. Besides, my sponsor says helping others helps me stay sober, so anytime you need to talk, call me. You've got my new number. I'm always here for you— just a phone call away."

The rain beat a steady patter against the windows, lending a somber backdrop as I hung up. More confused now than before, I glanced about the cabin's gloomy interior. *One candle doesn't shed much light…either in here or on the situation.* I twisted my engagement around my finger, studying it in the candlelight.

The door squeaked open, and I jumped.

"Sorry, didn't mean to startle you." Luke crossed the room. "And I'm sorry for stomping off. The Pierce's Disease, the hail, and now the rain have taken their toll." He sighed. "But I shouldn't take out my frustrations on you." Holding out his arms, he moved a step closer. "If you'll have me, do you still want to get married?"

Chapter 18

I wanted to wrap my arms around him, but I sat rooted to my chair, squirming as I replayed the phone call. *Cody called* me. *I didn't call him, so why do I feel I've been unfaithful?*

Luke's shoulders slumped as his arms fell to his sides. "That's no?"

"No." Guilt or no guilt, I jumped off the chair, snuggling against him until his arms enfolded me. "That's definitely *not* no." Conforming my body to his, I kissed him, communing nonverbally.

As he came up for air, he smiled. "That's more like it." Then looking about the cabin, he noticed the candle. "Why are all the lights off?" He tightened his grip. "Planning a romantic evening?"

"No, the power went out."

"It did?" His arms fell to his sides. "When?"

"Right after you left." I narrowed my eyes. "Where were you?"

"In the shed, but it never lost power." He flicked the switch, and the room flooded with light.

"What the…?" I shook my head, questioning my memory. "After the lights went out, a shadow crossed the room, then lifted a veil—"

"Veil…Valentina?"

"Maybe." I shrugged. "Maybe the candlelight was playing tricks on my eyes, but I'd swear a see-through figure showed me its face before it floated through the door."

"Not this again." He met my gaze. "I thought we were rid of ghosts."

"Me, too, but that's what I saw." I chewed my lip, debating whether to bring up another topic. "And speaking of ghosts…from the past…" Already regretting it, I hesitated.

"Yeah."

"Cody called tonight."

"And you answered?" His eyes burned into me.

"I thought it was you. The phone rang moments after you stormed out—"

"What did he want?"

"He said a sixth sense told him to call me, which is odd—"

"So now he's simpatico?" His scowl telegraphed his scorn. "Do you still have feelings for him?"

"No, Cody's just an old friend." *Isn't he?*

My phone rang.

Rather than interrupt our conversation, I turned off the ringer, but the vibration continued.

"Are you going to get that?" Luke gave me a withering glare. "Or won't you answer Lover Boy while I'm here?"

Rolling my eyes, I pressed connect. "Hello."

The line was dead.

Disconnecting, I shrugged. "Whoever it was hung up."

"Lover Boy?"

"No." I let out an exasperated sigh. "Probably a wrong number."

"Likely story…"

My phone rang again.

"Who is this?"

Static crackled, and Caller ID displayed 00000000. "Hello?"

The white noise morphed into a mechanical vocalization of raspy vowels and consonants. "Guh…eeeeh…tuh…ooo…uuuu…tuh."

I put the phone on speaker.

"Guheeehtuh oouuutuh." The decibel level escalating from a whisper to a roar, the sounds continued until they formed words. "Get out! Get—"

My hand trembling, I disconnected. "What was that?"

"Valentina?"

"That'd be my guess. The way Marianna and Mateo wanted us together, maybe she wants us apart." Recalling Luke's depression and the tension between us, I winced. "Granted, we're stressed about the wedding—"

"And the vineyard…"

"But I can't help wondering if our bickering isn't related to the bugs and weather."

"Bugs?" He gave a skeptical laugh.

"Remember those swarms of horse flies and maggots on Valentina's veil? Then the next day you found leafhoppers spreading Pierce's Disease."

"Probably coincidental, though the timing *is* uncanny." He rubbed his jaw. "Okay, but you can't blame her for the weather."

"Maybe I can." I tossed my chin. "I read an article about electromagnetic energy. To manifest, spirits have to pull heat from the surrounding air, causing the temperature to plummet. Think cold spots." Recollecting the most recent event, I shook off a chill.

"Okay, heat's a form of energy. I'll give you that, but what do ghosts have to do with hail, rain, or lightning?"

"That same article said spirits feed off another form of energy—negative ions—and thunderstorms create negative ions. Think. These events all began after I found Valentina's veil. I can't help but believe she's responsible for the storms and infestations." *Not to mention temptations.* Cody's hunch came to mind. *Who or what was behind that call?* Recalling Rosie's warning, I faced Luke. "What did you do with that veil?"

"Threw it in the garbage. Why?"

"If that veil's the link to Valentina, we need to burn it." I grabbed the matches from the breakfast bar, then opened the door. "Come on."

The wind swept the rain inside, drenching me and puddling on the floor.

"Wait 'til the storm ends." He tried to shut the door.

"No, *now*." Despite the deluge, I held my ground.

"Another few minutes won't matter." He shut the door.

"I'm not so sure. Ever since I bought that veil, it's been one thing after another: flies, maggots, leafhoppers spreading Pierce's Disease, wind, rain, hail, and..." *Luke's depression, my temptation.* "Worst of all, our bickering." I stared him down. "Let's get rid of it, *now*, before it causes any more damage."

"If you feel that strongly about it—"

"I do. Now, *come on!*" I pushed open the door.

Rain pounded the portico as a bolt of lightning struck the tombstone.

My adrenaline pumping, I yelped.

"Wait here, under the overhang. I'll get the garbage can." He dashed into the rain.

The air sizzled, and another bolt of lightning struck where he had stood.

His hackles rising, Teddy howled.

"Luke?" My heart pounded as I shouted into the storm.

The air hissed and crackled. Static electricity made my hair stand on end. A third bolt of lightning crashed beside the portico, forcing me back.

"Luke, are you all right?" The sky blazed with forked lightning while the rain hammered sideways, soaking me. The thunder deafening, my ears rang as I shouted into the darkness. "Luke?"

The rain sheeted off him as he sloshed the metal can through the mud. Another thunderbolt clapped and, on its heels, another just as he reached the overhang. He lifted the metal lid. "Go for it."

I lit a match, and the wind blew it out. I lit a second, cupping my hand around the flame to protect it.

Thunder bellowed, while lightning floodlit the sky.

I tossed the match into the garbage can's dry interior.

As the flames caught, took hold, and began engulfing the tulle, the wind howled like a wounded animal.

Thick, black smoke forced me back, choking me. But as the blaze ran out of fuel, the flames flickered, sputtered, and finally expired.

The embers dying, the wind stopped, and the rain dwindled to a drizzle.

I tucked my arm around Luke's waist, hooking my thumb in his jeans' belt loop. "Think this will free us of

Valentina?"

****

The next morning, I pointed to a break in the clouds. "Look, a patch of blue."

"The first I've seen in days. Maybe you were right about the veil." His smile tender, he pulled me close. "Sorry I've been so detached the past few days. Now, what wedding plans did you want to discuss?"

I drew back my head, studying him. "You're *sure* you want to discuss wedding plans?"

"Absolutely, and you'll be happy to hear I've sent the invitations."

"You did?" I breathed a sigh of relief, mentally checking it off our to-do list. "What about the wedding arch?"

"What do you think I was doing yesterday in the shed?"

"Really?" *Why did I ever question his love?* I threw my arms around his neck and kissed him. "Thank you!"

"It's almost done—except for the post brackets I ordered, which are scheduled to be delivered this morning."

Luke's cell phone buzzed.

"Scratch that"—he scanned the message—"which just *were* delivered. How's that for timing?" He reached for my hand. "Let's check the mailbox."

Our arms swinging between us like kids, I nearly skipped down the driveway.

But when he opened the box, his face fell.

"What's wrong?"

Fingering the small package, he sighed. "They sent the wrong-sized brackets."

"How can you be sure?"

"The wedding arch calls for seventeen-inch brackets." He measured the package against his hand. "These are roughly seven inches."

"Now what?"

He gave a dispirited shrug as he filed the report and reordered the brackets. Then he turned to me. "Just hope they arrive in time."

****

That afternoon, I stopped by the local bakery. The front window displayed a Mexican embroidery cake, its piped buttercream mimicking Mexican floral patterns.

I sent Luke a snapshot.

Maeve—*How's this for our wedding cake?*—

When he replied with a thumbs-up emoticon, I stepped inside to place the order.

Not five minutes later, Bea walked in, her cinnamon perfume overpowering the bakery's sweet, yeasty aroma.

I turned my back, breathing shallowly to avoid the stench, as well as confrontation.

Making no attempt to recognize boundaries, Bea shouldered into my personal space, elbowing me as she eavesdropped.

Silently fuming, I shrugged her off.

"Be with you in a moment." The shopkeeper grazed the newcomer with a perfunctory smile as she concluded my order. "We'll deliver the cake next Friday morning at ten."

"Better make that nine to be safe. Thanks." I turned to leave.

"Don't think your wedding will be any cakewalk." Bea blocked my escape.

"*Excuse* me." I sidestepped her.

"Never in a million years…" Bea smiled through her hiss.

****

I found Luke in the vineyard. "How's the pesticide spraying going?"

"Done." His relaxed smile spoke volumes.

"I'm so glad." I took a deep breath before asking the next question. "Think you sprayed in time to save the vines?"

"Too early to say, but the odds are good."

"Thank God." Reassured, I hugged him.

"How'd it go with the wedding plans?"

"The to-do list is getting shorter." Enjoying the security of his arms, I rattled off the morning's accomplishments. "Besides ordering the cake, I stopped at the rental center. They'll take care of the tent, tables, chairs, table linens, runners, napkins, disposable dishes, flatware, and glasses—both the set up *and* the cleanup." I breathed a sigh of relief.

"Good, that translates to more fun and less work on our big day." His arms squeezed around me.

Despite our progress, a vague thought nagged. "I just feel we're overlooking something. What are we forgetting?"

"Can't think of anything." He shook his head. "We've reconfirmed with the minister, sent the invitations—"

"And booked the venue…" I chuckled before snuggling against him. "Good thing we have an 'in' with the owners."

"Isn't it, though?" A warm chuckle tumbled from his lips.

My happiness was complete except for that one

niggling thought. *What haven't we crossed off our list?*
****

The reordered parts arrived Monday, and Luke assembled the wedding arch at the vineyard's entrance near the patio's far edge.

"It's beautiful." I raised my hands in a prayerful pose. "Once I trim it with off-white netting and add the flowers, it'll be the perfect backdrop for our wedding."

"No rain's in the forecast so far." Luke caught my gaze as he closed his phone's app. "We don't want any 'clouds' overshadowing our day."

"Wish we could take out rain insurance." I snickered at the idea.

"A weather permit." He cackled at the thought.

"*Permit! Crap!*" I thumped my palm against my head. "*That's* what we forgot!"

"What?"

"Our wedding license, and Rosie said Texas has a three-day waiting period."

He checked his watch. "Too late to get it today. The county clerk's office closed ten minutes ago."

"No…" I began hyperventilating. "I can't think. What day is it?"

"Monday. Tomorrow is Tuesday." Wearing a gentle smile, Luke took me by the shoulders. "We'll have the license in plenty of time."

"Tomorrow's cutting it close." I shook my head, disgusted. "How could I forget?"
****

The next morning, when I tried to make coffee, the pipes gurgled, and the faucet ran dry. "What happened to the water?"

Luke turned on the bathroom faucet, and the pipes

hissed. "Air's trapped in the lines. I'll have to bleed them."

"Can you do that…in time, I mean?" I checked the clock. "The county clerk's office opens in two hours…Let's skip coffee. We can pick it up on the way."

"Trapped air in the pipes means no water anywhere, not just in the kitchen. The irrigation system's offline, and if the recovering vines aren't watered, we'll lose them for sure."

"But this is the last day to get the marriage license." My breathing became labored. "With the 72-hour wait, if we don't get it today, we can't be married Friday."

"Relax." His smile was sympathetic. "The office is open 'til noon and then again all afternoon."

"Okay…" I busied myself, but at nine, impatience took over. "Almost done?"

"Not yet." He wiped his brow, leaving a smudge on his face.

An hour later, I forced a smile. "Ready?"

He straightened his back. "Why don't you get the license without me?"

"Doesn't work that way." I shook my head. "We *both* have to appear in person."

He sighed. "I don't know why bleeding the lines is taking so long, but another few minutes should do it."

An hour later, I resorted to chewing my nails. "Done?"

His head and chest under the kitchen sink, he grunted. "Just about."

At 11:40, he climbed from beneath the sink, turned on the tap, washed his hands and face, and grinned. "Ready."

We hopped in the truck and, ten minutes later,

parked in front of the county clerk's office.

My heels clacking as I jogged along the sidewalk, I pulled Luke along. "Come on. The office closes in five minutes."

A sign posted at the entrance showed the office hours: nine to noon and one to five.

I checked my phone as I tugged at the door: 11:56. But it didn't budge. "Uh-oh…"

"Relax. We can have lunch and come back when they open at one."

The midday sun was bright. The sky was clear, and the Lincoln Mountains seemed near enough to touch.

Encouraged by their beauty, I took a deep breath, remembering the first time I'd seen them. "Was that only three months ago that we met?" I shook my head as we walked to the drugstore. "Seems I've known you all my life."

Five minutes later, we slid into a booth made from reclaimed wood. *The same booth where Cody and I sat.* My chest tightened. *Guilty conscience?*

"Coffee?" The question rhetorical, the waitress set two mugs and an urn on our table. "Want menus?"

Déjà vu—the same server that waited on Cody and me. I turned away.

As if on cue, my phone buzzed.

Without checking Caller ID, I knew who it was. *Cody's timing is more than a fluke.*

"Going to answer it?"

Glancing at the name, I pressed *decline*. "No one important." *Is it? Cody's timing is impeccable. Why did he call now? Valentina?* I ordered a club sandwich but, too upset to eat, barely nibbled at it. "Luke, if we don't get the license this afternoon, all our wedding plans—"

"Don't worry." He reached for my hand. "Worse comes to worst, we'll go through the motions, then get married the next day. This isn't the end of the world."

At 12:55, we walked back to the county clerk's office.

A note on the door read *Closed* with an emergency phone number listed.

No! Is this Valentina's work...or a sign we shouldn't get married? I breathed uneasily as I punched in the number, put my phone on speaker, and crossed my fingers.

A recording answered. "The office is closed Tuesday afternoon for a district meeting and reopens Wednesday morning at nine."

How could I leave the marriage license until the last minute? Dragging my feet as I stumbled toward the truck, I nearly bumped into Mamie.

"What a surprise running into you two." The woman's face lit up in a friendly smile. "What are you up to these days?"

"Luke and I were applying for a marriage license—"

"Congratulations!"

"*Were* applying...past tense."

While Luke shared the details, I recalled the woman's research skills. "Do you have any ideas?"

"As a matter of fact..." Mamie's puckered brow relaxed. "I'm headed to the library now. Come with me." Within moments, she sat at a computer and found the link to the state's online resources for licenses. "Fill out this application, while I check something."

Ten minutes later, the form was printing as she returned with a man in tow. "This is Benjamin Polk, the county clerk."

My jaw went slack. "Mamie, you're a miracle worker."

"Not really. The first Tuesday of every month, the district holds its meeting in the boardroom." She smiled as she clapped the clerk's shoulder. "Ben will take it from here."

"Good to see you again." The gray-haired man shook hands with Luke. "How can I help?"

"Can you issue us a marriage license?"

"I can as long as you both have your driver's licenses, the fee, and the signed form."

"Here's the form." I pulled the paper from the printer, signed it, and handed Luke the pen. "Your turn." Then I faced Ben. "More importantly, can we still get married as planned?"

"As long as your wedding takes place 72 hours from now." He checked his watch. "Which means after one thirty Friday…what time's your ceremony?"

****

I woke screaming.

"What's wrong?" Luke's voice breathless, he vaulted from his air mattress.

"I dreamt Valentina showed up at our wedding."

"How do you know it was Valentina?"

"I recognized her veil."

"It's just pre-wedding jitters." He leaned over the bed to kiss me. "Go back to sleep."

I nodded and lay in the dark, tossing and turning until I slipped into a fitful doze.

Again, Valentina visited my dreams, this time, lifting back her veil to reveal a pronounced cleft palate. Her scarred, upper lip hooked to her nose, and her bottom lip protruded. Then gradually her face morphed into Bea's, exposing a faint scar on Bea's upper lip, and the scent of cinnamon filled the air.

The microwave beeped, waking me with a start.

"Morning, sleepyhead." Luke brought me a coffee mug and a steaming cinnamon roll. "Thought you'd like to start the day with a sugar rush."

As I inhaled the aroma, my dream made sense. "Didn't know you were a pastry chef."

"I'm not." He snickered. "But I can open a can and pop 'em in the oven with the best of 'em."

I tried to smile my thanks but apparently didn't succeed.

His grin faded. "Rough night?"

****

Wednesday night, what started as a sweet dream soured. After the minister said, "Speak now or forever hold your peace," Bea stepped from behind the wedding arch and seized Luke's hand.

Instead of pulling away, he wrapped his arms around her and kissed her in front of the gaping assembly. Then they ran off through the vineyard, hand in hand, leaving me, staring.

The dream changed. Now, Luke and I were newlyweds at our reception, cutting our wedding cake together.

Bea appeared from nowhere, lifted the cake with both hands, and pitched it at us. Then she broke a wine bottle against the table and, using the sharp edge as a short-range weapon, lunged at Luke. "If I can't have you, no one will."

I sat up in bed, drenched in sweat. Trying to get my bearings, I glanced about the cabin. Luke's air mattress was empty, and Teddy was nowhere in sight. *Did I oversleep?* Slumping back against the pillows, I glanced at the time. *Six*. But the wall clock was crooked, as if someone had bumped into it, and the framed photo near the fireplace was askew.

The cabin door squeaked open with a drawn-out whine.

I scrambled to my feet.

As Teddy bounded inside, Luke poked his head in, then strode over. "Good, you're awake."

I took a deep breath and kissed him, preferring reality to my nightmare. "Were you redecorating?"

"What do you mean?"

I gestured at the wall-hangings. "Instead of noon at the top, the clock's tilted, so 11:55 is at the top—and the photo's crooked, too."

"That's odd." Straightening both, he shrugged. "Maybe a slamming door jolted them."

"Maybe…"

"Coffee?"

"Definitely, and in copious amounts."

He crossed to the kitchen, poured me a cup, then set a spoon and sugar bowl on the bar. "Another rough night?"

"The only good thing about nightmares is waking up from them." Chuckling as I reached for the sugar, I yelped.

Though the lid was still on the bowl, sugar had spilled across the bar and onto the floor.

I caught Luke's gaze. "Valentina?"

****

The next night, when I dreamt the minister said, "Speak now or forever hold your peace," Cody jumped up from the back row.

"Don't go through with this wedding, Maeve. I've never stopped loving you. Come with me to Las—"

Two groomsmen caught him under the arms and escorted him from the vineyard.

With his shouts still ringing through the air, Bea strode toward me in a white bridal gown. "Luke can't marry you." Carrying an enormous bouquet, she stared me down. "He's marrying me!"

Two guests tried to usher her from the ceremony.

But Bea broke free from their grasp. "If I can't have Luke, no one will." She pulled a handgun from her bouquet, aimed at Luke, and squeezed the trigger.

"No!" I woke on our wedding day in tears. *What's Bea planning?*

****

The morning flew by in a flurry of last-minute instructions and preparations.

The baker delivered the wedding cake, but instead of frothy white buttercream, the frosting was inky black and festooned with sugar skulls. In place of the traditional bride and groom figurines, two *Calavera-Catrina* skeletons topped the multilayered cake, and a banner across it read, *'Til Death Do Us Part.*

"A Day of the Dead cake?" I gasped. "Is this cake someone's idea of a joke?"

The delivery man pulled out the receipt. "Your name's Maeve Jackson, isn't it?"

"Yes, but this isn't the Mexican embroidery cake I ordered." Ready to burst into tears, I scrolled through my phone's photos. "How could you mistake that floral motif on white frosting for skeletons on black?"

He reread the receipt. "You cancelled that cake

Monday and placed this order instead."

Luke turned toward me. "More of Valentina's handiwork?"

Recalling Bea's behavior in the bakery, I shook my head. "My money's on her great-great-granddaughter."

"Wait a minute…" Luke moved in for a closer look. "We can fix this."

"How?" Groaning, I slumped into a chair. "This cake's for All Souls' Day—not a wedding."

He turned to the delivery man. "Can the bakery add a Y at the end?"

The man's eyes narrowed. "Why?"

"So instead of *'Til Death Do Us Part*, it reads *'Til Death Do Us Party*." Luke gave my shoulder a friendly shake. "What do you think?"

Torn between laughing and crying, I smiled through my tears. " 'Y' not?"

****

At noon, the bakery redelivered the cake. As that van drove off, a refrigerated flower truck arrived. But when the driver opened the back doors, he gasped from the blast of frigid air.

Afraid to ask, I steeled myself. "What's wrong?"

"I don't know how this happened, but the flowers froze." He checked the frost covered dial. "The thermometer's always set to 55 degrees Fahrenheit. Now it reads seventeen."

"Are the flowers salvageable?" I looked past him at the truck's wilted blooms.

He shook his head. "They're stiff now, but when they thaw, they'll be a slimy mess."

"The wedding's in four hours." I glanced at my watch, estimating the time to set up. "Can you deliver fresh floral centerpieces, boutonnieres, flower girl's rose petals, bridal bouquet, aisle decorations, and arch garlands in the next hour?" I waved Luke over.

"It's too late to order from the warehouse." The man stuttered. "All I can do is deliver what's in stock, and since we're short-staffed today, the best I can promise is two hours."

I turned as Luke approached. "Did you hear?"

Nodding, he shrugged. "It is what it is."

"Sorry..." The man closed the truck's back doors. "I'll make this a rush order, but..." He grimaced before stepping in his truck.

Luke put his arm around me as he gestured to the blue skies. "It's a beautiful morning. You're a lovely bride, and today's our wedding day. Let's not worry about details."

"You're right." Despite the setbacks, I forced a smile. "But I can't help wondering if Bea tampered with the thermostat." Then the cold spots, hail, and thunderstorms came to mind. *Or is this Valentina's handiwork?*

****

The rental company called, apologizing for the delay.

I breathed deeply, taking it in stride.

Two hours later, the florist delivered the flowers. But instead of roses with soft pink centers and champagne-colored petals, he brought orange mums and purple daisies.

The rental company arrived an hour before the wedding. As they set up the chairs, I rushed about, arranging the arch and aisle flowers. Then placing the centerpieces on the tables—the last task before getting dressed—I realized they had set up the tables on the grass. "What happened to the tent I ordered?"

The manager referred to her list. "Oops, my bad." She gestured toward the clear skies. "But don't worry. No rain's in the forecast."

What else? Though annoyed with the woman's cavalier attitude, I was too beat-down to object. I checked the time: 3:10 pm. *Fifty minutes until I walk down the aisle, and I haven't even showered.*

After tucking the boutonnieres, flower girl's petals, and bridal bouquet in the fridge, I showered, slipped into my antique tea dress, and checked my reflection in the mirror. *Something's missing...the brooch.* I pinned the cameo to my bodice and assessed the effect.

This time, instead of my outdoor glow and short bob, the mirror image showed a buttermilk complexion and upswept *Gibson Girl* hairdo.

Marianna?

Teddy barked.

I blinked, and my reflection appeared normal. *Overactive imagination?*

A rap at the door drew my attention, followed by Rosie's voice. "Knock-knock."

"Come in." I checked the time: 3:40 pm. "The door's unlocked."

Stepping inside, Rosie gasped as she spread her hands. "You look positively radiant."

"Bet you say that to all the brides." I felt the heat creep into my cheeks.

"I'm serious. You're glowing." Rosie gave an apologetic grin. "Sorry I'm late. We had a slight problem—"

"Oh, no!" My heart skipped a beat. "The staff

walked out? The kitchen caught fire?"

"No, no, nothing like that." Chuckling, she shook her head. "We had a power outage, and—"

"All the food spoiled?" I groaned. *What next?*

"No, the food prep just took a little longer than expected. That's all." Rosie rested her hands on my shoulders. "Everything's under control—I'm just running a few minutes late."

Recounting the day's mishaps, I gave a deep sigh. "I don't think I could handle another glitch."

"These are just pre-wedding jitters. Relax." Rosie gave my shoulder a friendly shake. "The weather's perfect for an outdoor wedding—and you look like you stepped out of a bride's magazine."

I brightened at the compliment.

"All you're missing is your veil."

"Which reminds me, can you anchor it, so it doesn't slide off?" I handed over the hair vine. "Be right back with the veil."

After several minutes, Rosie called, "Need any help?"

"Just a minute." I rummaged through the clothes closet. "I *know* I hung it here after ironing out the wrinkles." When I reached the end of the rack without finding it, I started at the far end, searching again, hanger by hanger.

After several minutes, Rosie joined me. "Maybe you left the veil at Luke's place, or would you have put it in the hope chest?"

"No." Frustrated at the delay, I shoved the clothes to one side and began sorting through them, one by one. "I put it *right here*."

"Mind if I look around?"

I glanced at my watch: 3:50 pm. I bit my lip. "Sure."

"Here it is!" Grinning, Rosie held up the veil.

"Where was it?" My head pounding, I pressed my fingers into my temples.

"In the hope chest…"

"What?"

Rosie's smile faded. "In the—"

"I heard you. I just can't believe it." My eyes brimming over with frustrated tears, I massaged my temples. "I *know* I hung it in the closet."

Rosie shrugged. "Somehow it got in the hope—"

A rap at the door interrupted. "Luke wants to know if you're ready."

I swiped at my tears. "Give me ten minutes." Then I recalled the flowers in the fridge. "Can you take the boutonnieres and give the flower girl these rose petals?" I handed over the flowers, set my bouquet on the table, and slumped into a chair.

Rosie gently shook my arm. "Come on. This is your big day. Don't let ants ruin the picnic."

"But it's been one thing after another…I think the universe is conspiring against our wedding."

"That's just stress talking."

I swallowed the lump in my throat. "Maybe you're right."

"Let me attach the veil. Then I'll wrap this bridal hair vine around your head like a tiara."

Ten minutes later, strains of Pachelbel's Canon in D drifted into the cabin.

"That's our cue." Rosie smiled. "Ready?"

Chapter 19

Ribbons cordoned off the rows of folding chairs, creating a central aisle, while tulle bows with orange mums and purple daisies festooned the end chairs. With the vineyard as the backdrop, the arch was the ceremony's focal point.

The minister entered from the side, leading Luke and his best man.

After a final tweak to ensure the bride's veil and hair vine were secure, Rosie started down the aisle.

The flower girl followed several measures later. Dressed in white, Luke's youngest cousin tossed multicolored rose petals from a basket.

The music swelled, and I began my journey. My heart singing, I caught Luke's gaze, where he waited beneath the floral arch.

Suddenly, a crash of thunder split the air.

From a cloudless, blue sky, lightning struck the arbor.

I closed my eyes against the brilliant white flash, and when I opened them, Luke lay crumpled beside the smoldering arch. I sprinted toward him. Then kneeling and cradling his head, I smothered him in kisses. "Are you all right?"

His eyes fluttering open, he gave me a wan smile and thumbs up while the best man helped him to his feet.

I said a silent prayer just as the heavens let loose a

cloudburst.

Roaring like a freight train, the wind flapped the tablecloths, overturned the chairs, and blew away the napkins.

Guests shrieked and scattered for cover.

"This way." Dripping wet, Luke led them to the covered patio. "Due to the unexpected wedding 'shower,' the nuptials are delayed. How about a pre-wedding toast while we wait out the storm?"

I chuckled despite the deluge, grateful he wasn't hurt.

He opened the Dutch door and brought out the wine. Then he leaned toward me in a whisper. "Why don't you take this opportunity to freshen up?"

"Freshen up?" My veil was plastered to my head, and my saturated dress clung to my legs, but I mustered a wry grin. "I need damage control."

****

Drenched from head to foot, I sloshed through the downpour and into the cabin.

As I dripped across the slate floor, something brushed against my cheek, and looking up, I screamed.

A feather wafted from Valentina's hanging beam.

Instantly, the temperature plummeted, and the petals of my bridal bouquet withered.

My breath fogged, and I shivered in my wet dress as much from fright as the frigid air. "Valentina?"

The wind moaned through the windows.

"Stop it!" I threw the shriveled daisies on the table. "Like it or not, this is *my* wedding, *my* life, and soon to be *my* house. Since *you* killed yourself, you have nothing to avenge and no one to blame but yourself." I stepped toward the door. "You've already gotten your justice, so get out!"

"And go where…?"

The tone was so plaintive, so frail, that I cocked my ear, straining to hear, but the only sound was the rain pelting the roof. *Did I imagine it?*

"Where would I go?" The nasal voice seemed stronger as a nearly transparent silhouette materialized.

I stepped back.

Barely visible, the image lifted its veil to reveal its face, then gave a coquettish leer, accentuating a split between its upper lip and nose. "Am I pretty?" The voice dripped with sarcasm.

"Valentina?" The name came out in a hoarse whisper.

"*Am I pretty?!*" The tone demanding now, the specter moved closer, bringing her cleft lip directly in line with my vision.

The stench of decay and mold overwhelming, I breathed through my mouth.

"How dare you say I have nothing to avenge and no one to blame but myself?" Valentina lisped.

I pulled back my head. "You committed suicide. No one harmed you *but you*, so why are you trying to ruin Luke's and my wedding?"

"Revenge."

"Against whom?"

"Marianna and her offspring."

"Why?" I gave a disbelieving laugh. "I read Marianna's diary. She was long gone before you married Mateo."

"Maybe gone but not forgotten." She glanced at the bed. "My husband never stopped loving her."

I followed her gaze, recalling the rumors.

"Do you have any idea what it's like growing up with a cleft lip and palate? The stares? The taunts? The pointing fingers? Just eating and drinking were daily challenges, but to be accepted...to be loved..." Valentina's laugh was contemptuous. "Mateo only married me for convenience."

How sad to know her husband loved another. I grimaced. *No wonder she resented Marianna.*

"Oh, no, you don't." Valentina tossed her chin, her sneer intensifying her deformity.

"What—"

"Don't you *dare* pity me." Jutting her face into mine, Valentina bared her teeth, exposing the gap in her palate.

Too hard to look, I shut my eyes.

The air became arctic.

"Sofia used to look at me that way. Can you imagine? My own daughter ashamed of—"

"Wait a minute." Trembling from the cold, I blinked. "You said Sofia? Sofia Ramirez?" I recalled the name from the library's records.

"Yes...why?"

A disbelieving grin tickling my lips, I studied the image in a new light. "Sofia Ramirez was my great-grandmother, which would make you my great-great-grandmother."

As the atmosphere lightened, the room lost its chill.

My breath no longer fogged the air, and I stopped chafing my arms to keep warm.

Valentina stepped back, studying my face. "Now that you mention it, I do see a family resemblance. Yes! You have Sofia's green eyes." Her face relaxing into a smile, she nodded.

I did a double take. *Is it my imagination, or is her cleft lip less noticeable?* Then speaking quietly, like a commentator's voiceover at a tennis match, I filled in the gaps of our family tree. "Sofia married Raymond Taylor, whose son Matt married my grandmother, Milly."

"Sofia had a son...?" Eyes wide, a look of wonder crossed Valentina's face.

I nodded. *Her cleft lip* is *less pronounced.* "Then you had two great-granddaughters, and now you have a great-great-granddaughter—actually,   two." Emphasizing the positive results, I glossed over my cousin. "See the good that came from your marriage?"

Valentina sneered. "Descendants don't change the fact that Mateo only tolerated me—never loved me."

"That's not true." A disembodied, masculine voice resonated. The air shimmered, and a translucent image in a blue campaign shirt and rusty-brown trousers materialized.

The specter was so transparent, the cabin's walls showed through him.

Mateo. I caught my breath.

"Maybe it began as a marriage of convenience, but over time, I came to love you."

"You did?" Her cheeks lifting in a smile, Valentina's cleft lip appeared less prominent.

"Yes, after the first few weeks, I"—he shrugged— "forgot your defect, for lack of a better word."

"How could you forget?" Shrinking, she touched her lips. "How could *anyone* forget this blemish?"

"Instead of the scar, I saw your gentle spirit." Mateo reached out his hand.

"I never knew..." Her lips and mouth intact, Valentina straightened her back as if a great weight had been lifted.

I blinked. *Her cleft palate is gone.*

"All this time, I thought you were ashamed of me—had settled for me." Valentina gazed at the viga beam overhead. "To escape the humiliation, I hanged myself, but instead of releasing me, my death *bound* me to these rafters…these walls."

I followed her line of vision, cringing at the despair that drove her to suicide.

"I loved you too much to blame you. Instead, I blamed Marianna. I thought, if you could forget her, you could love me."

"I *did* love you—"

"But you *wanted* Marianna." The charged air became glacial. "Calling her name in bed was the final humiliation." Her cleft lip again as prominent as a camel's, Valentina went purple with rage.

Mateo winced. "An innocent slip of the tongue—"

"Maybe unintentional, but not so innocent. You showed your true feelings."

"I can't deny I loved Marianna. Love is stubborn. You can't will it to come or go, but I did love you…*still* love you."

As the temperature warmed, I stopped shivering.

"You do?" Her voice as plaintive as a child's, Valentina gazed into his face. Again, her scar was barely visible.

Nodding, he held out his hand. "Come with me."

She leaned toward him as if tempted, then pulled back. "I can't."

"Why not?"

She glanced about the cabin's four walls before staring at the overhead beam. "I belong here…"

"No." Shaking his head, he again reached out. "You belong with me."

"I do?" Radiant, all traces of the scar gone, Valentina floated toward him and took his hand.

I closed my eyes as an earsplitting explosion of light consumed them.

Luke burst through the door, with Rosie close behind. "What was that?"

****

I filled them in as I dried my hair. "First Marianna, then Mateo, their baby, and now Valentina…"

Standing at the ironing board, Rosie pressed the wrinkles from the damp veil. "Think that's the last of the cabin's ghosts?"

"Knock on wood." I said a silent prayer while I rapped the wall.

"Maybe now we can get on with the wedding." Luke peeked out the window. "At least, the rain's stopped."

I handed him two rolls of paper towels. "Dry the chairs, and I'll be out in ten minutes."

He grinned at Rosie. "Not even married yet, and already she's giving me orders."

"Discipline is good for the soul." Chuckling, Rosie hung the veil over a chair as she crossed to the utility room. "Let's see if the dryer got the dress's wrinkles out."

The coast clear, I stole a kiss. "The next time we're alone, Mr. Kaylor, we'll be husband and wife."

"See you in ten, Mrs. Kaylor-to-be." He gave me a quick peck before breezing out the door.

I sighed as I glanced about. *So much life has been lived in this room.*

"The heat puckered the seams. Just needs a quick

pressing…was that a sigh I heard?" The cotton batiste dress in hand, Rosie paused as she returned from the utility room.

I nodded. "I've always loved this cabin, but I've never sensed such peace here."

"If only these walls could talk." Rosie slipped the dress over the ironing board. "Remember when you found the dime?"

The memories flooded back. "You said by finding my roots, I'd completed one circle and started the next."

"And by releasing the souls bound here, maybe you ended *that* circle"—she gestured to the wedding dress—"and are beginning another."

****

Instead of marching down the aisle, I simply stood beside Luke.

The ceremony went smoothly until the minister said, "Speak now or forever hold your peace."

My back to the guests, I gritted my teeth, anticipating Bea's objection. Or Cody's. The pause interminable, I cringed, waiting…

A loud, mournful howl broke the silence.

I turned as Teddy bayed at the sky. Comic relief to my pent-up tension, I began shaking with suppressed laughter, then chuckling aloud.

The minister swallowed a smile as he repeated the question.

Again, Teddy howled, and the wedding guests giggled.

Sharing a smile with Luke, I gave a shrill whistle. "Teddy, come here, boy."

The dog joined us, sitting between us in rapt attention.

The minister started a third time.

But ears up and chest out, Teddy held his peace throughout the vows.

Finally, the minister addressed him. "Do you, Teddy, take the bride and groom to be your lawfully wedded parents?"

Wagging his tail, Teddy gave one loud bark.

The pastor beamed from ear to ear. "In that case, the groom may kiss the bride."

Taking me in his arms, Luke leaned me backwards in a deep kiss.

I closed my eyes, basking in his embrace. Then sensing the sun's warmth on my eyelids, I peeked.

The sun broke through the clouds, refracting the light, and a double rainbow arced across the heavens in colors ranging from red to violet.

In love with life, I turned to my husband. "Valentina's gift?"

RECIPES

Simple Sponge Cake

The recipe mentioned in the story is one I found in my grandmother's 1930, handcrafted cookbook. Following, please find my three-ingredient version. It's as easy as one—two—three!

Ingredients
3 eggs, whipped until foamy

1/2 cup superfine sugar (or granulated sugar may be substituted)

2/3 cup self-rising flour (or all-purpose flour plus 1 teaspoon baking powder and 1/3 teaspoon salt may be substituted)

Directions
Preheat the oven to 375 degrees F. Grease an 8- or 9-inch round cake pan.

Using a medium bowl, gradually add the sugar to the eggs until fluffy. Fold in the flour. Pour into the greased cake pan.

Bake 20 minutes or until the cake springs back when lightly pressed.

Do *not* open the oven during baking. If the heat escapes quickly, the cake will fall.

Place the pan over a wire rack until cool.

Optional: Serve with whipped cream and berries, jam, or lemon curd.

Mother's Soft Gingerbread

Ingredients
2 eggs, lightly beaten
1 cup dark brown sugar (*granulated sugar plus 2 tablespoons molasses may be substituted)
¾ cup butter or shortening, melted
¾ cup molasses
3 cups flour, sifted
1 teaspoon soda
1 teaspoon ginger
1 teaspoon cinnamon
¼ teaspoon salt, or to taste
1 cup sour milk (*milk plus 1 tablespoon vinegar or lemon juice may be substituted)

Directions
Preheat oven to 350 degrees F. Generously grease and flour an 8-inch square baking pan.
Combine the beaten eggs with the brown sugar, shortening, and molasses. Sift the flour and blend with the spices. Alternating, add the egg mixture and milk to the flour mixture. Beat until smooth.
Pour the batter into baking pan. Bake for 45 to 50 minutes, or until the gingerbread springs back when lightly touched.
Optional: Top with whipped cream.

CHICKEN WITH HONEY-LOQUAT GLAZE

Ingredients
1/2 cup honey
3 tablespoons soy sauce
3 cups loquats, seeded and quartered
4 tablespoons ginger, minced, to taste
4 tablespoons butter
4 chicken breasts, boned and skinned
Salt, to taste
Ground black pepper, to taste

Directions
Combine the honey, soy sauce, loquats, ginger, and butter in a medium saucepan. Simmer, covered, for five minutes, or until loquats soften.

Purée the loquat mixture in a blender or food processor, pulsing until the consistency of applesauce. Set the mixture aside.

Preheat the grill. Season the chicken breasts with salt and pepper. Grill about five minutes per side, or until done, showing an internal temperature of 165 degrees F.

* (Or season the chicken and sear in butter in a skillet until browned. Transfer the chicken to a baking pan and bake at 350 degrees F for thirty minutes, or until done, showing an internal temperature of 165 degrees F.)

Add the chicken to the loquat purée in a medium skillet. Stir over low heat, simmering for 5-10 minutes, or until chicken is warmed through and evenly coated with the loquat purée.

* Optional: Serve over rice.
Makes 4 servings.

A word about the author…

Dr. Karen Hulene Bartell is a best-selling author, motivational keynote speaker, wife, and all-around pilgrim of life. She writes paranormal, mystery, and frontier romance, as well as multicultural, offbeat love stories that lift the spirit.

Dr. Bartell lives in the Piney Woods of East Texas with her husband and her 'mews' - three rescued cats and a rescued CATahoula Leopard dog.